Lesbian Sex Stories: 30 Steamy Sapphire Sex Tales

The Complete 2012-2013 Spirited Sapphire Catalog

Spirited Sapphire Publishing

Copyright

TABLE OF CONTENTS

STORY 1 –
OPEN RELATIONSHIP

Spirited Sapphire Publishing

Beth and Jill are one of those unique couples that are perfectly ok with bringing in a third party on occasion, to enjoy some sexual fun. That's where Kristen came in. They had met her a few months ago at a lesbian event that they had attended. They were all about the same age, late 20's, and agreed that sex should be a pleasurable experience shared by consenting participants no matter how many there may be involved. Both Beth and Jill are very confident and secure in their commitment to each other, and feel that this type of open relationship can actually rev up a couples' sex life, preventing it from becoming routine and lackluster.

It was Saturday and the three women had attended an outdoor arts and music festival, ending at Beth and Jill's home. They decided to order pizza and see what movies were on cable. The pizza arrived and they all settled down with some floor pillows. They chose a raunchy lesbian prison movie, and ordered it from the cable network.

While the movie was a bit rough in some places, there were some pretty hot scenes thrown in there, too. All three girls were starting to get really turned on. Beth started caressing Jill's legs as they were all fixated on the television. Kristen started watching their interaction, trying not to be obvious. However, Beth and Jill both saw that Kristen was pretty interested in what they were doing. Jill glanced at Beth and Beth gave her a slight nod.

"Hey, Kristen," Jill said. "Do you like what you see?"

"Um, oh, I'm sorry, I wasn't trying to stare."

"No, baby, that's not what I meant. Come over here."

"Seriously? You both really want me to?"

Beth and Jill started to laugh and both reached out simultaneously to pull Kristen over to them. The next thing Kristen knew is that she was laying back on a couple of those floor pillows while Beth was on one side of her and Jill was on the other. Together, the girls started to undress their friend, all the while sucking on her earlobes and kissing and licking her neck on either side. They glanced at each other with slight smiles as they moved their way down to Kristen's luscious, round breasts. Her nipples were a dusky rose color and they stood up prominently, showing their excitement. Those pouty, erect nipples just made the girls start to lick and suck on them more, until Kristen was moaning and squirming all over the place. They reached their hands across Kristen's tone, naked body, and clasped them together while they continued to pleasure her tits with their much talented tongues.

As they moved down her body, together they removed her jeans and thong. Again, they used their tongues, only this time it was to trace a path up the insides of Kristen's well sculpted thighs, and didn't stop until they were at that delicious little fold that concealed her very precious pleasure center. Beth parted those folds with her tongue and started to suck Kristen's stiff and swelling clit. Jill moved her mouth down a little further south and used both her tongue and finger to slide into Kristen's moistening pussy. She could taste that musky flavor of desire the more she used her tongue and finger to fuck Kristen. Suddenly, the first of many orgasms slammed into Kristen. Beth and Jill held on and continued their ministrations until Kristen had crested and started to come down on the other side. Wanting to give Kristen an experience she'd never forget, the girls didn't stop but instead just picked up the pace again.

By this time, Beth and Jill are getting wildly

excited, as they both continue sucking Kristen's clit and finger fucking her pussy together. She started to cum again, and this time it was so hard that Kristen actually started to scream. They girls went back up to her face and took turns kissing her mouth, letting Kristen taste her sweetness off of their lips. When Kristen had calmed down some, they girls again focused their attention between Kristen's parted thighs.

"Beth," Jill whispered. "Lick her pussy. Look how wet she is."

Beth didn't have to be asked twice. She first used her very talented tongue to give some gentle lip love to the outside of Kristen's swollen pussy lips, before plunging her tongue in as deep as she could manage. Tongue fucking Kristen was really getting Beth excited, and she reached over to get Jill's hand. This time Beth guided Jill's fingers into her own soaking wet pussy with no problem, and Jill started to slide her fingers in and out of her. Beth was keeping the same rhythm with her tongue in Kristen's pussy as Jill's fingers were using in Beth's pussy. Both women started to cum at the same time, leaving lots of wetness all over those pillows.

Beth moved up so that she could straddle Kristen's face. Jill also straddled Kristen's body, and positioned herself on all fours, so that she could finger fuck her while Beth leaned down and tongued Jill's stiff little clit. Jill was more than ready for a good tongue lashing. She started moaning as soon as she felt Beth's tongue touch her in the way that only Beth could. Driving her fingers inside of Kristen's pussy, she continued to finger fuck her as Beth tongue fucked her while riding Kristen's mouth.

No one was sure who started this amazing Daisy Chain of sex, but they all started to moan, scream and gyrating together, pretty much at the same time. All three girls were gasping as they collapsed in a heap on the floor. After recovering, each of the women exchanged a kiss with the others. Then, as if on cue, they all got to their feet and headed into the backyard to dive into the cool water of the swimming pool. They all splashed each other playfully with the water and smiled secret little satisfied smiles at each other. It was if they knew this was only the first of many pleasurable encounters to come.

Inside the house, the credits from the movie were starting to roll unseen by any of them.

STORY 2 –
SENSUAL MASSAGE

Copyright © 2012 Spirited Sapphire Publishing

Finally! Sara thought as she stretched her arms over her head and arched her back a bit. It was a hard case for the law firm that she worked as a paralegal for, but in the end, they had all pulled together to for the big win. Oh, who am I kidding? Sara thought, I love my job! Still, she had to admit to herself that now that it was over, she was ready for some much needed 'Sara time'.

Strolling down the hallway to the client lounge, Sara found a bottle of decent merlot and decided to treat herself to glass. She suddenly realized just how tense her body felt. It had to be from the stress of working so many long hours. A massage would be oh so perfect right now. Seeing that it was almost 10pm already, she knew that all of the day spas in downtown Chicago would be closed by now, but she decided to browse the web to see what might be available anyway.

After sifting through the ads for the larger spas only to find all of them all closed, just as she suspected, she started to see some ads for some "outcall" massages. Well, this looks interesting, Sara thought. Also, she couldn't help but notice the photos of beautiful women that seemed to come attached to these ads. What could be nicer than having a gorgeous woman render me helpless with a full body massage? Sara thought to herself.

"I'm going to do it!" Sara announced out loud to the empty lounge as she reached for her cell phone. Having chosen one randomly, she called and made an appointment with a masseuse named Toni. After giving the address of her law firm, Sara poured another glass of wine, her body already feeling the effects from the first glass, and sat back to wait.

Within half an hour, someone rang the front bell of the building. Sara pushed the button on the intercom system.

"Yes?" she said.

"Hi, my name is Toni. I'm here to see Sara," came the reply.

"Sure, just a second," Sara said. She hurried down the hallway to the front of the office. After punching in the code for the alarm, she quickly opened the door and motioned the woman inside. Then she reset the alarm and led the way to the client lounge. Once in the soft light of the lounge, Sara turned and faced Toni, and nearly stopped breathing.

"I'm Sara," she said. "I hope it doesn't make you uncomfortable if I tell you how absolutely stunning you are. I also happen to be gay, and am attracted to sexy, feminine type women. Hopefully, that won't be a problem."

Toni laughed in a rather sultry voice.

"No, that doesn't make me feel uncomfortable." she said as she took off the light weight coat she was wearing. "And, as for you being gay, it might please you to know that I too am a lesbian, which means I know how to touch a woman in all the right places. I guess you could say, teasing and pleasing is what I do best!"

Sara took in the vision that was now standing before her. Toni was tall, probably 5' 9" to 5' 10", with long brown hair, deep brown eyes, and a slender yet curvaceous body. Her waist cinched in, which accented full rounded hips. A set of luscious bouncy breasts stood out from her chest, and Sara's mouth started watering just looking at them. Her fingers itched to be touching those nipples that were clearly erect under the sheer black tank top Toni was wearing. Toni continued to get comfortable by peeling off her tight black yoga pants, giving Sara a perfect view of her shapely toned legs and nice plump ass, adorned by a pair of black laced panties.

Smiling mischievously, Toni asked, "Where should I set up?"

"Oh, well, right over here is fine," Sara replied as she walked to a vacant space in the client lounge.

"Great!" Toni said as she sat up her table and got things ready. "If you want, you can start disrobing while I do this. There are some towels in that bag over there that you can use to cover up with."

Sara did as was requested of her, and slipped out of her clothes. She was grateful now that she had kept up with her gym membership. Even though she was a bit shorter than Toni at 5' 7", she was still in excellent shape. Her body was a bit muscular, but not in an unflattering way. Her ass was round and tight; her legs toned and muscled in just the right places. Heavy but firm breasts were in place above a slightly rounded stomach. It was without shame or modesty that she faced Toni completely nude.

A sly smile teased Toni's full lips as she took in Sara's beautiful and naked body.

"Ok, then," she said. "No towels. That works for me."

She motioned for Sara to get on the table. Sara sauntered over slowly, carrying her bottle of wine along with her half full glass. Sitting both of them down on a small end table that she had pulled within reach of the massage table, she hopped up on it and lay on her stomach.

"So we're doing your back first?" Toni asked, secretly getting aroused by the sight of Sara's naked body on her massage table. "That's perfect."

She chose a bottle from the group of oils she had brought with her and squeezed it into her hands. Starting at Sara's shoulders, she applied the oil with her very talented hands. Toni kneaded the tension out of Sara's upper back and then traveled south to her lower back. As she worked, Sara periodically continued to sip her wine, completely unaware that Toni was visually taking in every curve of her body and waiting for just the slightest of cues to take the massage to a whole new level.

Toni had now moved to Sara's feet and was massaging each toe and working up toward her calves. As she moved her hands up to Sara's thighs, she applied just the right amount of pressure to the muscles there. Sara moaned ever so slightly as Toni massaged her way up to the tops of her thighs, wishing that those fingers would travel even further upward.

"How does that feel?" asked Toni.

"Mmmm, it feels heavenly!" Sara whispered. "Didn't you forget a place?", giving Toni the very cue she was hoping for.

Toni laughed and said, "No, sexy. I didn't forget. I'm going to leave that part till right before you turn over."

With those words, Toni began seriously massaging each of Sara's rounded ass cheeks, letting her fingers brush ever-so-lightly along her inner thighs, making a barely there contact with Sara's soft pussy lips with each gentle pass. She spent enough time there that she could tell it was having the desired effect. Finally, with a light little tap on Sara's backside, and a stirring in her own pussy lips, she told her it was time to turn over.

As soon as Sara was lying on her back, Toni could spot a little glistening spot between her thighs as she settled on the table. Using different massage oil this time, she started at Sara's neck and slowly worked her way down. Skipping the very intimate areas, Toni decided to tease Sara a little by going to her feet and moving her way up the front of her legs. Sara's eyes were closed and her breathing was uneven. Toni moved her hands up Sara's sides, then onto her breasts, where she started to lightly tease her nipples.

Hoping for approval, Toni asked "Is this ok?".

Sara moaned in answer as she managed to nod. That told Toni that it was time to move in for a little more sensual touching. Sara's nipples were now like hard little pebbles and Toni kept making little circles around them.

"Oh god," Sara whispered. "That's so good."

"You just relax into it and enjoy," Toni said. "That's why I'm here. You have such a beautiful body that it's a pleasure for me to be able to touch you like this."

Sara was floating on a fluffy cloud with little bits of electricity surrounding it. Toni's fingers felt like magic as they traced a trail from her nipples down across her bare stomach and further down still across the outer folds of her smooth pussy lips. When Toni teased her nipples, Sara was jolted all the way to the center of her pleasure core. She had always had this feeling that something in her nipples was connected to that very special part of her body. There were times that she had reached an orgasm just from having her nipples sucked and teased.

Now, Sara felt Toni's light feathery touch on her shaved mound. She parted her thighs slightly to encourage Toni to touch her where she really wanted it. Her juices were starting to gather and slip down her inner thighs. Toni understood what Sara wanted. Slowly, she parted Sara's most intimate folds so she could amp up the pleasure that she knew Sara was ready to receive.

As soon as Sara felt Toni's fingers making small slow circles around her stiff little rosebud of pleasure, she arched her back so that her hips were pushing against Toni's fingers. She hoped that this movement would encourage Toni to move faster because she could feel the tightening in her abdomen and the slight contractions in her pretty pink love tunnel. Sara was very ready to go over that edge of complete ecstasy. She knew that she was moaning louder now, but she didn't care.

Toni slipped a couple fingers inside of Sara as she continued to tease her pleasure center. Keeping pace with the circles she was making, she slid her finger in and out in the same rhythm. Oh yes, yes, thought Sara. It may have been something she said aloud, but she was so caught up in the fever that was seizing her down below, that she wasn't sure. Something she was sure about was that she was riding Toni's fingers with everything that was in her. Ohhhh yes, yes, yes! She was going over that edge now and nothing could stop her. Sara's body writhed as her orgasm slammed into her. It felt like a never ending shock wave, jolting like orgasmic lightening through Sara's body.

When she finally crested that last wave, Sara found her naked body wrapped in Toni's arms, sweat soaked and gasping for breath. She was utterly spent, yet felt on top of the world!

"Wow!" Sara said. "You weren't kidding. You really do know how to tease and please! That was absolutely amazing!"

Still not worrying about covering her nakedness, Toni enjoyed the view of Sara's luscious ass as she walked across the room and got her purse. She paid Toni and included a hefty tip. Toni thanked her, packed up her supplies, and left smiling over her shoulder.

As for Sara, she got dressed and went to her car. She thought about Toni all the way home as well as what plans she would make for this weekend. It seemed to already be off to a grand start and she was going to do everything possible to build on that.

STORY 3 –
LAST CALL

Copyright © 2012 Spirited Sapphire Publishing

"Can I get you another one of these, babe?" Maya, the bartender, asked Lisa.

"Sure, why not? I can use an extra dose of relaxation tonight," Lisa replied.

As Maya poured Lisa another glass of red wine, she glanced at Lisa. Giving her a sexy smile, she set the drink in front of her. Damn, that woman is hot! Lisa thought. Her tall curvaceous body moved lithely as she hurried around behind the bar waiting on patrons. Maya's skin was smooth and the color of cream in your coffee. She had the most amazing golden green eyes that she had ever seen in her life. Lisa had been lost in those eyes many times. Maya's full lips could form the perfect pout, as well as a seductive smile that would drop a woman from a mile away. I wonder if it's ever going to happen between us, Lisa thought. She seems interested, but I've given her plenty of chances to show me she wants more, and she never follows through. That damn silent dance that lesbians often do. Both wanting to make a move, yet wanting the other to do it first.

"Last call, everyone!" Maya suddenly called out.

The few people that were still drinking quickly put in their orders and Maya was scurrying around filling them. Her energy amazed Lisa. She was on her feet at least eight hours a night and she never seemed to tire. This job is probably what helps keep her in such amazing shape, Lisa thought, as she drank in the sight of Maya's sexy figure. Maya's mini skirt showed off her toned tanned legs that Lisa longed to run her tongue all the way from her ankles to the inner most curves of her thighs. Not to mention, that Lisa was near hypnotized by Maya's breasts as they jiggled about in her always skimpy tops. Lisa was grateful that Maya seldom ever wore a bra.

Awakening from her lustful trance, Lisa suddenly thought to herself out loud "When did it get to be so late?". I've been sitting here drooling over Maya and dreaming of touching her. I could swear she's actually flirting back with me tonight, Lisa wishfully thought. She continued to take her time sipping her wine while risking a side glance at Maya. Just as she did so, she caught Maya glancing back at her. Actually, Maya wasn't just glancing back at her, she was boldly checking Lisa out. Ok, Lisa thought. I did not imagine that! She's totally flirting with me!

Gradually, the lingering patrons started to make their way out of the bar. Lisa stood up and reached for her wallet in her purse to pay for tonight's drinks.

"Hey, you don't have to take off just yet, do you?" Maya asked. "Why don't you hang out and keep me company while I close up?"

"Um sure, ok," Lisa said, smiling. She sat back down and Maya handed her another glass of wine before she headed over and locked the door. Turning off the OPEN sign, she went back over to the bar and started wiping it down.

"You know, I'm glad you're sticking around. I've wanted a chance to get to know you a little better," Maya said as she stood directly across the bar from Lisa, staring at her with those gorgeous golden green eyes.

Suddenly suffering from a dry mouth, Lisa picked up her glass of wine and took a sip. She was so nervous, however, that some of it dribbled down her chin. Before she could react, Maya leaned over the bar and quickly licked the offending drip of wine from Lisa's chin and slid up to kiss her fully on the mouth. Lisa was in a bit of shock but she totally went with it. Maya's lips felt just as soft and full as she had imagined. She could taste the wine on Maya's tongue that she had just licked from her chin. The kiss went from a tentative exploration to a full-fledged tongue tango within seconds.

Then, Maya broke the kiss and fairly flew around from the backside of the bar. Once she reached the other side, she twirled Lisa around and slid her off of the bar stool, leaning her back against the bar. The women continued to kiss as if their very air depended upon it. Lisa could feel Maya's hands all over her body. While kissing her, Maya slipped her hands under Lisa's t-shirt and pushed it up over her head. Now, Lisa was standing in only her jeans and a French cut bra.

Oh god, Lisa thought as she felt Maya's tongue tracing a trail from her mouth down her neck and over the tops of her heaving breasts. With her head buried in Lisa's cleavage, she discreetly unhooked the front of her bra. Lisa's full breasts sprang out into Maya's hands. Moving back up to Lisa's face, Maya started to kiss her all over again while moving her thumbs over Lisa's nipples. Lisa's back was arched, which caused her breasts to become completely Maya's property. She leaned her head over and ran the tip of her tongue around Lisa's right nipple first and then moved to her left one.

Lisa's body was melting like butter, as this woman whom she has been lusting over for weeks, has suddenly taken full command of her very willing and wanton body. As Maya continued to lick and suck on Lisa's nipples, she unclasped the hair tie that was holding her long, thick black hair in a ponytail and released it. Now, Maya's hair was cascading over her shoulders and down her back, and Lisa loved running her fingers through it as Maya kept playing with her exposed tits.

The bra hit the floor along with the t-shirt. Maya was now unzipping Lisa's jeans while her mouth was still working its magic on the upper part of Lisa's body. She felt Maya's finger sliding inside the open zipper and down the front of her bikini panties. Is this really happening, she thought? I couldn't stop her if an atomic bomb dropped right now. As Maya's hand slid over Lisa's shaved mound and parted the folds between her legs, Lisa moaned.

Maya took that as encouragement and slid the jeans all the way down her legs until Lisa was able to step out of them. Then she led Lisa over by the jukebox and lowered them both to the carpeted floor there. Now, she could position herself over Lisa's body so that the friction between them would be physical. As Maya started to work her way down over Lisa's stomach, Lisa suddenly stopped her.

"Hey," she said in a husky whisper. "Let's get you naked, too." She started to help Maya out of her clothes, an exercise that became a bit frantic with need. Lisa first untied Maya's halter top and tossed it to the side. She then unzipped the back of her mini skirt, and with ease, let it slide off of Maya's beautiful hips. Lastly, Lisa tugged off the pair of silk pink panties that Maya had been wearing and gasped with unbridled excitement as she felt Maya's naked body press against her own naked skin.

Maya went back to kissing her way down Lisa's body, when Lisa started to turn around. Now, Maya totally understood. Soon, they were in a position that allows two women to fully enjoy each other. Lisa licked her way up the inside of Maya's thighs until she found those precious little folds that hid her stiff, little rosebud of pleasure. I'm going to make her feel like she's never been properly licked in her life, thought Lisa. As her tongue touched the tip of Maya's bud, she felt Maya's hips jerk a little and heard moaning from her. Lisa's tongue traced gentle circles around Maya's hardened clit, as her fingers spread and caressed her lips. Maya's hips were rocking as Lisa was now gently sucking on Maya's clit, while at the same time she was slowly guiding a finger in and out of Maya's very hot, very moist pussy.

"Is that good baby?" Lisa asked. "Oh god, you taste so good!"

Maya suddenly kicked back into high gear and started to return the favor that Lisa was doing for her. She could feel Lisa's wetness covering her face as she started to suck on her clit. Soon, they were both riding each other's faces, and Lisa could feel her orgasm building. She wasn't ready for it to be over, yet, but there wasn't going to be anything she could do to stop it. She was losing all control as she felt the sudden heat in her belly, and her love juices start to flow.

As Lisa's orgasm hit, she screamed out with pleasure, while her head was still between Maya's moistened lips. This seemed to set off a similar response in Maya, who also started to moan wildly and gyrate against Lisa's tongue. It was Maya's turn to climax, and Lisa resumed her tongue fucking as Maya's body stiffened and shivered to her own waves of ecstasy. When the contractions subsided, they laid against one another's sweat covered body and basked in the moment, while catching their breath..

Lisa suddenly started to laugh, and turned to look Maya in the eyes.

"Do you know how long I've wanted to do that?" she asked Maya.

"Probably about as long as I've wanted it," Maya replied.

"Let's not wait so long to repeat it, ok?"

"Oh, you better believe it won't!"

They kissed each other deeply and got to their feet. After locating their clothes, they got dressed and called a taxi. Since it was really late, getting a cab was fairly easy in Manhattan. Few people were out and about at this hour through the week. They both climbed into the backseat when the taxi arrived. Clasping hands, they smiled at each other. Lisa was still a little shaky from all the excitement. She also couldn't believe that she had just made love with this beautiful woman who she could still taste. I definitely do want this to happen again, she thought. She also knew that she would dream of the way Maya's mouth, tongue, and hands had felt on her body tonight, when she hit the bed for sleep.

Lisa's apartment was first. She turned to Maya and they kissed a deep and passionate kiss while the taxi driver silently watched in his rear view mirror. They both glanced at him and then giggled with each other. Maya got back into the cab and waved as she rode away. Lisa stood there watching the back of the cab until it disappeared. Yep, she thought. I'm going to have that woman again very soon!

STORY 4 –
INTIMATE COUNSELING

Spirited Sapphire Publishing

Holly sits on the plush brown couch in the waiting room of the life coach that she is going to be seeing in just a few minutes, nervously sipping some cold mineral water that the receptionist has brought her. She was a bit relieved because she was feeling unexpectedly agitated and her mouth was rather dry, so the cool mineral water tickling down her throat felt refreshing. Linda had come highly recommended to Holly as someone that would be able to help her calm down and bring more balance into her life. Holly has always been an over achiever and was very successful in her business. But, Holly's friends often worry about her because she never takes time for herself, to do something just for fun or for sheer relaxation. So, she has agreed to meet with Linda to see if she could do anything to teach Holly about the finer points of enjoying life.

Holly sits back and tries to get comfortable as she waits. She crosses her well-toned and shapely legs as her business skirt rides up a bit. It was good that she decided to wear that blazer over her sleeveless blouse because the air conditioning in the waiting room area felt like it was on full throttle, and she could feel her nipples stiffen against the smooth fabric of her blouse. She tossed her long, thick brown hair back and took another sip of her water. Dammit, she thought. Now, I'm starting to get too warm.

A few minutes later Holly is called into Linda's office. As Holly enters Linda's office their eyes meet, and BAM! - there is an instantaneous electric connection between them, and both women do a quick whole body scan to take in the sight of the other. Shit, now Holly is really hot, and practically forgets why she's there, as all sorts of lustful thoughts are zooming through her overactive mind. After introducing herself to Holly, Linda invites her to sit down and make herself comfortable on the office couch, while trying to maintain her professional composure and not let on how attracted she is to her new client. Holly can't wait to take off her blazer, and as she does, she also coyly undoes a few buttons at the top of her blouse providing a clear view of her cleavage. As she settles onto the oversized couch in the office, she can't help but wonder if those sexual vibes she's picking up are all in her mind, or if her new life coach was equally as attracted and turned on as she was. Holly was quite suddenly very interested in whatever guidance Linda might have to offer, hoping it would be more than just how to balance out her chaotic life.

It's soon clear that both women are making supreme efforts to stay focused on what was actually supposed to be happening here. All Linda seems to be able to do is stare at Holly's curvaceous body and perky breasts, as they now reveal themselves through her half-buttoned blouse, wishing she could fully expose and fondle them. Holly is having difficulties as well, and is trying her best not to stare at Linda like a sex-crazed cat, but she's feeling nothing but total lust with every glance she takes. And, the subtle scent of musk oil that Linda is wearing is only contributing to the matter, and Holly finds herself trying not to squirm as desire is enveloping her entire body.

Linda finally starts to ask some questions. Holly confirms that her age is 34. To Holly, Linda appears to be about the same age, and notices that she has the most amazing Angelina Jolie-like full lips. As Linda forms her words, Holly can't seem to take her eyes off of that mouth. She blushes as she thinks to herself how much she would love to feel that mouth moving over her entire body. Oh how she'd love to feel those pouty lips kiss her deeply, suck on her tits and lick her to orgasm heaven.

'Holly? Holly, are you ok?' Linda asks.

Holly suddenly realizes that Linda has just asked her a question but she has no idea as to what it was. So she asks her to please repeat it. Linda has just asked her why she's come in. Holly begins explaining about how much of an over achiever she is and how her friends are all worried about how she never relaxes, and she never does anything just for the sheer fun of it, and she needs to learn how to let her hair down and have some fun. This prompts Linda to suddenly ask Holly about her sex life. Linda is horrified that those words have just leapt out of her mouth, but Holly doesn't seem to notice anything unusual. Instead, she replies honestly in saying that she really could handle some slow, sensual sex to kind of take the edge off of things in her overly busy life.

Thinking she knows just the right form of 'fun' to take that edge off that Holly wishes for, Linda slowly gets up from her chair and walks over to where Holly is sitting. She smiles at Holly and gently brushes a strand of Holly's hair from her face. They stare at each other for the briefest of minutes before Linda leans over with those sexy, pouty lips and kisses Holly slowly, gently and fully on her mouth. In no time though, that kiss turns into a very heated exchange between the two women, and their tongues and lips are dancing feverously with one another. Holly has never been kissed in this way by anyone in her life and her body immediately responds. She doesn't even think that this may not be the way a therapy session is supposed to go. In fact, Holly is thinking this is going better than she could have ever anticipated, and she is loving the results already!

Linda doesn't stop with just kissing Holly. She slowly moves her tongue down her neck and over to her ear lobe, sucking very gently before moving down across her breastbone to her luscious, perfect breasts. She slowly pushes Holly back onto the couch so that she can finish unbuttoning her blouse. Holly sighs deeply as Linda pushes back her blouse and unhooks the front closure of her bra. When she does so, Holly's breasts spring into Linda's hands, and she lightly kneads them before leaning down and placing her pouty, full lips around one of Holly's dark rosy nipples. Using her tongue as well as her lips, Linda causes Holly's nipple to grow hard and stand up inside Linda's mouth. She can feel Holly's heartbeat speed up, her breathing accelerates and her whole body starts to arch upward towards Linda's as if silently screaming 'take me'. It was obvious, Linda's suggest method of relaxation and fun were being well received by her client.

As Linda continues to play with and caress Holly's breasts, she realizes that she's also becoming very excited herself. She loves Holly's breasts and she loves the feeling of those luscious orbs under her hands and her mouth. In fact, never has Linda had access to such completely perfect breasts. However, it is quickly becoming obvious to Linda that Holly needs to receive attention elsewhere, so as to properly balance out her 'therapy'.

As Linda continues to play with Holly's magnificent breasts, she slowly slides her hand under Holly's skirt, gliding her fingers across her ultra soft skin, and starts to tease the inner most part of her thighs. Holly's legs part a little to give Linda easier access and Linda takes it. Her fingers graze lightly over the crotch of Holly's panties and she finds the dampness there that she had expected. Holly is moaning now and arching her hips against Linda's hand.

Yes, Linda is ready to give Holly exactly what she wants. Slowly, she slips Holly's panties down to her ankles and off of her feet. She can smell the muskiness of Holly's desire as she runs the tip of her tongue up her thigh, ending at the folds that hide Holly's pleasure center. Instead of using her fingers, she uses her tongue to part those folds to discover the stiff little rosebud there that is just waiting to be suckled. Linda gently wraps her lips around it and Holly gasps, spreading her thighs open even further. She places her hands on Linda's head and slightly pushes it into her center even more as she starts to slowly rotate her aching little clit on Linda's face.

Linda is fully enjoying being used for dispensing some much needed pleasure to her client, and she continues to lick and suck Holly's clit while slipping a finger just inside of her soaking wet love tunnel, which was already beginning to contract around her finger. At the moment, Holly is beyond any function of thought, except feeling all of these sexual sensations vibrating through her body all at once. She starts to feel herself climbing up that mountain of pleasure. Linda continues her therapeutic ministrations as she feels Holly getting closer and closer to her point of no return.

Suddenly, Holly begins to gyrate against Linda very quickly and starts moaning. Linda knows that she is going over that climax cliff now, as she feels Holly's pussy tighten and pulsate around her fingers. When Holly stops moving, she lays there with Linda still between her legs. Breathing deeply, Holly strokes Linda's hair, and thanks her for such a wonderful experience. She had to admit, she couldn't remember the last time she had this much uninhibited fun. Additionally, Holly also had to admit that she felt incredibly relaxed and enjoying an almost Zen-like moment. When Linda finally sits up, the two women engage in one last, long deep kiss before starting to readjust their clothes.

Before Holly starts for the office door, she tells Linda that she is quite happy with Linda's suggested therapy of fun and relaxation to help balance out her life and enjoy it more, and will be scheduling an appointment to see her weekly for a while. Linda smiles at Holly, as she secretly anticipates their next client appointment.

STORY 5 –
STRAP-ON FUN

I really wish I could figure out a way to tell Cheryl what I want, thought Jamie. It's just that everything had been so great in their relationship during the year and a half they had been together. She never wanted Cheryl to think that she didn't love or want her anymore. But, there was something she wanted to at least try sexually with Cheryl, and she has been waiting for just the right moment to share her secret fantasy with her, never yet quite getting up the nerve. They were going out tonight to a local rock concert. Maybe, Jamie thought, I can tell her tonight after we're both relaxed from the concert and some dancing.

The concert was great, and afterwards they drove to one of their favorite bars to do a little drinking and, hopefully, a lot of dancing. Jamie wasn't a hard drinker and after a couple of glasses of gin and tonic, she had loosened up quite a bit. Dressed in ass-contouring jeans, a tight white tank top with no bra and 'fuck me' high heels, Jamie's body was glued next to Cheryl's on the dance floor. Cheryl was enjoying watching Jamie 'dirty dance' for her during the fast songs, and loved feeling her breasts pressed against hers when they were dancing to the slower R&B tunes. Jamie was sexy as hell, and Cheryl loved showing her off wherever they went. Whether dancing fast and dirty or slow and romantic, Jamie and Cheryl's bodies were ever entwined and both of them were feeling more than a little horny by now. A slow song came on that they both loved, and as their bodies were pressed close together swaying in time to the music, without actually thinking about it, Jamie put her mouth to Cheryl's ear and whispered the request of her secret sexual fantasy into it.

"Seriously?" Cheryl pulled back and looked at Jamie.

Jamie nodded. "Is that ok?" she asked.

Instead of answering her, she grabbed Jamie's hand and pulled her hurriedly out of the bar. They got in the car and drove to a 24 hour adult toy superstore that was local to them. On the way, Cheryl told Jamie that she couldn't be more excited to learn of her secret sexual fantasy, and was actually quite turned on by it. After arriving at the superstore for adult toys, both of them started browsing all of the dildos and strap-ons that this store carried. There were just so many of them that it was difficult to decide which one was best. Finally, Cheryl spied an awesome leather strap-on belt covered in silver studs. It fit perfectly with Cheryl's rocker chick image. Jamie selected the perfect dildo to go with it. Not too big, not too small, and made of a natural feeling silicone. They picked out some pina colada flavored lube to complete the purchase, and hurried to pay for everything. The sales girl who rang up their purchase smiled at them, and told them to enjoy their new 'toy'. Jamie and Cheryl rush back out to the car to go home and play.

Cheryl pulled Jamie into the bedroom where they strip and climb into their oversized shower together. The foreplay begins, as they soap up each other's bodies and kiss and fondle one another under the warm cascading water. As Cheryl presses Jamie's soapy, slippery body against the shower wall, kissing her intently, Jamie closes her eyes and envisions what it might feel like if Cheryl was already wearing her new 'appendage' and guiding it slowly into her hot hole. As if reading her mind, Cheryl props one of Jamie's legs up on the ledge in the shower, kneels in front of her and starts teasing the folds of her lips with her warm tongue. Jamie's legs start to quiver, as Cheryl continues on with her tongue teasing, giving her a few minutes of lip love before turning off the shower.

By the time they had toweled dried off, they were both horny as hell over the new experience that they were about to share. Both of them donned some sexy lingerie, and Cheryl popped in one of their favorite rock CDs to help set the mood for some dominant loving. Jamie wore a black satin bra and panty set with a red netting teddy over it. Cheryl put on a pair of black panties and a bra with silver studs that would match her new silver studded strap on belt. The hard pulsing of the music made them want to move, so they started dancing and grinding their bodies together. Cheryl started nibbling on Jamie's neck while gently pulling her hair. Their hips started grinding together in time to the music as Cheryl ran her hands over Jamie's full breasts, pinching and pulling on her nipples before moving her hand downward and running her fingers between Jamie's thighs.

It was evident from her closed eyes and parted lips that Jamie was quite turned on. Cheryl gave Jamie a little push backward until she was backed up against one of the arms of the couch. She turned Jamie around and bent her over the couch. Using a cat o' nine tails that she slyly purchased along with their new strap on at the adult store, she began giving Jamie a light spanking on her pretty upturned ass cheeks. After a few slaps with the cat tails, Jamie's ass cheeks started to form a bright rosy glow, and Cheryl quickly soothed away the slight stinging by gently running her hands across them, before then sliding a finger slowly around Jamie's moist pussy opening. First teasing her with slow, deliberate circles all around her soft parted lips, Cheryl finally slipped the tip of her finger just inside of Jamie's soaked pussy. As Cheryl slides her finger deeper inside of Jamie, she can feel her love juices running down her finger. She knew that Jamie was more than ready for some special attention, so she laid down underneath Jamie and spread her thighs apart. Taking the pina colada lube they had bought, she put some on her finger and spread it slowly over Jamie's clit, which made Jamie moan and move her body against Cheryl's hand.

Cheryl brought Jamie's clit down to her face and used her tongue to tease it and her lips to suck it as it became like a tiny stiff little 'cock'. Jamie started grinding her hips against Cheryl's mouth now and moaned even more loudly while also encouraging Cheryl verbally to continue what she was doing. Jamie announced that she was going to cum all over Cheryl's face and then she spasmed while howling at the top of her lungs.

While Jamie starts to recover from the intense experience that Cheryl has just given her, Cheryl quickly put on the studded strap on attire and lay on her back on the floor. Crooking her finger at Jamie, she said, "Come here you sexy thing. I want to give you something." Jamie smiled slightly at what she knew was to come and she sauntered over to Cheryl and straddled her.

With her pussy still contracting from her recent explosive orgasm, Jamie wasn't prepared for the intense electric sensation she felt upon sliding her hot, wet little pussy all the way down on Cheryl's "cock." Before she even knew what was happening, Jamie was instantly rendered helpless as she felt another intense orgasm permeate her entire body. She keeps moving up and down on Cheryl's appendage, while leaning down and nibbling Cheryl's neck and tits, as she pulls them free from the studded bra. Jamie bites lightly on Cheryl's hard nipples while continuing to grind into her hips.

Suddenly, Cheryl lifts Jamie up off of her and removed her artificial cock from her pussy. Flipping Jamie over, she put her in a doggy style position. This allowed Cheryl to slide her "cock" inside Jamie from behind and fuck her slow and deep. As Jamie's moans and cries became louder, Cheryl started pumping her pussy harder and faster, power fucking Jamie until yet another orgasm hit her and made her legs buckle in complete surrender. This last orgasm was so intense and even harder than the other two, and Jamie is done for the moment. She collapses in an exhausted heap on the floor.

After a moment, Cheryl pulled out of Jamie and discarded the strap-on, dildo and all. She cuddled up to Jamie and put her arms around her.

"So, was it all that you hoped it would be?" she asked.

Jamie started to laugh a little before answering. Finally, she turned onto her side so that she could pull Cheryl's arms around her even more.

"What do you think?" Jamie asked. "Only next time, I'll do you so you can see just how hot it is!"

Spirited Sapphire Publishing

STORY 6 –
MARDI GRAS

This was an excellent idea, thought Tina. I'm so glad that I let my friends talk me into coming to Mardi Gras this year. Tina always wanted to experience this ever-popular New Orleans tradition, but either always had to work or simply was too shy to participate in the exhibitionist fun. And now, she was here. Tina leaned back in her chair and sipped her cocktail called 'blue lightening', while enjoying her friends chat and laughter over the remains of their dinner. Soon it would be time to get into their costumes and hit the colorful and noisy streets. They had all had plenty to drink so it was a good thing that they weren't driving back to their hotel. In fact, it was just down the block from where they were eating.

They paid their bill and the girls started their short walk back to the French Colonial hotel they were staying at. Tina couldn't believe all of the wildness that was already going on in the streets of New Orleans. There were beautiful, mostly naked, women all over the place, which didn't do a lot for her current celibate state. Her last relationship had ended more than a year ago and she hadn't met anyone since that she was interested in, not even for a one night stand. That was one of the many reasons that her friends insisted she join them on this little trek of naughty anonymous fun.

So far, she has really been having a blast, enjoying the lively music, the delicious food and entertaining street performers. Now, all those bared bouncing breasts and painted nude bodies were causing quite a stir in Tina's body, and quite frankly she was ready to act on it....tonight! She actually couldn't wait until it was completely dark and they could all be on the street in their own costumes. Thus far, everything had been just as wild and sexy as she had been told it would be. Tina couldn't recall ever seeing a sea of naked women like she's already bared witness to, and she was in tits and ass heaven. And, she had actually let herself be talked into doing something so daring that she was rather shocked at herself. Maybe it was the alcohol, maybe it was just being in New Orleans, or maybe it was a combination of things, but Tina had allowed herself to be talked into forgoing her costume top, and having her breasts air-brush painted and going topless. They were all doing it and Tina's friends insisted that she join them. Honestly, just standing in front of the girl who was air-brushing her and her friends tits was exhilarating in itself, and she was already having visions of the possibilities of things to come.

The rest of her costume was very beautiful and quite sexy. There were lots of gold and violet colored feathers, as well as glitter and sequins. A see-through violet colored skirt hit her mid-thigh and she had a traditional but elaborate mask also done in violet and gold. Her shoulder-length auburn hair looked amazing with the violet colors of her costume. Tina had always kept herself fit, which was emphasized as her costume covered very little of her thin, lean body. Her breasts, now painted with an elaborate design of purple, black and silver flowers and swirls, were full, perky and adorned with large dark nipples that were temporarily painted with glitter.

Walking down the crowded streets of the French Quarter, the ladies were having a wonderful time as they giggled, waved and pointed at all of the various costumes and beautiful naked women. Since night fell, people were getting even more brazen in their public displays of lust, and, of course, this only served to near-push Tina off the deep end of sexual frustration and wantonness. As they got deeper into the Quarter, they started seeing couples not just kissing, but simulating sex, as well as actually having sex. These couples consisted of men and women, men and men, and women and women. There were even some trios that seemed to be having very heated encounters. Tina was awestruck as well as highly aroused. Oh, let me be taken by some beautiful female stranger, Tina thought to herself. Little did she know that she was mere moments, from having her wish fulfilled.

As the ladies were staring and squealing in delight at the sights, Tina suddenly caught a flash of silver and white from the corner of her eye. Whipping her head around for a better look, she spotted a tall woman wearing a silver and white mask accompanied by a see-through, barely there costume, giving Tina a perfect view of her small, firm breasts and sleek, long legs. This girl reminded Tina of a very provocative and somewhat futuristic Marie Antoinette. Tina could feel the sexual energy radiating off of her all the way across the street. Oh my god! She thought. I would love to kiss her, to feel her, to taste her! Tina turned around to see where her friends were heading and then looked back only to find the gorgeous stranger had vanished. Damn, Tina thought. The most exciting, enticing woman I've seen in a year and she just disappears. Disappointed, she walked a few feet further to catch up with her friends when, suddenly, she was pulled into a shadowed cobblestone alley. Just as she was about to scream for help, she saw that her captor was none other than the mystery woman she had just been eyeing from across the street, and her stunning blue eyes pierced right through her, from behind her silver adorned mask.

Tina suddenly found herself being pushed up against the side of a building and her mouth was covered with the full, sexy lips of this incredibly sexy woman in the white and silver mask. She really does look a lot like

Marie Antoinette, was Tina last cognizant thought before she lost herself to the open mouthed, tongue sucking kisses that she was suddenly involved in. Tina's blood was heated to the boiling point with pleasure and desire, and god knows how she was even able to remain standing, when all she wanted to do in that instant was lay on the cobblestone street with this near-naked goddess who was assaulting her, and let her have her way.

Marie Antoinette ran her hands up and over Tina's bare, painted breasts. Her nipples were erect and sensitive as this beautiful stranger teased them to an even more sensitive state, before leaning over and giving them a gentle tug with her teeth. Tina moaned and grabbed at her captors breasts as she gave into the attention she was receiving. Marie really knew what she was doing. Tina could feel her pussy throbbing and wanted nothing more than for this woman to touch and caress her lips in a special way. It was almost as if Marie could read her mind because at that moment, she lowered one hand so that she could move it up Tina's short see-through skirt.

Ah, yes, yes, thought Tina. That's just what I need. Touch me right there, as she struggled to keep herself balanced up against the building wall. Marie Antoinette deftly slipped a finger just inside of Tina's thong. The wetness that had gathered there helped that finger move easily just inside the soft lips covering her pleasure cove. Tina couldn't help but move her hips in rhythm with Marie's fingers. Suddenly, Marie broke their ravenous tongue tango and started to kiss her way down the curves of Tina's body. Getting on her knees, Marie lifted Tina's little skirt and her tongue quickly found what she was seeking. As she started to suckle gently on Tina's aching and stiff little clit, Tina clutched at the brick wall with her hands as she took notice to the flashing lights of the parade floats that seemed to be like her own personal fireworks show. The lights and music darted around the two of them like the perfect backdrop, as Tina continued to relish the feel of Marie's soft mouth buried deep in her pussy with each vibrating beat of the music.

Marie continued to lick, suck and kiss that very intimate part of Tina until she could no longer control her response. Tina's orgasm approached, and overtook her body almost in perfect time to a band's drum solo taking place just out in the main street. Later, she would be grateful for the noise because it drowned out her screams of forbidden pleasure. Just as Tina was starting to come down off her cloud of ecstasy, Marie stood quickly and kissed her deeply and passionately. As she was sliding her tongue into Tina's mouth, she straddled Tina's knee and began riding it with hungry thrusts. Tina began to feel the wetness accumulating on her bare thigh and knew that Marie was close to her own erotic release. As Marie continued to gyrate against her knee, Tina could taste the sweet dew of herself on Marie's mouth.

Marie suddenly stiffened and then broke into a series of fast thrusts and hip gyrations. Tina could feel moisture sliding down her inner thigh as her beautiful mystery woman threw her head back and howled as her orgasm permeated her seductive body. And then it was over. The women readjusted their costumes, kissed once more and then Marie Antoinette disappeared back into the throngs of people in the street, leaving Tina breathless, wet, and quite satisfied. After taking a moment to process what just happened, Tina slipped out of the cobblestone alley and once again became a part of the massive sea of partying naked bodies.

STORY 7 –
PERSONAL TRAINER

Copyright © 2012 Spirited Sapphire Publishing

Spirited Sapphire Publishing

Well, this is going to be different, thought Janice as she pulled her car into a parking spot at the gym. She always trained alone but she really wanted to have a decent chance of at least placing in the marathon she signed up for. Her body was pretty toned already, but she wanted to build up her strength, endurance and a bit more muscle to give herself the extra edge she knew she would need against her race competitors. Janice was meeting with her personal trainer today who was going to help her do those things, and as quickly as possible.

When Janice walked into the gym, she was floored by the number of gorgeous women that were in various stages of working out. She couldn't help but watch them for a few minutes. Some of them were wearing workout pants with tank tops, and others were wearing little more than shorts and a sports bra. Janice decided that she might just like this gym experience after all. Who wouldn't love to take in the sights and sounds of grunting, sweating, toned women?

While she was standing there and enjoying the scenery of sweaty shirts with erects nipples and teasing peaks of ass cheeks as women were bending over their exercise equipment, a woman walked up to her and asked if she could help her. Janice snapped back into reality and replied that she was meeting with a personal trainer.

"Oh, you must be Janice!" exclaimed the woman. "I'm Monica and I'm going to be your personal trainer." They shook hands and Monica led Janice into the weight room, where she explained to Janice how to use each piece of the equipment. The entire time she was explaining things, Monica was also making a detailed assessment of her new client and she was very impressed with what she saw.

Janice was a bit on the short side, but her body was lean and firm. Monica was especially mesmerized by Janice's enormous breasts, which were struggling to stay contained in her sports bra, and her tight and toned ass that, yes, you could probably literally bounce a quarter off of it. Monica could only think about what it would feel like to touch Janice's very hot body. Little did she know that while she was taking a mind trip through erotic dreamland, that Janice was having her own silent sensual escapade.

Janice was instantly attracted to Monica as soon as she saw her, and their eyes met. When they shook hands, she felt a jolt of excitement travel through her body, and she tried her damndest not to blatantly scan every detail of her delicious body from head to toe. Each time Monica showed Janice another piece of equipment, it seemed as if she stood in just the right position for Janice to not only see her very attractive assets, but also to take in the ever-so-subtle spicy floral scent she was wearing. It's probably a good thing that I have an idea what this equipment does, Janice thought, because I can't concentrate for a damn with this sexy woman's body just inches away from me. In fact, she started to wonder if this was her trainers passive-aggressive offering of some sexual fun, or just her own wishful thinking.

As Janice worked out on each piece of equipment, Monica spots her so that the workout is safe. That wasn't the only reason that she wanted to stand so closely to Janice, though. The sweat was glistening on Janice's skin now, and mixed with her own natural skin pheromones, the combination was creating a unique scent that was secretly driving Monica absolutely wild. She had some sweating of her own going on, as she could feel her panties start to stick to her moistening pussy.

At the end of the hour-long session, Monica gave Janice a slight smack on her ass and congratulated her on a job well done. She then suggested that Janice hit the showers and then enjoy a cool, refreshing glass of wheatgrass juice to replenish the energy that she had used up while working out. Janice was so sweaty that she actually couldn't wait to jump into a nice, cool shower. She headed to the locker room, stripped off her sweaty workout gear and headed with soap and towel in hand to the community shower. No one else was currently using it, so she turned on the water and started to soap her body. As she stood under the jet of cool spraying water, there was suddenly a pair of hands sliding around her from behind and cupping her heavy breasts. She also felt another set of breasts pressing into her back. Janice flew around and came face to face with Monica, who was also naked, wet and needing to be cooled down herself.

"Oh my!" Janice exclaimed. "You startled me!"

"I didn't mean to startle you, Janice. I just wanted to make sure that you were doing ok after your workout since you haven't been used to actual machines. I know how tough it can be on your body the first few times, so I wanted to see if you needed any sore spots massaged."

With that, she started to kiss Janice deeply and with growing hunger. Janice responded passionately, and with that, Monica steered them both into a private shower stall on the other side of the lockers. They continued to kiss and move their hands over each other's slippery bodies. Monica was now able to touch and fondle Janice's magnificent breasts, and Janice had no problem with letting her do so. As the two slid down onto the bench in the shower stall, Monica traced her fingers slowly down Janice's tight stomach, across her smooth, shaved pussy, and then parting her soft delicate lips to locate her pretty pink clit.

Janice was moaning as she felt Monica's fingers skillfully part the folds of her lips to expose her aching little clit. She started to move her hips back and forth as she rode Monica's finger. As she did so, Janice started to kiss and suck on Monica's nipples, which only made Monica even more dedicated in her efforts to please Janice. She slid down Janice's body until she was on her knees in front of her. Moving her hand so that she could see Janice's clit, she saw that it was a bit oversized, much like a tiny cock. Monica was quite excited to get her mouth wrapped around it and started to suck it ever-so-gently, while at the same time, tracing Janice's outer pussy lips with her fingers.

Not only was Janice's clit rather large, but it was also ultra-sensitive. So, when Monica's mouth descended upon it, a low moan rose from Janice's throat, and her hips arched as if she was riding a bucking horse. She placed her hands on Monica's head and pushed against it to make her take in her clit even more. Monica slipped a couple fingers into Janice's eager pussy and started to finger fuck her slowly and deeply.

Janice was in sexual paradise, enjoying the way that Monica was licking and fingering her. She didn't want it to end, but it had been such a long time since she had had such passionate sex with anyone that this was wearing her down pretty quickly. Monica picked up on Janice's dilemma and started to speed up both her mouth and finger. She also added another finger as she fucked Janice's pretty wet little hole, which was now start to pulse and contract around her fingers.

Janice could feel the pressure and heat building in

her pussy. Already the little spasms were starting to take hold, and Monica's mouth and fingers were keeping time with the pulsing sensations. When it hit, Janice lost all control. Suddenly, her entire body tensed and she felt herself cumming over Monica's face and fingers. Monica supported Janice physically, and held her until her body relaxed and slumped back up against the shower wall. Monica leaned forward and gave Janice another of those amazing slow, deep kisses, then started to rise.

"No, wait," Janice said. "There's something I want to do."

With those words, Janice started to fondle Monica's firm tits and draw them into her mouth. Monica was already quite aroused from her sexual exploration of Janice's body, so this was certainly a treat she wasn't about to turn down. She hadn't expected Janice to reciprocate, but she was very happy and grateful that it seemed to be the case. Janice was kissing and sucking Monica's firm little nipples, then started to work her way downward. Her hands slid down around Monica's back and her firm ass, as she kneaded it lovingly. It was now Janice's turn to go to her knees, as she buried her face deep into Monica's clean-shaven mound. Gingerly parting her swollen lips, Janice began licking her, making small little circles around her stiffening clit. As she continued to give Monica the same type of tongue lovin' she had just been the recipient of, it didn't take long for Monica to succumb to her own wild ride of pleasure. In no time, she was moaning and grasping Janice's hair as she rode her face during the climactic finale.

Minutes passed, then Janice slowly rose back to her feet, and the two women kissed once more under the shower spray that was rinsing away all traces of their sexual encounter. They stepped out of the shower, toweled off and got dressed again. Monica left Janice with a look over her shoulder and a mischievous grin.

"I look forward to seeing you at your next training session sexy," she said in a husky voice.

"So do I," Janice responded with a smile. "So do I!"

STORY 8 –
MAY I SEE YOUR LICENSE

Copyright © 2012 Spirited Sapphire Publishing

This is going to be one long trip, thought Hannah, as she drove along the I-10 freeway heading towards Los Angeles from Phoenix. Between the heat, the late hour and her super horny state, Hannah was anxious to reach her destination. I so need this vacation, she thought, as she sipped on the large iced tea that she purchased at the last truck stop. Pulling up her sundress high on her thighs to allow the car's air-conditioning to better cool down her overheated body, she then popped in one of her favorite jazz CD's to help calm her tension, and settled in for another long stretch of highway to get through. Her friends were expecting her by morning and she was hoping to make it before the early morning rush hour. She never liked driving in that mess.

The next couple of hundred miles went by in a pleasant blur thanks to the music. However, the non-stop sexy jazz tunes put her in an even hornier state than she was in before, and she became acutely aware of the growing sensations between her thighs. Hannah was definitely looking forward to seeing her friends and enjoying a week of spontaneous fun with the girls. As her thoughts started to become scattered, Hannah leaned her neck back against the head rest on the seat, and she let her mind drift a little in anticipation of what potential fun was waiting for her at the end of this drive. To help herself along a bit, she moved one of her hands underneath her lavender mini sundress. She quickly slipped a finger inside the crotch of her matching lavender G-string, and sighed out loud as her fingers brushed against her swelling lips. Lazily, she parted those lips to expose her throbbing clit. "Ah yes", she said out loud to herself, that's it right there baby!" She was so horny now, that Hannah was starting to feel herself getting wet, and her clit harden, under the touch of her fingers, as she swirled them all along those soft, smooth pussy lips.

Suddenly, Hannah sees a blue light flashing in her rearview mirror. Slammed back to reality, Hannah's mind is racing. "Is that the cops? Oh shit, shit, shit! What the hell was I doing? I don't think I was speeding. I'm wearing my seatbelt and I'm not drinking." Hannah signaled and pulled over to the side of the highway. She watched as the police car pulled over and right up behind her. Stories started running through her mind about women being pulled over on lonely night roads by police impersonators. Oh god! What if that's what is happening to me? She was fighting down her panic when she saw the officer get out of the car. She looked a little closer and saw that this police officer was a woman, a smoking hot, sexy as hell police woman!

Hannah quickly readjusted her dress and waited for the officer to approach. She couldn't help but notice how well the woman filled out her uniform in spite of her nervousness. Even though it was dark, the lights from the flashing police bar revealed that the lady officer had blond hair, appeared to be above average height, and had this confident, sexy strut as she walked up to Hannah's vehicle. The police woman leaned into Hannah's window and swept the light from her flashlight first all through the car, before then shining it down onto Hannah's body, making her squirm a little in her seat.

"May I see your driver's license and registration, please?"

Hannah didn't feel that it sounded much like a request, though. She started to fumble around in her purse and then her glove compartment to get the required documents.

Handing them over to the law official, she asked "What did I do, officer?", also, noticing that the female officer was doing a head to toe assessment of her, from her vantage point through the window.

"Do you know how fast you were going?" the female officer asked instead of replying.

"No, I don't know for sure but I'm fairly sure that I wasn't speeding." Hannah replied.

"Step out of the car please." The female officer responded, as she stepped back a couple feet to give Hannah room to exit her vehicle.

Hannah was mixed with emotions. She was chasing down lustful thoughts of this gorgeous woman police officer, who stood before her like a Greek goddess, while at the same time, feeling her body start to shake from growing nervousness. What was going on? Since she had always been taught to obey the law, Hannah slowly got out of her car, being extra careful not to make any too sudden movements. The police woman then directed her to walk back toward the police car, walking just a few inches directly behind Hannah. Hannah could almost feel the officer's body touching her own. When they reached the front of the police car, the officer reached inside of it, and shut off the lights and engine in one fell swoop.

"Place your hands on the hood of the car," the officer instructed, in an almost soft and gentle voice. Now officially terrified, Hannah did as she was told. Moving her hands briskly up and down Hannah's body, the officer suddenly slapped a pair of handcuffs on her wrists.

"No! Wait!" Hannah yelled.

Coming up behind her, the officer whispered into her ear telling her that she didn't have to worry, that she was just getting a "warning." With that, Hannah suddenly found her body somewhat unceremoniously sprawled on the hood of the police car. The next thing she knew was that her sundress was pulled quickly up and over her head, leaving her braless, chest bare and the only left covering her body was her lavender G-string.

"Oh, you are incredibly sexy my dear," the officer whispered, looking at Hannah like a hormone enraged alley cat. Then, she began using her mouth, tongue and hands on Hannah's exposed skin. Holding her body against the hood of the police car, the officer began kissing her mouth. Hannah actually responded back to the officers deep, hungry kisses, while at the same time, trying to grasp the surrealness of the moment. The officer then licked a tongue trail down to Hannah's pert little breasts and started sucking on her dark brown nipples. Hannah's body began to respond in spite of herself and she found her hips arching and pressing against the officers utility belt. Her nipples were growing harder with each lick and suckle of the officer's tongue, and, even though she was still in a state of puzzlement, she had to admit that she was wanting to be straight-up fucked by this incredible highway patrolling beauty.

While the officer was sucking and biting on Hannah's left nipple, she was squeezing and fondling the right breast giving Hannah some of the most amazing sensations she's experienced in quite a while. She loved the way that the inner electricity was moving from her nipples straight to her pussy. As the officer goddess continued with the stimulation of Hannah's nipples and breasts, Hannah hips were now gyrating up and down off the hood of the police car. She was now past consciously moving her body, and instead she was just getting lost in the sensations that were flowing through her naked, sprawled form.

Suddenly, her seducing officer started moving her

mouth downward across Hannah's belly. Oh god, was she really going to be feeling this incredible woman's tongue on her pussy? Hannah wanted that more than she wanted anything else right then in this crazy moment and she arched her hips even higher, freely offering herself to her officer goddess. She could already feel the dampness from her pussy moistening the sides of her thighs, and, before she knew it, her silent plea had been answered. She could feel the feathery-light licking of that tongue as it worked on tasting her juices. Not only that, the officer was nibbling her way up towards that precious part of her that she was so praying would soon be receiving attention, because she couldn't take too much more teasing.

Just as that last thought completed itself in Hannah's mind, she felt the tip of the officer's tongue parting her pussy lips, and her mouth carefully wrapped itself around her sweet, rosy clit. As she expertly sucked on Hannah's swollen bud, she slipped a single finger inside of Hannah's now dripping hot pussy. Hannah gasped involuntarily and cried out. She was no longer aware of the occasional truck passing by on the highway, but, she was very aware that her hands were still in cuffs, because she wanted so bad to wrap them around the woman who was bringing her so much pleasure, and feel her curves beneath her hands.

Apparently, that wasn't meant to be, though. Lady officer had a great rhythm going with the way she sucked on Hannah's now very sensitive little clit, while at the same time finger fucking her now pulsating pussy. As horny as Hannah had already been when the police officer first stopped her, there was no way that she was going to last any longer to the sensual play she was receiving. She could feel herself fast approaching her peak and knew she would take her any second.

And, it did. With one hand free, lady officer held Hannah's body down, as it bucked and writhed on the hood of the police car. She rode the officer's finger and mouth over and over until the waves of her orgasm subsided and she came down on the other side, her cries echoing in the night air. While Hannah was still recovering from one of the most intense orgasms she had ever had, not to mention, under the most unusual of circumstances, the female police officer stood up. She pulled up Hannah's G-string and pulled down her sundress to cover up her previously exposed body. She helped her up from the hood of the car, turned her around and unlocked the handcuffs.

With a coy smile on her face, lady police officer then escorted a still weak-kneed Hannah back to her car. She opened the door and helped Hannah back into her car and closed the door.

"You have a nice night gorgeous, and don't forget to drive carefully." The officer stood back from the car and nodded to Hannah.

As Hannah guided her car back onto the freeway, she watched her officer goddess from her rearview mirror get back into her police car. Damn, she is one sexy ass cop, and that was one hell of a 'warning'! Hannah still could hardly believe what had just happened to her. A slow smile started to spread over her face, and she laughed out loud to herself in the car. The girls are never going to believe this!

STORY 9 –
OFFICE ROMANCE

Copyright © 2012 Spirited Sapphire Publishing

Becky and Amy had just enjoyed another wonderful weekend together at their favorite casino. They did a lot of things together socially outside of the advertising agency they both worked for in Dallas. They had become fast friends during the last several months, sharing dinner at their favorite restaurants, checking out live music on the weekends, enjoying cultural events and even helping each other shop for family gifts. The chemistry and comfort level that they both shared was off the charts, and they were both all-too-aware of this fact every time they were together, and even when they were apart. They would probably be even more involved in their relationship, except for the fact that both of them seemed to be a little wary of pursuing a full-fledged relationship since they worked together. You just never knew what was going to happen with office romances. Still, they shared hotel rooms whenever they went away for weekend or overnight business trips, and there was lots of teasing. Lots and lots of teasing and innuendos that continuously caused both of them to silently wonder.........."What if?".

Both women were quite attractive as well as fit. Becky at 36 is very slender with the body of a swimmer, and she favors sexy outfits that show a lot of skin whenever she and Amy go out. Amy, on the other hand, had recently turned 40 and looks a lot like the actress Julianne Moore, right down to her hair color. She prefers outfits that are retro, yet sexy. Both women turn heads whenever they go out, or walk into a room, including each other's.

Since both women were very much into each other, neither of them had formed other romantic relationships with anyone. Therefore, they would each be attending this year's annual holiday office party alone, yet secretly desiring to be there with the other. The annual holiday office party has been known to get more than a little wild in the past, especially between office co-workers that have been feeling those sparks. Becky and Amy might think they're fooling everyone else about their own sparks, but they've only been fooling themselves.

On the night of the party, both women sat at their respective homes sipping cocktails and trying to figure out what to wear. They were both thinking about each other, too. Could this be 'The Night'? Neither could think of a better holiday gift, than the gift of them being together. There was certainly a better chance of something happening tonight than it ever had before, because if anything actually did happened it could just be brushed off as a drunken party incident if necessary, although, they both knew in their hearts that wouldn't be the case.

The women arrived separately but within minutes of each other, and immediately started seeking each other out in the crowd. Becky wore a strapless, red sequined, knee length dress with black heels and simple pearl jewelry. Her blond hair, which she usually wore straight, was done in long, sexy waves, and framed her thin facial features and long neck beautifully. Her outfit emphasized her small but firm breasts and long, lean legs. She was a stunning sight to behold, and everyone took notice. Amy chose a tight, vintage A-line skirt in red and paired it with a white silk blouse and black heels. Her ensemble highlighted her small waist and curvaceous hips and ass. Her magnificent red hair was in a sexy retro upsweep and was adorned by mistletoe. Everyone kept watch of the two from their locations in the private ballroom, as they waited to see if anything was finally going to happen between these sexy, love-struck women. And, because everyone knew how 'things' just sort of have a way of happening at the annual holiday party, everyone watching and waiting was counting on it, as if it was a much anticipated climatic finale of a television series.

At least they watched for the first portion of the party. Eventually, between champagne and harder liquor, the party was in full swing, and co-workers were chatting each other up with lively conversation, dancing uninhibitedly on the dance floor and tables, and spilling their secret desires to their intended object of affection. As can often be the case with office parties, they can sometime turn into drunken orgies of a sort. Many co-workers were starting to sneak off into different dark corners and into whatever private places they could find off of the hotel's ballroom.

Amy had just refilled her martini at the bar, and was going to head to the DJ booth to request a song. As she turned around, she came face to face with Becky, and they stood there silently, staring into each other's eyes. Long, heavy moments passed, as their eyes stayed glued to the others, silently communicating their deepest and truest of feelings. Amy kept thinking how much she wanted Becky and finally decided they were being ridiculous by denying themselves what they both so badly wanted, and what they both knew was so right. And, what Amy also knew was right, was that she was going to take care of this matter, right this moment!

She suddenly grabbed Becky's hand and led her outside and onto the candlelit deck that surrounded the hotel pool. Almost instantly, she spied a two person lounge, enclosed in a 3 sided cabana, and it was close to one of the outdoor fire pits. It's perfect, she thought. Pulling Becky into this space, Amy brought her up against her body, and after a moment's hesitation, did what she had been wanting to do for many long months. Amy gently and passionately began to kiss Becky, in a way that would fully convey her desire for her. Becky responded eagerly, sliding her tongue into Amy's mouth and kissing her full soft lips with alternating kisses of fury, then slow, deep, lingering lip embraces. Their arms found their way around each others bodies, hands roaming, and strained against each other as the softness of their mouths continued their sensual exploration. Their kissing frenzy lasted for several minutes, as they got used to the explosive sensations of being together at last.

Gradually, they started to move their hands as they cautiously, yet enthusiastically explored each other's body. Amy peeled down the front of Becky's sequined dress to expose her tits, and firmly grasped one of her perfectly formed breasts. She could feel her nipple growing hard under the playful toying of her fingers. Becky responded by gasping and kissing Amy even more deeply. Amy then pushed Becky back onto the chaise lounge, and crawled on top of her. She continued kissing Becky as she slid her hands under her dress, and in one fell swoop, slipped off her panties like a magician would rip off a tablecloth from underneath a table full of dishes.

Admiring Becky's silky smooth legs with her hands, Amy now slowly slid down the length of Becky's body and spread her thighs apart to reveal those satiny lips she has so longed to feel and taste. Burying her face directly in Becky's crotch, she used the tip of her tongue to part those satiny folds, and was rewarded with a stiff little rosebud just waiting to be stimulated. That's just what I was looking for, thought Amy, as she started to methodically seduce Becky's clit with her tongue. The more she licked, the more Becky moaned and squirmed in the lounge chair above her.

Those tantalizing, yet tortuous months of longing,

waiting and wondering were now behind the two women, and Amy was going to please her fairytale woman in every way she knew how. She continued on, by wrapping her lips around Becky's clit and sucked and tugged on it ever-so-gently, causing jolts of electrical pleasure to run through Becky from head to toe. No woman had ever taken the time to orally please her, the way Amy was pleasing her in this very moment. Becky both loved and desired the woman before her with all her being, and the fact that their coming together was finally becoming a reality, made her lose control faster and harder than she ever had in her life. Her orgasm hit her out of nowhere and she was trying to stifle her cries from the party happenings going on nearby, as wave after wave of ecstasy rippled through her body.

Becky pulled Amy up, and quickly unbuttoned her blouse and satin white bra, so that she could free and play with her luscious breasts. Sucking a woman's nipples was something that she totally enjoyed and she wanted nothing more than to taste and nibble on Amy's nipples right now. Amy threw her head back and started rubbing her moistening pussy against Becky's thigh, as Becky continued to suck and play with Amy's tits.

Amy's pent-up sexual desire for Becky also caused her to cum rather quickly, and she climaxed within a few minutes, just from Becky's seductive mouth play and rubbing her panty covered pussy against her thigh. She wanted more, though, and moved back down between Becky's thighs once more. Using her tongue once more on Becky's clit, this time she slid a finger into her soaking, contracting little pussy. Just as Becky started to cum once more, they heard their names being called from across the other side of the pool area.

"Oh great, it's time for the Holiday Grab Bag!" said Amy a bit sarcastically.

"Yes, we definitely wouldn't want to miss that!" Becky said, giggling and pulling up her panties.

They quickly both fixed their clothes and headed back to the party wearing a glow that neither of them could deny, or hide. As they walked back into the hotel, they were met with lots of knowing looks and smiles. It was as if their co-workers had indeed just witnessed their desired climatic ending, and new beginning, of the love saga between Amy and Becky.

Amy looked over at Becky and smiled at her. "Happy holidays, baby," she said.

Becky smiled back, and replied, "Happy holidays beautiful!"

STORY 10 – ESCORT

Wow, thought Liz. I can finally relax! It had been such a long turbulent flight from Los Angeles to New York City, so she didn't really mind the two day layover in New York. And, the hotel where the flight crew was being put-up had amazing amenities to enjoy right there. The rest of the flight crew was already making plans for a wild, all-nighter on the town, but Liz wasn't in the mood for bar hopping, loud music and drunken madness this evening.

She had gone straight to her room, threw her bags in the closet and stripped. Now, lying nude and exhausted across the bed, she was reflecting just how often she was away from home as compared to when she was there. Yes, she did get to see the world, and that was all great, but she also found it difficult to maintain a true relationship. She was also bored and lonely a lot in all ways. At 28, she figured she still had some time before she needed to revamp her lifestyle. But for now, she really was longing to enjoy the company of a beautiful, intelligent, and sexy woman, even if it was for just one night.

As she relaxed on the bed, Liz started to thumb through the entertainment books that were supplied by the hotel. She looked through several of them before she came upon a full page color ad for an upscale escort agency. There were photos of scantily clad, available women that were just a phone call away from giving someone some one on one pleasure. The photos themselves literally made Liz breathless, and, just looking at some of them gave her instant tingles between her legs. Then there was the whole one-on-one pleasure thing. Liz's body was buzzing with arousal and she started to seriously contemplate calling one of these escort agencies, for some woman-to-woman fun this evening.

After pondering this delicious thought for a minute, Liz decided to call and see if she could get a girl. Men did it all the time, so why couldn't she? But what if they didn't service lesbians? Well, it didn't say anything about it being a men only service. There was only one way to find out.

Liz called the agency and was thrilled to find out that there were more than a dozen women that provided outcall services to women. The receptionist that Liz spoke with asked her for any preferences she had, and promised to send the perfect woman to spend some time with her that night. So Liz booked the appointment and started to get ready for some quality sensual time with her professional Lady of the Evening. She took a shower, and then spent some time re-styling her hair, and putting on fresh makeup. Finally, she donned a sexy black satin bra and panty set, spritzed on some heedy Egyptian musk, and put on some long, silver hoop earrings that accented her jet black hair perfectly. Glancing in the mirror, to check that all was in place, Liz had to admire her well kept, feminine figure. Her dark, black hair accentuated the creamy white tone of her skin. Her long, lean legs triggered compliments from passengers daily. And, her breasts certainly didn't need a bra for support, as they were firm and perky with pale pink nipples, that silently commanded to be touched by anyone who had the privilege of seeing them bared.

In just a little over an hour, Liz heard a soft knock on her hotel room door. She leapt up and quickly went to the door. Peeking through the security hole in the door, she saw that her lady had arrived. Her pulse suddenly racing, she took a deep breath and opened the door.

What she saw standing before her, sent sensations zooming straight to her crotch. While Liz continued to stand there, the lovely creature introduced herself.

"You must be Liz," she said in a sultry voice. "I'm Miranda."

"Oh yes, of course! I'm Liz. Please come in! It's wonderful to meet you, Miranda!"

Liz nervously finally was able to arrange her face into a welcoming smile. But she just couldn't stop staring. Miranda was tall with long blonde hair and dark, hypnotic brown eyes. She was wearing a light colored, long trench coat and a pair of black stiletto heels. Slowly, she removed the trench coat and treated Liz to view of her form, which included a pair of ample breasts sitting on a perfectly toned, slim body. Liz had no problem noticing this because Miranda wore only a black fishnet teddy underneath the coat.

Tossing her coat onto one of the chairs in the sitting area, Miranda walked over to the in-room bar. As she looked inside to see what was available, she happened to spy a bottle of unopened champagne that was still chilling in a bucket of ice on the table next to the mini bar. It was compliments of the hotel.

"Wow, this is actually pretty good champagne," she said. "Let me pour us some, and let's relax and enjoy ourselves."

Liz got comfortable on the king sized bed and watched Miranda's sexy body move about in her see-through teddy as she opened the champagne and poured them each a glass. Holding up her champagne flute to Liz, they clinked and toasted each other. Miranda got comfortable next to Liz on the bed, and as they sipped champagne and made small talk, they soon realized that there was a powerful attraction happening between the two. As they chatted, Miranda slowly started to rub Liz's leg with her hand. The more she talked the higher her hand traveled up Liz's thigh, and Liz was all too aware of how close her fingers were to her throbbing pussy.

Stopping just short of the crotch of Liz's pretty little black panties, she reached over and took Liz's glass from her hand and sat it on the nightstand. Leaning in close to her face, Miranda whispered, "You're so very beautiful." Then she started to gently paint her lips with tender, passionate kisses.

Those tender kisses soon transformed into a sultry, lioness-style mouth and tongue party, and the women were sliding their tongues in and out of each other mouths, while sucking and nibbling on each others lips. Pushing Liz back onto the bed, Miranda then did a slow cat crawl up her body. Still kissing Liz, Miranda took one of her hands up and over head. Before Liz knew what was going on, she was slipped into a fuzzy pair of handcuffs.

"Now," Miranda whispered. "You have to be very still so that I can give you what you know you want."

Miranda started to kiss and lick her way down to Liz's firm, round breasts. When she reached them, she slipped her long, red fingernail under the front opening of Liz's sexy bra. Her breasts sprang forward like they were escaping. Miranda started to run her tongue all around each of Liz's nipples and suckled them into hardened little peaks, until Liz was practically whimpering.

"Shhh," Miranda said. "Save your strength kitten, because you're going to need it."

Then, she continued to kiss and lick her way down Liz's body until she got to the top of her panties. Using her teeth, she pulled Liz's panties down all the way down to her ankles. Now, she had Liz completely naked. It made her want to taste her, which is just what she did as she slid her tongue between the glistening folds that cloaked Liz's pleasure bud. Licking all around Liz's lips and clit started producing lots of moisture from her neglected pussy. Miranda giggled low and crawled back up to Liz's face. Kissing her full on the mouth, she allowed Liz to share in the tasting of the sweet honey her pussy was producing.

Liz loved everything that Miranda was doing to her and it wasn't all just because she hadn't had any physical pleasure in such a long time. She felt as if Miranda had her captured in a seductive prison and was holding her hostage to the sweet sensual torment that she was dealing her. Miranda renewed her pussy play, and her warm tongue and lips felt so damn good against Liz's aching and stiff little clit. Liz arched her hips upward in an effort to receive more of Miranda's ever-skilled mouth and tongue.

Miranda licked small slow circles around it at first, and only picked up the pace when she knew that Liz was getting close. That's when she started to lick faster and faster as she slid a finger into Liz's already pulsating pussy, finger fucking her in rhythm with her tongue. Liz's body was stiffening, and Miranda knew she was getting ready to cum. Handcuffed to the bed, Liz couldn't move much, but she certainly started bucking wildly when those currents of orgasm started to run through her body. It seemed to go on wave after wave. Just when she thought she would die from pleasure, Miranda un-cuffed her, and turned her over.

She helped her get onto all fours on the bed and got behind her. Slowly, Miranda slid three of her fingers deep into Liz's soaking pussy from behind. Oh god, thought Liz. I can't get enough of this woman! She smells so sexy and I love the way she's finger fucking me! She's going to make me cum again!

Miranda had many sexual talents, and her finger-fucking talents were grade A! Liz's next orgasm hit her with all of the subtlety of a tidal wave. Her pussy sucked in Miranda's fingers and held them there until her inner contractions subsided. With that, she collapsed onto the bed and turned over. Miranda leaned over Liz and kissed her long and deep, and with a sexy, confident look of accomplishment.

"I better get going, sexy," she said. "But I'm going to leave my card for you on the nightstand, so you can look me up the next time you come back in town."

"You're quite the temptress, Miranda," said Liz, smiling. She reached over and picked up her purse from the nightstand and got out her wallet.

"Oh, you already took care of that on the phone," said Miranda quickly.

"Yes, I know. But I want to give you a tip for the most amazing sex I've had in a very long time."

Miranda took the money and kissed Liz once more. Smiling, she covered her curvaceous, naked body with her trench coat, and out the door she went. Liz fell very contently to sleep, knowing that she had something, or rather someone, to look forward to on her future layovers in New York!

STORY 11 –
THE WATCHER

Copyright © 2012 Spirited Sapphire Publishing

Ah, there they are! The Watcher thought. Such a beautiful couple they were, her Maggie and Sue. It's been so wonderful since they moved into the apartment building across the way from hers. It's also wonderful that they rarely close the drapes over their floor-to-ceiling windows of their living room. She knows that they find the view of Chicago amazing, just as she does, but they have no idea that she finds the view of the two of them just as amazing!

The Watcher's parents couldn't have given her a better gift for Christmas. The high-powered telescope, intended to be for viewing the fabulous star constellations of the night skies, gave The Watcher an accidental....ok, not so accidental....view of some of her neighbors a few months back, and ever since she first laid eyes on the beautiful female couple across the way, she's been hooked. And, after the first time The Watcher bore witness to Maggie and Sue walking around naked and having sex, she has been a dedicated and very appreciative voyeur. Yeah, stars are wonderful to look at, but those sexy bare breasts and firm round asses of her obsessions were much more titillating then whatever the current zodiac star alignment happened to be.

It's Friday night, and The Watcher thought she saw Maggie and Sue leaving earlier and headed in the direction of what she knew was their favorite restaurant. She wondered if they'd be back soon to enjoy each others company at home, or if they were going to make it an all-nighter out on the town. Sometimes they did that. Oh wait! Is that them coming home now? Yes, yes it is them! The Watcher was suddenly quite excited, and aroused, as she realized it just might turn out to be a tantalizing evening of 'star body' gazing after all.

Ah, it looks like Maggie is putting on some music. Where did Sue go? Maybe she went to bathroom. There she is! She's coming back now. The Watcher notices that Sue is carrying a bottle of wine, or maybe champagne, and a couple of glasses. She is wearing a silky black robe, that is barely covering her perfect round ass cheeks, and as she bends over to fill the two glasses, The Watcher gets a grade-A view of that ass that sends some tingling sensations coursing through her belly. The girls take a sip of their wine and start to move in close to each other. Oh, it looks like they're going to undress each other. Sue pulled what looked to be a one-piece sundress over Maggie's head and....Wow! The Watcher gasped in a whisper to herself. Maggie had on a really sexy, see-through black teddy that revealed her ample firm breasts! The Watcher had on so many occasions, fantasized about sucking, nibbling and fondling those gorgeous orbs. That body of Maggie's just didn't quit. Add with those long legs and high tight ass of hers, it was the perfect fantasy recipe that had given The Watcher many happy dreams.

Maggie untied the sash from Sue's robe and helped glide it over her shoulders, where it then fell onto the floor around her feet. Sue was wearing red tonight, in the form of a corset with a lace up front. Her body was rather petite in comparison to Maggie's, but it was still breathtakingly gorgeous. Sue had pert little breasts where Maggie's were full and round, and Sue's legs were incredibly toned, probably because she took those ballet exercise classes. The Watcher guessed she did this for fitness rather than any real desire to be a professional dancer. Her shoulder length auburn hair was pulled back at the moment and The Watcher took notice of Sue's stunning almond-shaped green eyes. She could imagine that Maggie often got lost in those beautiful eyes, and it made The Watcher feel envious of the obvious harmony and connection of the two beauties across the way.

Maggie struck a wonderful contrast to Sue. Her hair was a wheat-blonde and cut in a short but stylish fashion. Her piercing blue eyes 'spoke' with depth and passion, as The Watcher had seen on many occasions when she was watching the two of them make love through her telescope. She watched them now as they toasted each other, and wrapped their arms around one another, face and lips only a breath apart. Their eyes appeared locked, and they seemed to be so totally into each other. The Watcher guessed that a slow song was playing now, because the women moved closer to the windows, and bodies pressed together, they began swaying slowly in an erotic hip grinding fashion. This was definitely worth all of the rushing The Watcher did to get home tonight.

Maggie and Sue looked so sexy dancing together like that, but it was nothing compared to the sparks that started flying when they began kissing each other. The kisses turned deep and passionate, as their bodies sank to the living room floor. Oh yes, yes, The Watcher thought enthusiastically. They're going to have sex! This was just what she had hoped for. She readjusted her telescope lens so that she was getting the closest, most intimate possible view of the two women, as their bodies entwined with one another on the floor.

Maggie seemed to be taking the lead this time, as she moved her lips down Sue's neck and spent some time on each of her nipples, sucking them and gently pulling on them with her teeth. The Watcher absently moved her hand up to her own breasts, and started to lightly caress and tug on one her already hardening nipples through her thin blouse. She continued to watch as Maggie now moved her mouth from Sue's breasts down across her taut stomach, while at the same time unlacing Sue's corset, until she finally completed her journey across skin and lace, and Sue's naked body lay sprawled and glistening with moisture from Maggie's kissing and suckling. The area between The Watcher's thighs started to tighten and tingle, as if she could feel Maggie's mouth doing the same erotic dance across her own body.

Thinking in those terms, The Watcher moved her own hand down across her stomach, and then back up, as she started to unbuttoned her blouse. She managed to get it completely unbuttoned and removed while never taking her eye from the telescope and her unfettered view of Maggie and Sue. Now, she was able to unclasp her bra, free her aching tits and start playing with her nipples, while she watched the couple in her view finder as things really started to get hot and steamy between them.

Maggie was spreading Sue's thighs apart, as she slid the matching red thong down and off her legs. The Watcher felt a thrill of excitement pulse through her own body, as she watched Maggie skillfully use her tongue to begin licking and sucking on Sue's smooth pussy lips. As she continued to watch, she moved her hand down to where she could slide it up under her skirt. Reaching her destination, The Watcher wasn't surprised to find the crotch of her panties already slightly moistened from her growing arousal. She quickly removed her skirt and panties to have better access to her own pussy lips, and as she stood there naked looking through her telescope, she heard herself moan as her body was filled with mounting sexual arousal and tension.

Sue was moving her hips in a way that The Watcher could tell she was riding against Maggie's mouth. Ah, yes, she thought. She could almost feel Maggie's sweet mouth on her own pussy, as she spread her swollen lips with her fingers and gently began circling her hardened clit. Suddenly, there was a change in the scene. Sue seemed to be saying something to Maggie and tugging on her lightly. Then, The Watcher understood. Sue felt like she was missing out on the action a bit, so she was having Maggie change positions. Now, the women were in a perfect 69 position, and The Watcher could barely keep standing as she simultaneously watched the pair through the lens while stroking her now very wanton pussy.

Soon, it was easy to see that Maggie and Sue were using their mouths, tongues and fingers on each other. The Watcher could tell that there was lots of movement, and it seemed to be getting a bit more frantic. It only made sense that Sue was the first to reach her pivotal moment since Maggie had been stimulating her for a while. The Watcher saw Sue throw back her head, with her mouth formed in the shape of an 'O', and even though she couldn't actually hear her, it was more than obvious that she was in the throes of a very intense orgasm. The Watcher slipped a finger into her soaking pussy as she witnessed Sue's pleasure, and within just a couple minutes, her own orgasmic contractions began. Holding onto the telescope, The Watcher continued to view Sue thrashing as she, herself, clinched her thighs together, squeezing her hand as she rode wave after wave of pleasure.

Sue calmed finally, and went back to pleasing Maggie with her mouth and tongue. It was clear that Maggie was also getting close to falling over the edge of that cliff of ecstasy. The Watcher tried to keep her focus, but as soon as Maggie started to ride Sue's face, it was just too much for her. Rapidly finger fucking her dripping pussy, The Watcher lost all control as her knees grew too weak to hold her up and she collapsed to the floor in another, even more intense orgasm.

The Watcher tried to catch her breath quickly, but that just wasn't going to happen. It was several minutes before she had returned to reality, and was able to stand once again. She put her eye back to the telescope to get one more peek at her lovely ladies. The Watcher smiled slightly as she watched Maggie and Sue, naked and arms around each other, turning off the lights as they strolled out of the living room together. Oh, how she so enjoyed these secret Friday night rendezvous!

STORY 12 – LAP DANCE

Copyright © 2012 Spirited Sapphire Publishing

Gwen looked at her face critically in the mirror after completing her makeup. I don't actually look 30, she thought. She had actually been carded the day before when she bought a bottle of wine. So she knew she was holding up well.

She knew this birthday had to come, but for some reason she was feeling old, even though 30 is so very far from being old and 'over-the-hill'. Was it because she had been single for far too long? Was it because she hadn't had sex in well over 6 months, and she was longing for the physical company of a beautiful woman? She wasn't sure, but, now that her birthday was here, Gwenn was pretty much ok with it. Besides, her friends were taking her out for what they called a "proper celebration." It sounded like it was going to be a fun evening, as it always is when they go out, even though they hadn't told her where exactly they were going. They did instruct her to dress "hot" though, and Gwenn complied. She now stood viewing herself in the full-length mirror of her bedroom wearing a sexy, white mini-skirt and a halter style top showing generous cleavage, and a toned bare back. Her sandals were Grecian style with lace ups winding around her calves almost up to her knees. The gold hoop earrings and bracelets helped complete her Greek goddess look for the evening, and with the contrast of her long, jet-black hair, she had to admit she looked pretty damn good for just turning 30.

Gwen checked her appearance once more, and with a nod of inner-approval, decided that she was ready for her fun birthday night out with the girls. She sat back on her plush living room couch and thumbed through a magazine while waiting for her friends to arrive. While waiting, she pondered just where they could possibly be taking her. She was hoping it was someplace fun and different, and perhaps even packed with sexy, available women.

When they girls arrived, they insisted that Gwenn wear a blindfold because they wanted the destination to be a complete surprise. So, after admonishing them to be careful of her makeup, she allowed them to blindfold her. They all had a great time in the car giggling and making jokes until Sharon, the driver, finally stopped and parked the car. Gwen was then led out of the car and across what seemed to be a paved parking lot. Suddenly, she was told to be careful because they were going down several steps. Her friends helped her navigate the steps, and Gwen's curiosity was definitely peaking, especially as she heard the growing noise of music. After what seemed like a forever-long few minutes, the group stopped and Gwen's blindfold was whisked off of her face.

"Surprise!" they all cried.

Gwen's mouth fell open when she saw where they were standing. They were at the entrance of The Grecian Garden!

"Oh my god!" screamed Gwen. This was exactly the sort of night she was hoping that her naughty girlfriends had planned for her. At 30, she really needed to cut loose and let her hair down. She wanted, and needed, to feel young and this was the perfect place to do it. What an amazing coincidence, that she chose to don her Greek goddess look for the evening, as she fit right in with all the other Grecian-dressed beauties.

The Grecian Garden was an underground strip club for lesbians, and was very popular among her friends. She had never been here before but always wanted to visit it. Now, she hugged each of her friends in turn and told them how thrilled she was with their choice of birthday celebration venue.

"Come on! Let's get in there and have some fun!" Gwen cried.

They all laughed and headed toward the entrance where there were male bouncers, the only males in sight. These guys stamped their hands and took their money, then motioned for them to enter. The place is jam packed with women of all shapes, sizes, ages, and appearances. Gwen loved the Greek goddess theme that it was all decorated in. She was particularly enjoying the waitresses. They were wearing short, white mini-skirts, strappy heels, and golden leaved wreaths in their hair. The best part, though, is that these gorgeous women were all topless! Her eyes were all over the place because there was just so much activity and so much to see…...yes, so very much beautiful, naked flesh to see.

Gwen was, again, thrilled to see that her enterprising friends had somehow managed to reserve a table just for them right next to the stage. This was going to be so fantastic! They were just in time for a new dancer to enter the stage and as they're settling into their seats and giving their drink orders, the music changed into something darker and deeper with lots of drum beats.

Gwen looked up to watch as one of the most beautiful women she'd ever seen strutted onto the stage. She was probably close to 6 feet tall, and wearing an amazing, and very sultry, warrior outfit. It was made out of a type of dark brown leather, low cut and very short. With gold details and a red cape, it was topped off with a set of matching wrist cuffs and gold Venus shoes. She was carrying a sword. Her long black hair swung behind her almost down to her waist, and as she moved about the stage and looked out into the crowd, her dark brown eyes took command of every woman she laid them on, including Gwenn.

Gwen was completely mesmerized, and instantly in lust with this woman. That was nothing, though, compared to the electrical sensations she felt surging throughout her body as the first pieces of the warrior goddess's costume were removed. The music was perfect for the way this dancer powerfully, yet seductively, moved her way across the stage. Her name was, appropriately enough, Aphrodite, and she was every bit as perfect as one would expect. As she whipped off the top part of her costume, she exposed a golden push up bra that she used to show off her round, luscious breasts. The skirt part was the next to go. Underneath she was wearing a golden G-string that matched her bra.

Soon, Aphrodite was spinning around the dancing pole that was placed in the center of the stage for just that purpose. Coming off of the pole, she gyrated her sexy full hips and perfectly rounded ass, while swiveling her sword in a very suggestive manner. She made her way very close to Gwen and leaned over just as she unsnapped the back of her gold bra. Gwen ended up with two large, bouncy breasts inches from her face, and, as if in a trance, she took a $5 bill and placed it between this goddess's breasts, taking the opportunity to brush the back of her hand across those smooth, luscious orbs.

Encouraged by the $5 bill, Aphrodite stood up and danced her way all over the stage once more with her long, toned and muscular legs before making her way back to Gwen. She spread her thighs just over Gwen's head and posed her near-naked, glistening body above her. Sure enough, Gwen took another $5 and tucked it into the side of the golden G-string.

Gwen's friends were watching the interaction

between their friend and Aphrodite. Sharon's eyes started gleaming with the beginning of an idea. She whispered something to Sabrina, who got up and left the table. In the meantime, Aphrodite was coming to the end of her performance and taking a final bow amid the whistles, applause and catcalls. The expression on Gwen's face was priceless, and her friends covertly sprung into action.

Sabrina had discreetly returned to the table and nodded slightly at Sharon. Gwen missed it all, because she was still looking towards the elevated dance floor and dreaming about the very beautiful Aphrodite who had just adorned the stage with her presence. Gwenn looked over at her friends and said," Was she not the hottest creature that you've ever seen?"

"Oh yes, she's a looker alright!"

"Totally gorgeous!"

"I wouldn't mind having some of that!"

There was a lot more murmuring over the incredible stripper. Suddenly, Gwen looked up to see Aphrodite approaching their table and her eyes lit right up!

"Good evening, ladies," Aphrodite said in a sultry voice. "I'm looking for a birthday girl named Gwen."

While her friends all pointed to her, Gwen was struck speechless. Oh, what had her crazy, wonderful friends done to her now? Aphrodite made her way over to Gwen and took her by the hand.

"Come on, Baby," she said. "You've got a birthday gift waiting in the VIP Lounge."

With that, she led Gwen away from her table of cheering friends, and went up a set of stairs at the back of the club. Aphrodite was wearing the cape from her outfit but Gwen could tell that she was still only wearing her gold G-string and Venus shoes. They walked into a main room in the VIP Lounge that held another, smaller stage, and it was like another complete club upstairs. There were fewer patrons up here, as well as all of these little rooms that cut off of the main VIP Lounge. It was to one of these smaller rooms that Aphrodite led Gwen.

There was a purple, velvet cushioned chair sitting almost in the middle of the room as well as a matching purple velvet loveseat and end table sitting against one wall. Aphrodite locked the door and led Gwen over to the chair. The room was seductively lit by flickering flame light bulbs on the wall, and sultry Moroccan-like music was playing through speakers hidden flush in the walls.

"Sit down, sweetheart," she said. "I'm going to give you a full 30 minutes of the best birthday present you've ever had."

Aphrodite started to dance up close and personal in front of her. Oh my god, thought Gwen, as her body immediately responded to the dancer's musky-like perfume and nakedness slithering just inches away from her. Gwen's pussy was already responding and moistening with her own sweet dew, as her hips rocked gently back and forth on the chair. This beautiful Amazon Goddess straddled Gwen as she performed snake like moves just inches from Gwen's body. Gwen's mouth went dry as she was biting her bottom lip to contain any moaning, while she watched Aphrodite's nipples come closer and closer to her mouth. Those luscious tits were within licking range, and it took every ounce of self-control for Gwen to keep from touching her sexy, private dancer.

Gwen wasn't completely clear on the rules of

engagement in their private room, so she kept her hands and legs firmly planted and still. Ok, not so still, they were trembling with want. It got even worse when Aphrodite put a leg up on the chair and poised her crotch just inches from Gwen's face. She was so close, that Gwen could see the outline of her lips through the thin gold G-string, and she longed to explore them with her mouth and tongue. Still, Gwen stayed in place, trying to calm her breathing so she wouldn't hyperventilate from sexual tension and frustration.

Just when she thought she might die of pent-up pleasure, Gwen got another shock. While Aphrodite was dancing over her, she suddenly started to run her fingers over the outside of Gwen's halter top and teasing her nipples through it. Gwen gasped and arched her back against the chair, letting her body language signal the 'go ahead' to Aphrodite, however, Aphrodite didn't' stay there. She moved her hands even further down Gwen's body as she danced her way down to her knees.

She slid her hand up Gwen's mini-skirt and slipped a finger just inside of Gwen's thong panties. Instantly, she found Gwen's stiff little clit and started moving circles around it.

"Mmm," Aphrodite murmured. "You're so nice and wet. You must really like me, hmm? I bet you'd like nothing more than to feel my mouth on your pussy right now, am I right?"

Gwen managed to nod and groan at the same time. Immediately, Aphrodite slipped her head under Gwen's skirt and flicked the tip of her tongue across Gwen's warm swollen clit. Gwen gasped again and moved her hips so that she was riding Aphrodite's tongue. She still wasn't sure if she was allowed to touch Aphrodite or not, but she put her hands lightly on the back of her head. However, she quickly removed them because she was afraid she would lose control and push Aphrodite's head into her pussy.

Gwen was so far off in pussy wonderland, literally dazed and confused into a blissful state as she leaned back and received the most expert of tongue lashings. Just when she was sure it couldn't get any better, Aphrodite added another touch. She slid two fingers inside of Gwen's now very wet tunnel of love, and started to slide them in-and-out in time with the circles she was making with her tongue around her clit.

Gwen was starting to squirm uncontrollably, as Aphrodite rhythmically continued plunging her fingers deep inside of her. Oh my god, I'm going to cum, Gwen thought. I hope that's not against the rules! Just as quickly as that thought entered her mind, it left, as her body stiffened to the sudden onset of climax. She couldn't have stopped it if her life depended upon it. Instead, she grasped the sides of the chair, wrapped her legs around Aphrodite's shoulders, and rode her face and fingers for all she was worth.

As Gwen was catching her breath, Aphrodite gave her clit and pussy a final teasing lick and straightened up her skirt. Then she stood up and leaned down to give Gwen a kiss. Gwen could taste herself on Aphrodite's mouth. Aphrodite straightened up and smiled down at Gwen.

"Happy Birthday sweetheart. Now I better return you to your friends before they send out a search party." Aphrodite took Gwen's hand and helped her stand. With another quick kiss, she led the way in the same direction that they had come in, and back downstairs. She delivered Gwen, who was still in a daze, to her table near the stage and waved at the girls.

Gwen's friends started talking all at once, bombarding her with questions. She simply held up a hand to silence them.

"This has been an exceptionally happy birthday, and I've got to thank you for the greatest present ever. Now, order me a drink, and I'll tell you all about it." Then she smiled a private little smile because she knew she would remember this birthday for the rest of her life.

Spirited Sapphire Publishing

STORY 13 –
ANNUAL CHECK-UP

I wonder if other women actually look forward to their yearly gynecological checkup, Abby thought, as she made the 45 minute drive to Dr. Nichols' office. I really should have changed doctors when I moved last year, she thought. But I'm so comfortable with Dr. Nichols. She's perfect for me. She's a tremendous doctor; never mind that I'm unbelievably attracted to her. Again, she had to laugh at herself. Every time she heard women talking about how much they dreaded their gynecological exams, all she could think about, was how hard she had to try to not get sexually turned on during hers.

At 42, you would think that I should be past all of this "crush" stuff, Abby thought. It just wasn't that easy, though. Dr. Nichols bore a striking resemblance to the gorgeous actress, Maria Bello, only taller. Not only that, Dr. Nichols was British and that sexy accent drove Abby absolutely wild. Abby even played with the idea of getting check-ups every 6 months, just so she could feel Dr. Nichols gently hands against her skin.

Trying to tamp down her excitement, Abby checked in with the receptionist and took a seat next to an oversized aquarium. Why do doctor's offices have aquariums? Abby pondered. Was it to calm the patients? Instead of having a fish tank, why not have a mermaid tank, which would be much more hypnotic, she thought, while letting out a slight chuckle. Within just a few minutes, Abby was called back to an examination room. The nurse left her with one of those fashionable paper gowns, and told her the doctor would be in to see her shortly. She undressed and donned the paper barrier that is intended to afford the patient a bit of privacy and dignity. Sitting on the edge of the examination table, Abby mindlessly caressed the sides of her thighs while fantasizing of what it might be like if Dr. Nichols and she had some quality time together......sans the paper gown. The very thought hardened Abby's nipples, and she could feel them chafing against the slightly rough paper material, which only served to arouse her more.

Suddenly, there was a quick knock on the door, and Dr. Nichols entered the room. She greeted Abby and sat down on the rolling stool next to the exam table. Her very presence was intoxicating to Abby, and she could immediately feel the heat of arousal flush her body. Dr. Nichols had an air of confidence and stature that was damn sexy. Then there were those breathtaking facial features of slightly plump lips, deep brown eyes and high check bones that made Abby just want to lean in and kiss the hell out of her. Abby tried to remain composed, as she rather absentmindedly answered Dr. Nichols questions asking if anything had changed since her last exam. Dr. Nichols then instructed Abby to lie back on the table, put her feet in the stirrups and situate her butt at the edge of the table. As Abby positioned herself, she watched Dr. Nichols lithe form intently as she rose from the chair and stood by the table over Abby.

"Would you please open your gown Abby, so I can do a breast exam" Instructed Dr. Nichols. Abby was concerned that her now somewhat heavy breathing would be obvious, once Dr. Nichols hands began probing her breasts. Abby spread open her gown to bare her tits and still hard nipples, and tried to relax while secretly anticipating those gentle hands on her naked flesh.

As they continued to talk, Dr. Nichols performed a very thorough breast exam, which quite literally started the juices flowing in Abby's pleasure center by the time she had finished. Next, Dr. Nichols moved to the bottom of the exam table, and Abby took notice that Dr. Nichols had left her gown open, leaving her tits still bared. Not able to control her arousal, Abby flushed at the thought of Dr. Nichols about to discover her moistened pussy, when she continued on with the internal part of the exam. Nonchalantly, Dr. Nichols continued to chat with Abby as she put on a pair of latex gloves and slid a couple gloved fingers inside of Abby to check her ovaries and uterus. It may have been an exam to Dr. Nichols, but Abby could feel herself getting embarrassingly wet the more her gorgeous doctor probed her. She actually was afraid she might start groaning with pleasure if the exam went on much longer.

Finally, Dr. Nichols withdrew her fingers from Abby, and she started to sit up.

"No, no, Abby, can you please just stay there for a minute?" Dr. Nichols said as she got up from her little stool.

"Oh sure," Abby replied. "Is there something wrong?"

"No, no, Abby," Dr. Nichols said. "In fact, I think there just might be something truly right."

Abby watched as Dr. Nichols locked the door and then walked back over to her. Next, she took Abby's hand gently into hers and looked her directly in the eyes.

"Please call me Emma," she said, forming those lips into a seductive smile. "I noticed that you've become quite turned on during my examination of you, and I have to admit to a bit of an attraction to you as well. I can't possibly let you leave here until you've been fully and intimately examined."

With that, she started to unbutton her lab coat. The lab coat was quickly followed by the rest of her clothing, and in a matter of less than a minute, beautiful Dr.

Nichols......Emma, was standing in front of Abby completely naked. Abby found herself caught between shock and uncontainable lust. Did she nod off and start dreaming, or was her doctor-patient fantasy actually coming true?

Emma's body was just as gorgeous as Abby had often imagined it might be. Full, teardrop-shaped breasts with dusky rose areolas and suckable, puffy nipples that jutted out from a body with a curved in waist, slim hips and a toned, tight ass. All Abby could do was stare in wonder as this beautiful woman instructed her to keep her feet in the stirrups and lay back down.

Abby gasped as Emma bent over her and placed her lips against Abby's. This is something that Abby had only ever dreamed of, and the moment was so surreal, she wasn't even certain what was happening was reality. As soon as Emma slipped the tip of her tongue into Abby's mouth, she knew that this was definitely real. It was a moment in time that she would always remember. As Emma deepened their kiss, she ran her hands over Abby's exposed breasts and gently tweaked and tugged on her nipples. Abby could also feel Emma's own nipples, as they were brushing back and forth against her sides.

Only then did Emma break their kiss, and it was so that she could focus on gently sucking and nibbling Abby's nipples. Abby's response was to arch her back and put a hand behind Emma's head so that she could take her nipples into her mouth even further. Then, Emma broke contact with Abby's nipples and started to lick a trail down across her stomach.

Abby prayed that Emma's mouth might soon be on that part of her body that was so aching for her touch. As if Emma read her mind, she moved in that very direction. Reseating herself on the stool she had so recently vacated, she had clear access to Abby's neatly shaven, pretty pink lips. She didn't even need to part the folds that usually hid her clit. With her feet still in the stirrups and her legs spread open, Abby's pussy lips were already parted, allowing Emma to put her mouth directly on Abby's erect little bud and start alternating between licking and sucking.

Abby was biting her bottom lip so that she wouldn't cry out in ecstasy. Emma certainly knew exactly where and how to touch her. Maybe she picked-up a few secret techniques during her residency. As she continued her attention on Abby's clit, Emma suddenly slid a finger into Abby's tight and soaking pussy. Being a gynecologist, it came as no surprise that Emma knew exactly where that delightful G-spot was located, and just how to manipulate it.

This became even clearer as Abby's pussy started contracting around Emma's finger. As her orgasm took control of her body, Abby's hips started to gyrate and she came completely off of the table several times. However, the thing that shocked her was that something happened to her that never had before. She actually squirted! To her total humiliation later, she realized that she had completely soaked Emma's face and chest. Emma laughed it off, though. In fact, she even thought that it was quite hot.

As the women cleaned up and got dressed, Emma slipped Abby a piece of paper with her personal cell number written on it.

"That's in case you don't want to wait a full year before seeing me again," she said as she winked at Abby. With that, Emma unlocked the door and went off to see her next patient.

Spirited Sapphire Publishing

STORY 14 – SUBMISSIVE PLAY

Copyright © 2012 Spirited Sapphire Publishing

Spirited Sapphire Publishing

Kelly was so happy to be done with her work day. Sure, it had been another win for her in the courtroom, but then, she never expected any less from herself. For that matter, neither did her clients. Kelly's much-sought-after services as a celebrity attorney did not come cheap. In fact, she charged some of the highest attorney fees in her state of California. People paid them without complaint, though; because they knew Kelly's reputation and that she got positive results for her clients. Yes, Kelly was a fireball in the courtroom. She was aggressive and very much like a mother lion where her clients were concerned. So, while she did charge high fees, she was worth every penny.

There was something missing in Kelly's life, though. More specifically her sex life, and she was taking notice to it more often these days, knowing it had to do with her always being "in charge" of everything in her life. And, while she knew she had to be in control in her professional world, in her personal world she wanted desperately to be submissive to someone and briefly surrender all of that 'I am She-Ra, hear me roar' business. No one knew that Kelly thought this way, though. She kept her fantasies about being dominated and told what to do to her self. That was the kind of information that could ruin her stellar career if it ever got out. Still, she really felt the need to unwind at the hands of a capable and demanding mistress.

Kelly passed by a newsstand on her way out of the courthouse on this particular Thursday afternoon, and spotted an alternative newspaper that she had often seen. It came out once a week, and contained all the latest entertainment news, food venues and alternative lifestyle happenings in the Los Angeles area. Suddenly drawn to what interesting tidbits she might extract from the artsy and culturally-diverse paper, she picked up a copy and carried it home with her. After pouring herself a tall gin and tonic and kicking her shoes off in the middle of the floor, she sat down on the sofa in her living room and started browsing through the paper. About halfway through, she spotted an ad for something called 'Madame's Den of Iniquity'. Now, that really got her attention, so she proceeded to read the entire ad.

It seemed that Madame's Den of Iniquity was in fact a high class lesbian dungeon, where women were invited to come and play out their fantasies of either domination or submission. Kelly felt her stomach tighten in excitement, as she read the general outline of 'dungeon play', and couldn't get to her phone fast enough. Making decisions on the fly is one of the things she did best, and calling to schedule herself for some 'dungeon play' was one of those in-the-moment, fly decisions. She called the number listed in the ad and made her reservation for the following evening, on Friday, for a play spot as a submissive slave. Kelly was given an address along with instructions to arrive at precisely 9PM. It would seem that her position of submissiveness was beginning already.

After 24 hours of intense anticipation, Kelly arrived at Madame's Den of Iniquity as directed, at exactly 9PM the following night. The address was located in an industrial park, and no one would have ever guessed this clandestine affair was housed here. It was easy enough to find, with an unassuming entrance to the establishment. Two other women arrived right behind Kelly, and the three of them walked in silence down a long, dark corridor lined with red lights, that opened up into a reception area.

The reception area was bare, except for a small table with a glowing lamp on it, and dozens of small mirrors that lined the walls, reflecting the red light from the lamp across the room like a dense red fog. Kelly was the first to step forward and check in with the Dungeon Madame, whom Kelly guessed to be about 50 years old, and still quite striking in appearance. She was assigned to a dungeon room and escorted there to wait for her mistress, being further instructed to remain standing in the middle of the room and not touch a thing. Kelly did as she was told, and as she stood there waiting in the dimly lit room, she took notice to the props, costumes and equipment that were lined along the walls. There was a collection of whips, masks, binding gear and gags spread across a long wooden table to her left. To her right, there was a smaller wooden table that was covered in various sized dildos and vibrators. And, in various locations on the walls, she noticed heavy-duty hooks that appeared to be designed for restraining purposes. I wonder which of these submissive supplies my mistress will be using with me tonight, Kelly thought.

Kelly's thoughts were interrupted by a door opening behind her, and a gorgeous, tall woman entered the room, stopping to stand just a few feet directly in front of her. This bewitching woman was a few inches taller than Kelly, had long dark hair, green eyes, and was dressed in a one-piece black patent leather jumpsuit, with matching black patent leather boots. The front of her jumpsuit was unzipped down to her mid-belly, teasing Kelly with a view of her half-exposed tits. Her mysterious mistress stood with her feet shoulder width apart, and looked Kelly up-and-down in a slow and deliberate assessment. This is what it must feel like to the many whom she has cross-examined in the courtroom, Kelly thought to herself. Now, the shoe was on the other foot, and it was Kelly's turn to be interrogated.

"So, you are Kelly?" the woman asked in a sexy,

husky voice.

"Yes, I'm Kelly", Kelly replied in a surprisingly subdued voice.

"I'm Mistress Nikki, and for the time you're here, you have no name. You're simply my slave, and you'll do what I tell you to do. You'll speak when told and not unless you're instructed to. Everything I instruct you to do, you will do immediately, and without question, or there will be consequences. Is that clear?"

Kelly nodded a bit apprehensively, but admittedly, she was already turned on by this' take control', hauntingly beautiful woman.

"You will address me as Mistress and answer any questions with Yes, Mistress or No, Mistress. Is that clear?"

"Yes, Mistress," Kelly answered.

"Very good. Now, I want you to undress down to your underwear and then get on your knees."

Kelly didn't dare argue and undressed in record time. She was in nothing but her black push up bra and thong panties when she knelt on her bare knees on the cold, stone floor. She was vaguely aware of Mistress Nikki moving around in the dungeon play room, but she kept her eyes on the floor and waited for her first instructions.

Mistress Nikki approached Kelly and stood before her. As Kelly stared at the high heeled boots that were in front of her face, she wondering if she was about to get stepped on by them. She also heard what sounded like slapping or popping against the palm of Mistress Nikki's hand, but Kelly didn't look up to see what it was.

"Get to your feet, Slave," Mistress Nikki finally

spoke. "Go over to the back wall and face it."

Kelly rose to her feet and went to the back wall as instructed. The same wall she spotted before, with all the hooks and straps attached to it. Oh god, Kelly thought, I'm about to be restrained. She was instructed to put her hands on the wall and to spread her legs apart, in a 'spread eagle' fashion. As Kelly assumed the position, suddenly feeling quite vulnerable, Mistress Nikki tightly fastened straps to both Kelly's wrists and ankles, securing her position against the cold brick wall. A hand came around her chest, and aggressively squeezed her right breast, while some type of object was being brush against her ass cheeks. What is that?, Kelly thought.

"Stick your ass out for me", Mistress Nikki demanded. Kelly obliged, and while still holding Kelly's breast in a vice grip, Mistress Nikki christened those ass cheeks with a snap of her cat-o-nine-tails, and Kelly felt the sting vibrate all the way down through her legs. Something told her that she shouldn't object, so she gritted her teeth together and bore that one along with several more.

"Now, Slave, that's a little introduction of what your punishment will be if you displease me. You're going to tell me "Thank you, Mistress! May I please have another?" after each lick. Do you understand?"

"Yes, Mistress," Kelly replied in a subdued voice. And, to her delightful surprise, even though her ass was stinging and hot from her slave spankings, Kelly's pussy was starting to throb....with excitement! She was starting to get very turned on, and was amazed that she was getting quite wet while enduring her Mistress's 'tool of discipline'. Being submissive was indeed, even hotter than she had ever imagined it could be.

"Now, I'm going to be untying you so that you can

move to that long table over there. Go to that table and lay down on your back."

Kelly gave her wrists a quick rub upon her release, did as she was told, and lay down on the table. Kelly let out a silent gasp, because the table she thought was made out of wood was actually made of a dark colored steel. The coldness seared through her body when Kelly first climbed onto it, but her bare skin adjusted to it, the longer she lay there. She looked up and saw that Mistress Nikki had approached the table and was holding some material in her hands. She proceeded to use pink velvet drapery cord to tie Kelly's wrists to the table through special holes that Kelly hadn't noticed before. She repeated the process with Kelly's ankles. When Kelly was once again immobile, Mistress Nikki brought out a very dark black blindfold that she tied around Kelly's eyes.

"Now, Slave, you're going to be having a bit of a tactile lesson. I've always thought it to be so much more interesting when you can't see what's coming."

Kelly started to tense, but she was also very excited that she was completely helpless and not in control of herself or the situation. The next thing she felt was her bra and panties being cut away from her body, which left her totally naked and even more vulnerable. Oh god, she thought, What's about to happen?

Just as that thought hit her, she felt something hot and sticky hit her nipples. She bit her bottom lip to keep from crying out. The hot substance quickly cooled and left her nipples with a rather numb, pulsing feeling. After this happened a few more times, Kelly realized that her Mistress was dripping hot candle wax on her. This was really turning her on! The initial pain, followed by the tightening of the cooling wax, was intense and pleasurable, and made her nipples quite erect. Kelly loved the way it all felt. Hot wax connecting to her flesh from nowhere, and her having no clue when it was coming, or where it was going to be landing. By the time Mistress Nikki had completed the lesson in tactile experience, Kelly was amazed at how thoroughly wet her pussy was.

Suddenly, out of nowhere, Kelly felt the smooth head of what felt suspiciously like a dildo, teasing the pouty folds that hid her now throbbing clit. She was so aroused and wet at this point, that she welcomed whatever Mistress Nikki might have in store for her, and she hoped it would include a climactic ending. Kelly tried to relax as she felt the slow insertion of what was definitely a dildo, slide into her thoroughly moistened, already contracting tight pussy. Mistress Nikki dildo-fucked Kelly thoroughly as she squirmed about on the table. And, when she could tell that Kelly was approaching her point of no return, she abruptly stopped.

Kelly involuntarily whimpered but caught herself just short of begging for more. Mistress Nikki spoke to her softy but firmly.

"Slave, if you want more of this, and you want to be allowed to reach an orgasm, you're going to have to convince me that you're worthy of it. You may speak."

Kelly let loose a torrent of begging, and said anything that she thought might work. She told her Mistress that she wasn't just a Mistress, that she was a Goddess and that she was privileged to be her slave. Then she told her that she wanted her Mistress to see how much she adored her and that reaching an orgasm would show her how much she meant to Kelly.

Kelly wasn't sure if Mistress Nikki bought any of it or not, but after an intense pause that seemed like eternity, she did go back to fucking Kelly with the dildo. And, this time she also used the fingers of her other hand to simultaneously play with her swollen clit. It didn't take long for Kelly to succumb, and her whole body arched off the table, pulling against the restraints, as she cried out and rode the pulsating sensations of her orgasm.

Mistress Nikki untied Kelly's blindfold and removed her restraints. She then instructed her to get up and get dressed. Kelly did as she was told, but she wasn't sure how she was supposed to take her leave. So, she took a guess and knelt once more before Mistress Nikki.

"Thank you, Mistress," she said. "I'm forever in your debt."

Mistress Nikki acknowledged Kelly with a nod, and opened the play room door, so that Kelly could take her leave. As Kelly made the drive home, she replayed the events of the evening over and over in her head. The verdict was clear.....submissive personal play was the perfect antidote to too much professional power play!

STORY 15 –
SISTER-IN-LAW

Tammy gave her apartment one last look to be sure that it looked nice enough for the arrival of her brother Matt and his wife Rebecca. They had moved away from Colorado Springs, Colorado after they had married three years ago, but they visited Tammy often, and during these years Tammy and Rebecca had become very close. Every time they came out to visit; Tammy always insisted that they stay with her. She had a three bedroom apartment in Colorado Springs, and she used one for her own room and a second one for a home office. Her guest room was always kept in good order, and she made sure that it was warm and welcoming whenever Matt and Rebecca came to visit.

It was funny how Rebecca and Tammy had started getting along so well that they no longer needed Matt around them as a buffer to feel comfortable and have fun together. Most of the time, the three of them did a lot of outdoor activities together, like hiking and kayaking. They also had talked about going camping in the near future. Tammy thought that would be an awesome idea, because it would give her a chance to explore what was going on with Rebecca. During the past few months, she could swear that Rebecca had been flirting with her, and making innuendos whenever Matt wasn't around. It definitely had peaked Tammy's curiosity, and she wanted to find out more about what was going on inside Rebecca's mind.

Things like long stares at Tammy, along with Rebecca double and triple checking with Tammy to make sure that she liked what Rebecca was wearing if they went out. Then, there was the way that Rebecca was always complimenting Tammy on her outfits, as well as her body. She was always asking Tammy if she had been working out, and telling her how toned and shapely her body was. Yeah, something was definitely afoot here and Tammy was determined to find out what it was.

Matt and Rebecca arrived right on schedule. Tammy had lunch already prepared, so they all sat down in the kitchen to eat. As they chatted over salad and sandwiches about what was new and exciting, Tammy was silently recalling how Rebecca hugged her long and hard when they first arrived. And, when Rebecca hugged her, she had pressed her body against Tammy's not in a way that a family member would, but in a way that someone's lover would.

"You look amazing, Tam," Rebecca said. "Did you do something new to your hair? It looks fantastic! Doesn't she look fantastic, Matt?"

Tammy smiled at Rebecca.

"I got it streaked," Tammy replied. "I'm really glad you like it."

"Yeah, Sis," Matt chimed in. "It looks really cool."

As they sat there talking and eating, Tammy felt a sock clad foot gently rubbing her ankle. Ok, well, I know that's not Matt, thought Tammy. Sure enough, when she looked across the table at Rebecca, she was staring directly at Tammy with a slight little smile on her face. Oh my god! Tammy thought. Things could get really interesting here. Matt was oblivious to it all, or maybe he just didn't care. After all, he was aware of Tammy's sexual preferences, but he knew that she would never try to take his wife away from him.

Once lunch was finished, they all decided to load up their backpacks and go for a five mile hike along one of their favorite wooded hiking trails. The fall day was gorgeous and warm, so it didn't matter that the hike took most of their afternoon. Throughout the entire walking journey, Rebecca kept close to Tammy, giving her lots of little touches on the arms and looking at her like she couldn't wait to tell her a secret. At the end of the hiking trail, they took a break in a grassy clearing at the edge of a small lake, where they laid out a large blanket so they could enjoy the snacks and water they brought with them. Matt finished eating before the women and decided to go for a swim.

"Why don't you girls come, too?" he asked.

"You know," said Tammy, "I think I'm just going to relax here for a little while, and enjoy the scenery. But you two go ahead."

"Um, I don't think I'm in the mood to swim right now, either," said Rebecca. "I'll just hang out here with Tammy."

With the girls deciding to stay behind, Matt took off to do some swimming and left the women together to chit chat about things that women like to talk about. They both watched him disappear over the hill, and soon they heard him splashing around in the water off in the distance. That's when Rebecca turned to Tammy.

"Tam, I've got a confession to make," she said.

"Oh really? Now this sounds intriguing. What's going on?" Tammy asked. Oh please do not tell me that you're cheating on my brother. She thought.

"Ok, here it goes," Rebecca said, as she took a deep breath, and let the words she'd been holding in, fly out of her mouth in one long-winded breath. "I've been fantasizing about you for months. And yes, I do mean fantasizing in a sexual sense. I don't get it, because you know how much I love your brother. But I can't stop thinking about you and wanting to be with you. Oh my god, I even think about you when Matt and I are having sex! I know that's horrible! But I really am so freaking attracted to you!"

Tammy didn't speak for several long seconds, but she coyly was taking in Rebecca's beautiful features, and thinking how lovely it would be to touch and taste her amazing body. Tammy didn't know if she was caught up in a moment of thinking, or not thinking, and then, she suddenly grinned at Rebecca and leaned over to kiss her gently on the mouth.

"So you want to give it a shot right now? We're all alone."

Rebecca now leaned in to return Tammy's kiss. The kiss got deeper and more passionate the longer it went on. Both women were starting to breathe more quickly and their hands were starting to roam. Tammy pulled her shirt off over her head, exposing her braless perky tits, so that Rebecca could experience putting her mouth on a woman's breasts for the very first time.

"Oh god," Rebecca whispered, as she hesitantly started to squeeze and fondle Tammy's tits with slightly shaky hands. "I've dreamed of touching you and kissing you like this for so long!" After Rebecca dared to explore Tammy's tits and nipples with her mouth and tongue, she looked up at her and said, "Your breasts are so beautiful and I love the way your nipples feel in my mouth."

She kept kissing and exploring Tammy's breasts while Tammy was starting to move her hands under Rebecca's t shirt. Being an expert at navigating a woman's body, Tammy knew just how to touch Rebecca to make her gasp and moan.

"Shhh," Tammy said. "Matt's just over the hill. We don't want him to catch us like this."

Rebecca attempted to silence her moans, but she

was getting so turned on, she literally almost couldn't help herself. Tammy guided Rebecca's hand down to the crotch of her jeans and helped her to unzip them. Then she gently pushed her hand inside her loosened jeans and encouraged Rebecca to explore what was inside her panties. Rebecca didn't have to be told twice. She slid her hand down beneath Tammy's bikini panties, asTammy spread her thighs apart to offer easier access for Rebecca.

Tammy felt that it was important to show Rebecca how to please another woman, and encouraged her do some finger exploration on her own. And with that, Tammy released her hand from Rebecca's and left her to navigate her smooth pussy lips and pleasure center on her own. She might not get this chance again, and she should have the experience of feeling her fingers inside a woman's pussy that was not her own. There was something else that Rebecca needed to learn, too.

"Do you want to taste me?" Tammy asked softly.

"Oh god, I so want to put my mouth on you," Rebecca moaned. "Please."

Tammy scooted her jeans down over her hips and lay back so that Rebecca could get her face where they both wanted it to be. She moved the crotch of her panties to the side and offered her stiff little clit to Rebecca. Instructing her patiently, Tammy told Rebecca exactly how to lick and then gently suck her clit. Once she got the hang of that, Tammy told Rebecca to gently slide a finger inside of her pussy.

"Here, just slide it in right here," Tammy whispered. "Ah yeah, that's it."

Incredibly, Rebecca was doing such a good job, that after only a few minutes, Tammy was so hot and turned on, that she felt herself very close to cumming.

"Ok, Becca," Tammy said in a shaky voice. "I'm about to cum and I didn't want to scare you. Just keep doing what you're doing, ok? Yeah, just …like… that."

Tammy's orgasm hit her and she bit her hand to keep her voice down, so that her cries of pleasure wouldn't carry all the way to Matt. To Rebecca's credit, she held on and did exactly what Tammy had told her to do. When she was coming down off of that last wave, and her body relaxed, Tammy realized that Rebecca's face and hand were soaked. She also realized that Rebecca was trembling with her own need now.

Gently, she pushed Rebecca onto her back, swiftly unzipped her jeans and pulled them down, along with her panties, around her ankles. Then Tammy expertly started to tongue Rebecca's clit, and tongue-fuck her. She had to remind Rebecca once more to keep her voice down, and then she slid two fingers inside of her pussy while sucking on her clit at the same time. It took only minutes for Rebecca's body to stiffen and twitch to the unexpected orgasm that washed over her.

Just as Tammy was about to show Rebecca some more tricks, they heard some more splashing, and then Matt's voice calling out to them as he was on his way back to them.

"Oh hell!" Tammy swore. Then she and Rebecca both started rapidly readjusting their clothes while giggling.

"Is my face still wet?" whispered Rebecca.

"No, not really. It just looks like you've been sweating."

Then both women started giggling again. They were all sorted out, just as Matt reappeared into the grass clearing.. Looking at them a bit oddly, he walked toward them.

"So, what have you two been up to?" he asked with raised eyebrows.

"Nothing special," said Tammy. "Just the usual girl talk.", as she and Rebecca looked at each other and exchanged a knowing glance.

STORY 16 –
PAGAN PLEASURES

Morgan was quite excited as she prepared for the night's Full Moon celebration with her pagan goddess spiritual coven. She loved that she and the other women switched around to different locations for these ceremonies and celebrations. It gave them a lot of variety in which to fully enjoy these celebrations. She was particularly excited for this evening, because they would be meeting at the home of Trinity, one of their members. Her home boasted a private well-manicured lawn as well as an Olympic size swimming pool. The entire backyard was enclosed with a high wooden privacy fence so there was no risk of being spied upon. But, the best part is that since it was a warm summer's night, they would be holding the celebration skyclad, which meant that all of the women would be participating in the nude and truly at one with Nature.

Morgan arrived at Trinity's house to find that she was the last one to get there. Lilith, Eve, Amethyst, Bronwyn, Lark, Raven, and Silver were already there. Trinity welcomed Morgan into her home, and then led her out to the backyard where the other women were already setting up flowers and candles for the circle. A small bonfire was started and the women enjoyed some drumming and music while waiting for the sun to set. When the sun finally did sink deep below the horizon, and darkness shrouded the night skies, a ceremonial circle was cast, and the full moon celebration began.

The moon was large and beautiful in the sky, and the ladies all gathered in a circle. At the same time, they dropped their long hooded cloaks to expose their gorgeous nude bodies to the firelight, moonlight and each other. They joined hands as they chanted and sang, while performing a special rhythmic dance, followed by a drawing down of the moon. As the women moved around the fire, the flickering shadows danced enticingly across their naked bodies, and all of the ladies partook in stealing glances at one another's lovely forms. Following this, they offered their special gifts to the Goddess, and closed the ceremony by giving thanks to Mother Earth.

After they broke the circle, the ladies all went onto the Florida room that was located at the back of Trinity's home, where they enjoyed the cakes and wine that Trinity had prepared and put out for them. As they drank the wine and nibbled on the food, the women started breaking off into small groups back out on the lawn, as well as around and in the pool. The night air was still quite warm, and the women were definitely in the mood to 'make merry'! These women knew each other very well, and there was always a lot of sexual tension and electricity flowing amongst them whenever they gathered. The fact that they were often nude for the ceremonies, only served to heightened the sexual energy that seemed to be ever present.

Raven, Lilith and Bronwyn were on a blanket out on the lawn as they drank wine, laughed and talked. Later, no one knew who started what, but suddenly, the women were joined in a three way kiss-fest of sorts. Lilith broke away from Raven and Bronwyn and started to work her way down a little bit, positioning herself directly between the women's bodies. Raven and Bronwyn were still kissing each other deeply, while Lilith moved back and forth between their luscious and beautiful breasts. Licking, nibbling and sucking on their nipples while using her hands to titillate and tease their outer pussy lips, heated things up even more, and it wasn't long before both Raven and Bronwyn decided they wanted to join Lilith in the fun she was having. Mutual kissing, touching, licking, and nibbling continued, with all three women thoroughly enjoying each others natural body delights. At some point, Raven was lying on her back and Lilith had kissed her way down between Raven's thighs, spreading them nice and wide so she could have full access to her pretty pink lips. Turning so that she was facing Raven's feet, Lilith was able to use her tongue to part those pouty little folds, as she then glided her tongue smoothly and slowly across every inch of Raven's clean-shaven pussy lips, which elicited much moaning and writhing.

Suddenly, Lilith emitted a little gasp and groan of her own, when she felt what turned out to be Bronwyn's tongue on her own wet little pussy. Looking back over her shoulder, she saw that Bronwyn was sitting on Raven's face while leaning forward to share her definite talents with Lilith. These ladies definitely knew how to have a good time with their special goddess daisy chain.

In the meantime, there was more goddess love going on, as Silver and Amethyst were enjoying some aqua pleasures in the shallow end of the pool. They were kissing each other deeply while their hands roamed over each other's naked body. And, in short order, their hands disappeared beneath the water as they started playing and fingering each other's pussy. Lark, who was sitting on the side of the pool watching them, was so completely aroused by this display of passionate affection, that she spread her thighs and began teasing her own swollen clit, and alternately finger-fucking her tight, soaked little pussy.

Somehow, Eve, Trinity and Morgan also ended up together on the lawn. As sort of a 'Thank You' to Trinity for hosting the Full Moon celebration, she was lying in between the other two women on her back, while Eve and Morgan were giving her stereo sex. Each woman was in charge of stimulating a side of Trinity, and they were doing it simultaneously. They started at the top of

Trinity's body, and Eve and Morgan each kissed and suckled on one of Trinity's earlobes. Then, they moved their mouths and tongues to either side of her neck, and, the totally fun part started when they made their way down to her tits and were squeezing, sucking and tugging on Trinity's nipples at the same time. Of course, things got even hotter when they both finally ended up between Trinity's thighs. After first receiving some simultaneous lip love from both of them along the crease between her thigh and outer pussy lips, her clit then got dual action from both Eve's and Morgan's mouths and tongues. As they continued their combined combustible actions on her clit, they each slid a finger into Trinity's tight, moist pussy, and it was then that Trinity was 'thanked' with a full moon celebratory orgasm.

As all of this sexual action reached a crescendo, there were various cries of pleasure coming from the lawn and pool areas. Some of the women even sounded as if they were howling at the moon, when their moments of climactic pleasure hit. It didn't happen all simultaneously, of course, but all that sexual baying into the midnight air was probably arousing whatever wildlife may be nearby.

Now, this was a perfect full moon celebration! These beautiful goddesses had shown their love and respect for Mother Nature, and had ended the evening with the giving and sharing of the most natural gifts of all....the gift of their sexuality.

After all of the women had shared their pleasures with one another, they drank more wine, relaxed and just enjoyed each other's company around the dying bonfire.

STORY 17 –
CAMP COUNSELOR TRAINING

Copyright © 2012 Spirited Sapphire Publishing

Denise had a lot going on in her life right now, and it was for those reasons that she was looking forward to being a camp counselor for an annual summer sports camp for girls. It would be 8 full weeks of hiking, swimming, and volleyball among all sorts of other outdoor sports related activities. She used to attend each year herself when she was 12 to 17. Now that she had turned 18, she had been invited to become a counselor. She was thrilled to have something to take her mind off of what she had recently realized about herself.

Denise had always been quite popular in high school. Guys were always asking her out, and she would usually go if she liked them. In fact, she even dated one guy exclusively in her senior year, but she wasn't sad to leave him behind after graduation. She had finally given in to having sex with him because she felt that she should, but she just didn't feel the 'earth move', like she was told it would. In fact, she didn't feel anything at all. No arousal during foreplay, no desire to feel his manhood, and no titillating sensations during intercourse. In fact, it just plain did nothing for her.

Denise wondered if there was something wrong with her. While her female friends always talked about how much they loved having sex with their boyfriends, Denise tried to pretend and go along with them, so she wouldn't appear to be an outcast, but she just didn't feel it. In fact, Denise just didn't feel that type of attraction to the opposite sex period. It wasn't that she hated boys, she just wasn't interested in them in a romantic or a sexual sense. The truth was, there were a couple of her female friends that she would often daydream and fantasize about. There were also some women celebrities that she was excited by, and she had even started masturbating to their pictures that she came across in magazines.

Denise had finally accepted, to herself at least, that she was attracted to women. She was attracted to them in a way that she had never felt for any guy. After coming to this realization, Denise got scared. Oh my god, she thought, how will I ever tell my parents? She figured that was something that could be put off for now, and she would wrestle with that challenge later. In the meantime, there was something a bit more pressing on her mind. She wanted more than anything to act on her feelings with another woman, but she didn't have the slightest clue as to how to go about it.

Wendy was Denise's camp counselor trainer, and has been Denise's obsession for the first 4 weeks of the camp. She was 20 years old and gorgeous. Her body was fit, toned and tan. She also had small, firm breasts, that she never seemed to feel the need to restrain with a bra. It had been exquisite torture for Denise to watch this woman bounce around in her tight little tank tops, and short shorts while leading the girls in their activities. It was all she could do to focus on what Wendy was trying to teach her.

Things were particularly difficult for Denise when they went swimming or got caught in the rain. Wendy's perky dark nipples stood out like sharp little diamonds through her soaked shirt, and she was so comfortable with her body, she never seemed to feel the need to cover up. Wendy has also been quite friendly to Denise, which only intensified her crush on the older girl. Denise's favorite part of the day, was after they saw all the camp girls off to their bunk houses for the night, and the camp counselors and counselor trainees would then all go to the counselors' bunk house. She would secretly watch Wendy undress and get ready for bed, all the while quietly masturbating under her covers.

On this particular night, the girls had retired early

because of an extra early wake-up call the next morning for an all-day rafting trip. They were all excited about the trip, but also really tired from their day, so most everyone was asleep in record time. Wendy entered the bunk house and started to undress for her shower. That's when Denise made an in the moment decision. She would follow Wendy and pretend that she was going to the toilets, which were just past the showers. In that way, she can get some clandestine looks at Wendy's nude and oh-so-perfectly fit body. Denise walked nonchalantly past the showers into the toilet, and when she re-emerged, she was stopped in her tracks by the sight of Wendy soaping up her naked body. Glancing over her shoulder, Wendy sees Denise starring at her. Then, Wendy drops a bombshell on Denise. She tells Denise that if she hasn't showered yet, she's more than welcome to join her. Feeling herself both aroused and now slightly panicky, Denise wasn't sure what she should say....or do. Is she flirting with me, Denise wondered, or is she just being nice and offering to share the shower?

As if in a dream, Denise slowly nods and starts to undress. Before she realized what was happening, she was standing naked in the shower with Wendy, both of them under the warm spray of water cascading down. Denise was floating somewhere between terrified and thrilled, and was actually trembling a little.

"What's wrong, sweetie?" asked Wendy. "Are you cold? Here, get closer so you can have more warm water."

She pulled Denise closer to her and put her arms around her. Then she smiled at her and picked up the soap. Lathering up her hands, Wendy started to slowly wash Denise's shoulders and her arms. Denise's trembling only increased, but not because she was cold. She was feeling so many things at once, lust being at the top of the list. Wendy had no idea that Denise had never been with a woman before. She had seen Denise watching her and just assumed that she loved women. However, given Denise's trembling, she was starting to realize that this just might Denise's first lesbian experience, and she better go easy on her.

So, that's just what Wendy did. Everything she did was slow and easy. Just as she started to wash Denise's chest, Wendy leaned in and started to kiss her gently on the mouth, while at the same time she began soaping up Denise's firm, round breasts. The second that Wendy's mouth touched hers, Denise immediately connected with that feeling of 'this is so right'. This, she thought, is the way that it should feel during intimacy. Not bland and benign, but electric and explosive. She began returning Wendy's kiss with all the hungry passion that was in her, suddenly feeling courageous enough to explore Wendy's mouth with her tongue.

Denise felt as if her nipples were connected to the pleasure center between her legs, because every touch that Wendy gave her there seemed to generate pulsating sensations inside her pussy. She wasn't sure what a real orgasm felt like, but she thought she might be pretty close to having one. For the moment, though, she just wanted Wendy to keep touching her naked, wet body and kissing her. She also wanted to touch Wendy and moved her hands so that they covered those pert, firm little breasts that Denise had been craving for weeks. Wendy encouraged her to play and she was starting to become a bit braver.

The two women continued to kiss and caress each other, as the water rained down upon them. Denise felt herself starting to lose control, and her legs weaken, from the explicit and expert guidance her counselor was giving her. Wendy's hand then began to trail over

Denise's stomach and straight down, until she found those soft smooth lips that hid her erect and very sensitive little clit. When Wendy's fingers made contact, Denise gasped out loud and groaned as she started to involuntarily move her clit back and forth against Wendy's fingers.

Oh god, thought Denise, I think I might be dying of pleasure! She became totally lost in kissing Wendy, as she felt Wendy's fingers working some amazing magic between her legs. Her breath started coming faster and faster, and her body, weak with pleasure, was being supported by Wendy's arms. Denise vaguely heard someone moaning, but was so overcome by all the physical sensations she was experiencing, that she didn't even realize that those moans were coming from her. Just as she started to feel that something was about to happen, Wendy slid a finger inside of her contracting hot pussy, while keeping her thumb pressed against her clit. And, then, it happened.......Denise was quickly pushed completely over the edge, and waves of pulsating contractions vibrated throughout her entire body. Wendy kept kissing her in an attempt to keep the sounds from carrying through the bunk house, as she gently guided both of their bodies down to the shower floor.

Finally, Denise came back down to earth and allowed herself to be cradled in Wendy's arms, enjoying those beautiful tits that were hovering just over her face.

"Oh god," Denise whispered. "Thank you! I feel validated, I feel exhilarated, and, I just had my first orgasm!"

"Well, sweetie, I'm honored I was the one who was able to provide you with your first female experience. If you're up for it, I've got some other things I can show you that I think you'll really like!" Wendy laughed softly.

"Oh, my gosh, do you mean there's more?" replied Denise. She knew that this was what she had been looking for, and no man would ever be able to give it to her. She would only find her pleasure in the arms of another woman. And that was more than ok with her!

STORY 18 – GLAMOUR SHOTS

I really hope Tracy likes this, thought Claire, as she entered the photography studio. She had always wanted to do something a little wild like have a private glamour shoot done, but now she had the perfect excuse to do it. She had a new love interest and wanted to make a sexy photo album of herself to give to Tracy. This can't help but heat things up a bit, she thought, even though things were pretty hot between them already.

"Hi there, you must be Claire," said the pretty receptionist at the front desk. "Just sign in right here and come with me."

The receptionist stopped them in front of a door marked Private and opened it. Standing aside, the receptionist motioned for Claire to enter. Inside was a huge dressing room. As in, dressing rooms you see in the movies huge! There was a full-length makeup counter with lights, and wall to wall racks of sexy lingerie and suggestive outfits that promised to show a lot of curves and skin. Claire already felt like a Hollywood glamour girl just being in this room.

"Ok, Claire," the receptionist said. "You will be choosing three outfits to wear for your shoot, and you can choose from whatever is available here in the dressing room. You'll also have two personal assistants. This is Kate, who will be doing your makeup, and Rayna, who will be in charge of making your hair look fabulous. So, relax, let the girls get you glammed up, and enjoy your shoot!"

With that, she turned and left the room, closing the door behind her, leaving Claire with her personal assistants Kate and Rayna. They women asked her if she had any idea what sort of look or persona she wanted to shoot today, so that they could assist her in choosing her outfits, and then fix her makeup and hair to match the outfits and intended look. It took close to an hour before Claire had chosen three outfits, and had her face done up as well as her hair.

Claire took a look at herself in the lighted makeup mirror, and couldn't believe what she saw. Her shoulder length dark brown hair was styled in large, slightly tousled waves that framed her face perfectly. Assessing her makeup, Claire had to admit that she had never seen her eyes 'pop' like that before. The shades of matte green eye shadow and black eyeliner, lined in a 60's 'cat-eye' look, gave such a depth to her dark brown eyes, that she almost couldn't believe it was her. Her lip color was a matted brown color, and because her skin had a natural olive overtone, instead of using a typical rose colored blush, Kate applied a more brownish-rose colored rouge, and the overall look made Claire look like a retro Italian beauty.

When Claire had put on her first ensemble and was ready to begin her photo shoot, the receptionist reappeared and escorted Claire to a studio set that was decorated like an upscale brothel. She couldn't believe how realistic everything was, right down to a sexy round bed covered with a red coverlet trimmed in black. Taking in account the sexy lingerie she was wearing, along with her new retro-glam look, Claire imagined herself to be a high-paid call girl, ready and waiting for her first client. The smooth sexy jazz music that was being piped in, certainly helped set the mood, and she couldn't wait to get started!

Suddenly, one of the most beautiful women Claire had ever seen entered the room. She had long dark blonde hair, bright blue eyes, and a body that instantly took Claire's breath away. She had to be at close to six feet tall and could have been a supermodel. Yet, she had a couple of expensive looking cameras hung casually around her neck, so Claire figured this must be her photographer.

"Hi, Claire, I'm Samantha, but please call me Sam," she said, extending her hand to Claire, who took it and they shook hands. "I've got to say you chose your costume wisely. You look quite incredible. I could almost eat you up myself!" She winked at Claire when she said that, and Claire had to remember that this was probably Sam's way of relaxing her clients and that she wasn't flirting with her. But it sure did feel like she had hit on her just a tiny bit.

"Thanks," replied Claire. "I was hoping it looked decent."

"Oh, I'd say it looks more than decent," Sam laughed. "Why don't you climb on the bed and let's get started?"

Claire got on the bed, and began striking the many poses that Sam was suggesting to her. While Sam was shooting pictures from every angle and distance from the bed, Claire was really getting into the moment, and embracing her inner sexual goddess. Sam was taking pictures in rapid fire succession as she crooned to her with things like "That's great, baby! Keep doing it just like that!" and "Come on, Beautiful, show me a little more thigh, there. That's it, Sexy, you're so freaking hot!"

Claire played right into her hands, and by the last frame, she was practically naked. She was down to wearing only a black velvet corset with garters and black fishnets stockings, and she was mostly topless, if you didn't count her arms crossed over her very ample breasts. Sam was easily able to make Claire feel quite comfortable during the shoot, and had talked her subject into some very provocative shots. Claire was tremendously turned on by Sam, and found herself fantasizing of what it might feel like to kiss her.

Sam approached the bed, and sat down at Claire's feet on the black shaggy rug that covered a part of the floor. She had some digital photo samples to show Claire, so Claire slid down to the floor beside her to take a look. As they went through the samples, Sam commented often on how hot Claire looked in the photos, and how incredibly sexy her body was. Claire kept giggling self-consciously, but she had to admit that Sam had done an amazing job of making her feel like a professional pinup model.

"Well, thank you for your compliments Sam. I have to admit, I've definitely channeled my inner diva today, and I can't remember the last time I felt this empowered and attractive." Claire laughed.

"Oh, you are definitely very powerful." Sam countered. "And, you're more than just attractive. You are downright alluring and hypnotic!"

The women's eyes met, as Sam leaned forward and pressed her mouth to Claire's as she put her hand on the back of her neck to pull her even closer. As they settled into a deep and passionate kiss, Sam slid her hand up the front of Claire's corset and began fondling and squeezing her plump soft breasts. Claire moaned a little and put her arms around Sam, pulling their bodies even closer, while caressing her back softly with her fingertips. Soon, those caresses turned into urgent groping, and Claire quickly helped free Sam of her shirt and bra, exposing her firm, small tits for Claire to enjoy.

The two women fell back onto one another on the black shaggy rug, and continued kissing and exploring each others bodies, with the fever of two lost lovers reunited. Sam then began removing the few remnants of

Claire's outfit, teasing Claire's naked skin with her mouth and tongue in the process. Sam then stood up to shed her hip-hugging jeans and panties, then pulled Claire up with her.

"Here, baby," Sam whispered. "Go sit in the vanity chair for me."

Claire stood up, walked to the chair and sat down. She sat back against the chair while spreading her thighs apart, with Sam on her knees in front of her grinning wickedly.

"That's just what I had in mind," Sam said, as she buried her face into Claire's pussy. Holding her lips apart while flicking her tongue in and out of her pussy a few times, Sam then licked her way all around those pink pouty folds, where she then began to suckle gently on Claire's erect little clit. Claire glanced sideways at the stand alone mirror on the studio set, and got a bird's eye view of Sam's naked form between her legs, and her hand pushing Sam's head further into the embrace of her pussy. Just as Claire was starting to feel herself lose control, Sam stood up and straddled her. She balanced against Claire's thighs just far back enough so that she could continue playing with Claire's clit, while also inviting Claire to play with hers.

Claire obliged, and her fingers quickly parted Sam's smooth lips and found her clit, while Sam slide a finger deep inside Claire's moist pussy, and began finger-fucking her at the same time. As the women continued to please each other, Claire's now soaking pussy started to contract, and she began riding Sam's finger faster and harder. Realizing what was about to happen, Sam grabbed Claire's other hand with her free hand, and sped up her actions as well. Suddenly, Sam's legs squeezed against Claire's legs, and they both came within seconds of each other. As Claire's body convulsed in climactic ecstasy, Sam shushed her moans with her mouth and tongue, while pressing her backwards against the chair.

After both of their bodies started to relax, Claire and Sam lay back down on the rug, waiting for their breathing to slow and the world of reality to return.

"I'm not sure I can walk just yet," Claire laughed.

"Oh, that's ok," Sam giggled wickedly. "I, uh, have something to show you. I accidentally left my camera switched on video, and…. well, here's a copy of our special 'glamour shoot session.' This one is for you…no charge."

STORY 19 – FOOD PLAY

Spirited Sapphire Publishing

Renee was so proud of Tanya for finally going after her dream of being an executive chef. She had been telling Tanya for a long time that she should just go for it. This was just one example of how great their relationship was. Renee and Tanya supported each other fully, and were so emotionally and sexually connected, that their relationship had withstood things that had caused the breakup of the relationships of many of their friends. These two women had learned that you just needed to work together if you wanted a relationship to last. And they really wanted theirs to not only be permanent, but fulfilling in aspects.

One area where their relationship excelled was in the bedroom, although their sexual escapades didn't always take place exclusively in their bedroom. They both loved to role play, and most of their role playing consisted of a variety of bondage and domination scenarios, and they switched off taking turns being the dominant one. With Tanya's graduation from culinary school coming up, Renee had put together a surprise that promised to be a whole lot of fun for both of them, and it involved some role playing in a whole new way.

Tanya came home one night from school totally worn out. She just wanted to unwind, and was looking forward to spending some quality time with Renee. When she came in the door, Renee was standing there to greet her. Tanya's mouth dropped open as she took in Renee's outfit. She was wearing a blood red mini skirt, black bra, black apron and red heels. The colors looked great against Renee's shoulder-length, golden blonde hair and the look transformed her into one smoking hot kitchen goddess.

Before Tanya could form any words, Renee spoke first.

"Go take your shower, Tanya. Then, I want you to come back out here to the kitchen completely naked. You've got 15 minutes to get out here, and get your bare ass in the chair that's waiting for you at the kitchen table. Do you understand?"

"Um yes ma'am!" And with that Tanya scurried off to the bathroom. Even though she hadn't completely grasped what Renee was doing, she had a feeling that it was going to end up in some sexy playtime for the two of them. So, Tanya quickly stripped and showered, being mindful of her time limit. As she soaped up her body, she couldn't help but fantasize about what Renee might have in store for them, and the possibilities alone started to get Tanya's juices flowing. She dried off her body, combed her hair, gave herself a quick spritz of perfume, and made it back to the kitchen clean and naked, in a little over 10 minutes.

"Sit down," ordered Renee.

Tanya obeyed, and instantly found her hands being tied behind the back of the chair.

"Now, spread your legs apart." Renee commanded.

Tanya didn't hesitate to obey. As she spread her legs wide, Renee tightly bound each of Tanya's ankles to the bottom of the chair legs. Naked, spread eagle and bound, Tanya was excited, but also a little anxious of what was getting ready to happen to her. After Renee finished securing Tanya's body to the chair, she stood back to take in the sight of Tanya's beautiful naked body, bound and waiting for her to take her pleasure with it. Tanya's plump soft breasts were heaving slightly with either apprehensive or arousal, and Renee was looking forward to paying great attention to them shortly. Renee also took in the site of Tanya's well manicured mound, and delighted in seeing her pussy lips already slightly parted due to her legs being spread open and tied down. Oh, I'll be giving you lots of attention shortly little pussy, thought Renee, as she then walked over to the other side of the kitchen to retrieve something.

As Tanya watched her, Renee brought over a tray containing fresh vegetables, fruits, and food toppings. "Now, I may not have the culinary skills you do sweetheart, but, I do know how to work a little magic with food in a different way." Renee said, as she placed the food tray on the table next to them.

As Tanya was taking inventory of the ingredients on the tray, Renee picked up a jar of honey, took out a spoonful of the sweet, sticky treat and dripped some onto Tanya's mouth. She then leaned down and slowly began lapping up the dripping honey from Tanya's lips, as Tanya let out some low moans of pleasure, as Renee's soft mouth kissed and suckled off the honey. Replacing the jar onto the tray, she next picked up some chocolate syrup, and drizzled it onto Tanya's plump breasts and diamond sharp nipples. Leaning down, Renee used her tongue to lick up every drop of the chocolate syrup then nibbled a bit on Tanya's erect nipples, while Tanya started to squirm in the chair.

"Mmm," Renee whispered in a husky voice. "So sweet you are. Let's see if this whipped cream will make you even sweeter."

Applying the dessert topping to Tanya's body from her mouth down across each of her breasts, Renee balanced herself by using Tanya's shoulders as a base, while leaning over her body and licking up every last bit of that whipped cream.

"Now that's what I'm talking about," Renee said in a very satisfied voice. "You make the most heavenly of desserts! But I've been a bad girl, and I've had my dessert before my dinner. I better not neglect my nutrition, so let's not forget our fruit and veggies."

As she talked, Renee picked up a sizeable carrot, cleaned and peeled to make it smooth, twirling it in between her fingers, as she knelt down on the floor in front of Tanya. With a wicked smile on her face, Renee turned the pointed end of the carrot toward Tanya's wide open little pussy. Touching the tip of the carrot to Tanya's pussy lips, she moved the vegetable around in slow, teasing circles around her hole a few times, before inserting the carrot slowly and fully into Tanya, who was looking down and could see the carrot as it disappeared into her most inner place.

Tanya was moaning and arching her body upwards, as Renee spent a few minutes slowly fucking her with that carrot, until Tanya's pussy was soaking wet. Renee suddenly removed the carrot from Tanya's pussy, and held it up to her mouth. After first sniffing it, Renee licked the moistened carrot up one side and down the other, enjoying the taste of Tanya's love juice left behind on it. Replacing the carrot on the tray, Renee then picked up a firm, unripe banana.

"I just wanted to get your warmed up baby," she said, winking at Tanya.

Spreading Tanya's pussy lips open further with the fingers of one hand, Renee used the other hand to gently glide in the banana, and as she did Tanya pulled against her restraints, trying to push her hips against Renee's hand. Renee pushed the banana in deeply, and then immediately pulled it almost all the way back out. She rhythmically continued to pleasure Tanya's pussy in-and-out with the 'food toy', as Tanya moaned and desperately tried gyrating her hips in the chair, as if trying to fuck the banana. Clearly, Tanya was totally turned on by Renee's 'food play', and Renee was getting quite aroused herself, as she watched Tanya's pussy lips grip around the fruit as it went in and out of her hole.

Renee withdrew the banana and Tanya actually whimpered in protest, causing Renee to laugh. She had saved her best surprise for last because she had an idea as to how it would be received.

"Close your eyes baby," Renee commanded Tanya, and of course, Tanya obeyed. Once Tanya's eyes were shut, Renee picked up a very frozen, and very cold Popsicle.

As soon as the tip of the Popsicle touched Tanya's pussy lips, she screamed and tilted the chair back, as she tried to pull her body away from this frozen assault. Renee managed to hold the Popsicle in place, gliding it inside even further, and started to lick up the dripping liquid as it immediately began thawing inside Tanya's hot pussy. Renee's tongue was moving back and forth very fast all around Tanya's pussy lips, and Tanya was trying desperately to maneuver her mound against Renee's mouth. As Tanya's clit now became the focus of attention from Renee's mouth, she could no longer manage to twist about against the hold her restraints, and instead, her body succumbed to the pulsing waves of contractions that first hit in the center of her belly, then deep within her pussy, followed by a whole body surge that caused her to limbs to stiffen and tremble. Her orgasm hit so suddenly, that even Renee hadn't felt it coming, yet she kept licking and suckling on Tanya's clit, while she managed to sneak the banana into her hand again. Continuing to work her tongue magic on Tanya's most sensitive areas, she also slid the banana in and out of Tanya's contracting pussy. After a few more minutes of intensive food-fucking, Tanya felt her excitement building once more. This excitement culminated in another rocket-launching orgasm for her, and when it did, Renee kept the banana moving steadily as she simultaneously stood up to plant a deep, passionate kiss on Tanya's mouth as she came, and came, and came.

Finally, Renee took the tray away and untied Tanya. Holding out her hands, she helped Tanya up out of the chair.

"Let's go jump in the shower baby, and rinse all of this food off," Renee said.

Tanya smiled at her in agreement, knowing that she would reward Renee's unique expertise with food play, with a sexy surprise or two in the shower.

STORY 20 – COUPLE SWAP

Zoe and Brenda were quite excited as they were packing up their car for a weekend camping trip that they were taking with their friends Paige and Diane. The two couples met last year at the annual Womyn's Festival, and the four of them had really hit it off. They were thrilled to find out that they actually lived quite close to each other, and they've since spent lots of time together participating in all kinds of outings, including some weekend getaways.

As the two women packed the car with all the necessary gear, Brenda started telling Zoe about a movie that she had seen the earlier in the week. It was about wife swapping, and Brenda asked Zoe outright what she thought about the whole partner swapping thing.

"Now why would you ask me that?" Zoe smiled.

"Well, you know I love you, right?" Brenda replied.

"Yes, baby, I know you love me. And I love you, too."

"Ok, well that movie kind of made me start thinking about some things."

"What sort of things," asked Zoe.

"Well, 'things' like maybe being with Paige and Diane, and, uh, you know, like sharing each other. Do you know what I mean?" Brenda finally managed to get out, suddenly feeling anxious and worried about how Zoe would react.

"Oh yeah, I know exactly what you mean." Zoe replied. "And, I have to admit, that I've actually given it a passing thought once or twice before myself. So, if Paige and Diane are up for a little swapping play, I'm open to trying it."

"Seriously?" squealed Brenda.

"Absolutely. I think it would be pretty hot!"

They hugged each other, finished loading up their gear, and then got in the car to go pick up Paige and Diane. The two couples headed up to north country, where it was higher and cooler, and there were lots of beautiful wooded areas that were perfect for a secluded and romantic camping trip. When they found just the right place, everyone jumped out with their arms full of equipment, and got busy setting up camp. Once everything was set up, all four of them went for a refreshing swim in the nearby lake. As the sun started to set, they climbed out of the water and Zoe and Diane got to work building a fire, so they could get dinner cooking. They had brought along some nice juicy steaks to cook, along with some potatoes to bake and a salad in the cooler. Of course, they also brought several bottles of good red wine.

The women had all put on some comfortable clothing, and while Brenda and Paige set up the blanket, plates, salad and wine, Zoe and Diane cooked the food over the fire. Once everything finished cooking, they sat back on the large blanket and enjoyed all the delicious food and wine, along with some titillating dinner conversation. All of the women starting glancing at each other from time to time, with extended mysterious looks, and Brenda started to wonder if Zoe had already said something to Paige and Diane. She hoped not, but she couldn't be sure. Once dinner was completed and the dishes taken care of, the women spread a couple extra blankets out close to the fire, and they all enjoyed some more wine, as the night sky turned dark, and the air of unspoken mystery and anticipation deepened amongst them.

Zoe cozied up to Brenda on the blanket, and began kissing and nibbling on her neck, while her hands squeezed and fondling Brenda's tits through her thin, tight t-shirt. Brenda's eyes were closed as she enjoyed Zoe's nibbling, and she pressed her body against Zoe's, while her hands roamed over the curves of her hips. Zoe looked up to see both Diane and Paige staring at them with a lustful look in their eyes, and Zoe could feel the sexual heat practically leaping off their bodies. Thus far, no one had said anything, but now all four women were staring at one another intensely, and the sexual tension was so thick in the air, you could cut it with a knife.

Zoe cleared her throat and spoke. "OK, I cannot stand the tension anymore, and I have a pretty good idea that we might all be thinking the same thing. Here's the deal. Brenda and I love each other very much, and we're also quite secure in our relationship. And, we've recently become interested in exploring some more 'open' sexual situations. Brenda and I are both really attracted to the two of you, and would like to ask you how would you feel about a little partner swapping tonight?"

Silence followed this little monologue, as if no one quite knew what to say next. However, all of the women began exchanging quick glances with each other, until finally, Diane broke the silence.

"Well, to be honest, Paige and I have actually taken part in a partner swapping encounter. We loved it and we would be very excited to do it again, if you're sure that you're up for it."

There were smiles and some giggling all around as the women 're-partnered', and Brenda moved onto the blanket with Paige, and Diane moved over to Zoe's. They had decided it would be better to keep everything out in the open on the blankets, instead of behind closed tent zippers. This way there would be no secrets amongst them, because they would all be able to see everything that was going on. Plus, adding the voyeurism factor, how hot it will be to watch their partners pleasing and being pleased by someone else.

Zoe and Brenda exchanged little smiles with one another, just before they each started kissing their 'new partners' for the first time. Brenda was completely lost in Paige the moment their lips touched. It had been a very long time since she had kissed anyone except Zoe, and she knew now that she had missed that feeling of newness that you get when kissing someone for the first time. She loved kissing Zoe, but there was something dangerously exciting about kissing someone new, especially when you know your partner is watching! Paige slid her tongue slowly into Brenda's mouth, and the tantalizing tongue tango that began between them, sent shivers of excitement throughout both of the bodies. The two women quickly undressed each other, and their naked bodies melded as one, as they lay on top of one another on the blanket.

On the other blanket, Zoe and Diane were also getting hot and heavy with each other. Those implied sexual sparks that were flying around during dinner were real, as Zoe found out quickly enough. Their kissing was deep and very passionate. These two didn't waste any time in getting their clothes off either, and soon they were lying naked in each other's arms, mouths connected and hands exploring tits and ass. Zoe and Diane were greedily trying to touch and taste each other's pussy, when Zoe happened to glance over at Brenda and Paige. Brenda was completely naked and lying on her back, thighs spread apart. Paige's head was buried between Brenda's thighs, and looked to be busily licking or sucking on Brenda's clit.

A jolt of unexpected excitement ran through Zoe's body, as she saw the love her life being pleased in such a way…...and, by someone other than her! It also made Zoe want to be doing the very same thing to Diane's pretty pink pussy. She flipped Diane onto her back and started to feast from her body, beginning with her perky, firm little tits. She licked and sucked and nibbled on those hard little nipples, as she kneaded each breast with alternating firm and gently pressure. Kissing her way down the rest of Diane's body, she landed just where she had longed to be. Diane's musky aroma rose to meet her, as Zoe placed her face between her tight and toned upper thighs. Nothing turned Zoe on more than that special scent of a woman, as she skillfully pleased her with her tongue.

Brenda looked over to see what Zoe was up to, and saw her beautiful woman busily pleasing Diane's clit as she slid two fingers into Diane's pussy. Knowing how masterful Zoe is with her mouth and tongue, Brenda knew the degree of pleasure that Diane was experiencing, and it suddenly, made her want to taste Paige in a most urgent way. She maneuvered the two of them into a perfect 69 position, so that she could part Paige's pretty pink folds and start sucking her clit. She was excited to find that Paige had an oversized clit and sucking it was almost like sucking a tiny cock. As Brenda and Paige continued to give lip love to each others pussy, their bodies started gryating against each others mouths, from the mounting sexual energy that was surging through them both.

Their symphony of moans became louder and more urgent, as their voices echoed off of the lake and the surrounding mountains into the night. Paige started to rhythmically ride Brenda's mouth, as Brenda held on, refusing to let go of that tiny erect appendage. When Paige's orgasm hit, Brenda got a huge surprise. Her face was suddenly and completely soaked in liquid. It was startling, but it was also really sexy. Even while Paige was climaxing, she continued to lick and suckle on Brenda's clit, and a few minutes later, her own orgasm flooded her body with wave after wave of pulsating pleasure.

Zoe had glanced over once again to see what was going on with Brenda, just in time to witness her lover's orgasm. This caused Zoe to suddenly fall over her own cliff of pleasure, as her and Diane were both finger-fucking each others moist pussies. Diane could no longer hold back, as the excitement of hearing and witnessing everyone else's orgasm finally got to her, and she let out her own ecstatic cry, as she rode Zoe's fingers into orgasmic bliss.

The women all lay back and held each other, and after agreeing that a good time was had by all, the women rejoined their partners and headed into their tents. The excitement still hung heavy in the air, but this time it was between the original partners, who would now be enjoying each other privately this time.

STORY 21 –
LESBIAN LOVE:
BEST FRIENDS TURNED
LESBIAN LOVERS

"So how did your session go today?" Amanda asked, as her friend Carrie got into the car.

"It wasn't that bad actually," Carrie said, as she buckled herself into the passenger seat of her best friend's car. "And, thanks Amanda for always being there for me and taking me to my appointments. I really do appreciate it."

"No problem. " Amanda replied with a warm smile. "You know I'd do anything for you."

Amanda glanced over at her friend inquisitively, as she pulled out of the parking lot of the medical office building. Wow, she thought, while scanning Carrie's facial expression for a sign of how her counseling session went. Carrie actually seemed a little upbeat, which is very different than how her friend has appeared to be for quite some time.

"Hey, that's great!" Amanda said enthusiastically. "It sounds like you're finding some clarity and direction."

"Yeah," Carrie agreed. "I am finding clarity, because I'm finally able to be honest with myself about a lot of things."

"Oh really?" Amanda asked curiously. "Anything you'd like to share?"

"Maybe," Carrie smiled secretly. "But not right now."

"Ok sweetie. You know I'm here for you whenever you're ready," Amanda said.

She knew that Carrie would open up to her when she was ready. There was no reason to rush her. As long as they have been friends the two women have shared absolutely everything with each other, the good, the bad, and the crazy. Amanda had no doubt that Carrie would eventually tell her what was going on, and she would be there for her no matter what it was.

Their friendship had started a number of years back in college, when they first met on campus. They quickly became very close friends, and shared all aspects of their lives with one another, including the fact that Amanda considered herself to be bi-sexual. Carrie had always been very understanding and accepting of Amanda's lifestyle and it never interfered with the closeness that the two women shared. Amanda had tried dating men, and she enjoyed herself, but the truth was that she much preferred the company of women and eventually came to the full realization that she was a lesbian and not bisexual. This revelation was fine by Carrie, and it didn't change their friendship in any way at all.

When Carrie married her college sweetheart, Amanda stood up with her as Carrie's maid of honor. The strong emotions Amanda had experienced that day as she watched the most important person in her life become permanently joined to someone else were not what she had expected, and she found her head and heart filled with a storm of surfacing feelings. Obviously, Carrie and Amanda cared deeply for each other, but Amanda suddenly felt as if she were losing a vital part of her life…..and heart. It was on this important day in her best friend's life, that Amanda came to the in-your-face realization that she loved Carrie. Not just a friend love, but a full-blown I am in love with you love. In fact, she loved Carrie so deeply and soulfully, that she wanted her to be her forever partner in life. And, because Amanda loved Carrie so deeply, for the first time ever, Amanda kept a secret from her best friend.

What Amanda had no real way of knowing was that Carrie never felt the way that she thought she should for her husband. She liked him and respected him, they shared lots of fun times together, and while the sex wasn't earth moving, it was ok and not too unpleasant. Carrie's life was secure and without domestic drama, and she thought this is what a marriage and partnership is all about. Or is it? Carrie constantly struggled with the feeling that something was missing, and often wondered to herself, 'Is this as good as it gets?".

In the meantime, Carrie found that the times she spent with Amanda were even more fulfilling to her than before, and nuggets of both confusion and awareness were starting to infiltrate her consciousness. Carrie loved how Amanda's eyes lit up whenever she saw her, and Carrie took great notice to those constant little butterfly feelings she felt in her stomach whenever she was with Amanda. Butterfly feelings she never felt with or for her husband. Carrie looked for any reason she could to talk or be with her friend, and in the 15 years that they have been friends, they spoke everyday no matter where either one of them happened to be in the world. In addition, they enjoyed vacations together, just the two of them, including trips to Hawaii, the Bahamas and even a few cruises.

Carrie knew she wanted to spend every moment she could with Amanda, yet during all those years, she had never once told Amanda about her confusion and feelings. Carrie didn't want to hurt her husband, even though the marriage wasn't exactly what she hoped it would be, and she also didn't know how Amanda would react if she told her. And so, even through all the truth and full-disclosure in the women's friendship, Amanda too had a secret that she was keeping from her best friend.

Once Amanda decided to settle down, she moved back to the northern suburbs of Chicago, which was coincidentally where Carrie and her husband had bought a home. Perhaps subconsciously Amanda was figuring out a way, any way, to be more geographically close to the secret love of her life. Amanda's move back to Chicago brought her exactly what she wanted, and their close proximity allowed the two women to spend even more time together. They went out frequently for lunch and dinner, did some volunteer work together and attended many social and cultural events together. Both Amanda and Carrie were happiest when they were together, which these days, seemed to be always.

At this point, Carrie's husband took notice to his wife's behavior, and Carrie's relationship with Amanda became a point of contention in their marriage. Then came the day that Carrie could just no longer deny that she simply wasn't in love with her husband, nor was she attracted to him sexually. While Carrie did have the security that she had always felt she needed in her life, she could no longer go on living this lie, and it just wasn't fair to either of them. Carrie knew they both deserved happiness, honesty and the opportunity to experience a partnership of true love. Of course, it was impossibly hard for Carrie to explain to her husband that she had realized that she just wasn't attracted to him, or even men in general, and in fact, she was also deeply in love with her best friend. Carrie practiced what she might say to her husband in the bathroom mirror over and over, but in the end, she just couldn't say what she wanted to say to him, and so she voiced what they both already knew to be true, that the two of them had grown apart and were cohabitating as friends, not as husband and wife, and certainly not as passionate lovers.

It hadn't been easy, and Carrie's husband wasn't initially willing to let go and wanted to try marriage counseling. Carrie knew that counseling wasn't going to help. She also knew that she wasn't ready to come out to anyone just yet about her newfound realization about her sexuality, so when her husband left, it was with many hurtful words. Carrie felt responsible for everything because she knew that she should never have married him in the first place, and she knew she also should have been more fully honest with him about the reasons why she wanted a divorce. More confusion and more awareness finally clogged Carrie's normally cheerful disposition, and she found herself at a very intense crossroads in her life.

Knowing that there was only one person she could trust and rely on, Carrie turned to Amanda for support during this precarious time of serious self-reconciliation. Amanda was the one that had found the counselor that Carrie was now seeing. Amanda was also the one that listened to Carrie without judgement whenever she needed to talk, and held and soothed her in her arms while she cried her guilty tears. Amanda even brought Carrie over to her own house for the first two weeks after her husband left, so she could keep a loving watch over her. Typically on counseling days, Amanda would pick Carrie up and take her to her appointment, and then pick her up afterwards. The two of them would have dinner together, and Carrie would oftentimes spend the night. Tonight was one of those nights.

Amanda and Carrie both enjoyed these nights together. Sometimes they would go out for dinner and enjoy a few drinks at one of their favorite intimate restaurants, and other nights they would dine in and sit around drinking wine and talking or watching a movie. Today, Carrie was silent on their drive back to Amanda's house, and deep in thought about what this night may bring. Today, in her counseling session, after two months of trying to dance around the subject, Carrie had finally admitted to her therapist the real reason that her marriage hadn't worked out, and the fact that there was no way it could have ever worked out, and that was because she has been in love with someone else the entire time. And, that someone else just happened to be Amanda.

This admission of her love for Amanda, spoken from her lips to someone else's ears was quite liberating for Carrie, and she embraced a sudden new sense of clarity, confidence and direction about the matter. Now that she finally spoke the words to her counselor, Carrie felt the great need to speak them to Amanda. She realized that she wasn't afraid after all of what Amanda's reaction might be, because she has deep-down known all along that even though things have never spoken between the two of them, Carrie and Amanda both knew they were right for each other, in love with each other, and meant to be with one another. That 'missing feeling' she always had during her marriage to her husband, was being fulfilled by Amanda. Amanda was sharing her passion, vulnerability, excitement and love with Carrie, being the perfect life partner that her heart truly desired. Carrie's body relaxed further into the car's bucket seat, as she smiled knowingly to herself.

Glancing over at Carrie as she maneuvered the street, Amanda was struck by the deep and genuine smile that had spread across her face that made Carrie absolutely glow. Now, what is Carrie thinking about that is causing her to smile like that, Amanda thought? Well, if it's important, she'll tell me when she's ready. As long as Carrie was coming to grips with her new life and finding happiness, that's all that matters. Even if she never knows the way in which I truly love her, Amanda thought, I want her to be happy.

"So what do you think about eating in tonight?"

Amanda asked, breaking the silence in the car.

"That actually sounds perfect," Carrie replied, as her smile grew even bigger.

"Great! What do you feel like?"

"How about Chinese food?" Carrie suggested

"Now you're reading my mind!" Amanda laughed.

When they arrived at Amanda's house, Carrie went up to the guest room that she stayed in whenever she spent the night, and jumped in to take a quick shower and freshen up while Amanda was downstairs ordering their dinner. Amanda knew everything Carrie liked and didn't like to eat, and always knew exactly what to order for her, whether it was Chinese food, Mexican food, or anything else. Tonight, Carrie took special care with her appearance, and after taking a quick shower, she applied some fresh makeup, arranged her hair in a sexy tousled look, and dressed in a pair of form fitting jeans with a snug low-neck sweater that accented her perky, rounded breasts. Then, she sprayed on some perfume that she knew Amanda loved, and after one last look in the mirror, she felt as ready as she ever would be and nervously went back downstairs.

Amanda was setting out some plates and wine glasses when Carrie entered the kitchen. She started helping Amanda, and the women chatted while they enjoyed a glass of wine and waited for their food to arrive. They both really loved these casual intimate times together, and there has never been anything complicated between them. Well, non-complicated except for the fact that Carrie has been keeping her feelings for Amanda to herself, but tonight there was an obvious sense of anticipation and electricity in the air, and she was going to change that. Carrie had always felt that what she and Amanda had between them was the way all relationships were meant to be, and she realized now that if you constantly had to struggle to make a relationship work, it just may mean that it's not meant to work. With her and Amanda, there has never been any 'trying to make things work', they just always magically did.

When the food arrived, they laughed and joked over their meal, and when neither one of them could eat another bite, they put the leftovers in the fridge and taking their wine with them, collapsed on the oversized couch in the adjoining family room. Propping their feet up on the coffee table, the women continued to laugh, talk and drink their wine, as Carrie was silently summonsing up the courage to confess her revelations and feelings to Amanda. Finally, Carrie sat down her glass on the table and turned to look over at Amanda with a somewhat serious expression. Well, she thought, it is now or never.

"Mandy, there's something that I need to say to you and I should have said it a long time ago."

"Sounds serious," Amanda said.

"Well, that depends on how you look at it. I suppose it could be considered serious," Carrie gave a short laugh. "Today, I had a huge breakthrough with my counselor. And, what I realized today, was that what I'm about to tell you I've known for a very long time, but today was the first time I was able to admit it out loud to both my self and someone else. I said it to my counselor, but I really need to say it to you."

"Of course, Carrie. You know you can tell me anything, right?" Amanda responded, as she straightened up on the couch and looked at her friend intently.

"Yeah, ok. Amanda, I'm a lesbian." Carrie blurted out. "But, that's not the most important part, so please let me finish before you say anything or I might lose my nerve. The important part of this, to me anyway, is that I'm in love with you. In fact, I finally realized that I've been in love with you for years, but just couldn't admit it. But I can now. You don't have to love me back in the same way or anything Amanda, I just needed to be clear to you and let know how I feel about you. Hell, I needed me to be clear about how I feel about you as well."

For several long moments, Amanda was unable to speak. She could feel the tears that filled her eyes and the huge lump in her throat that was keeping her from saying anything. Finally, she reached over and took Carrie's hands in hers and swallowed.

"Carrie," she managed to whisper huskily. "You've just, quite possibly, made me the happiest woman in the world. I've been in love with you for so long, but I never dreamed that you would return my feelings. It nearly killed me to watch you get married feeling the way I do for you. I can't imagine my life without you in it Carrie and nothing would make me happier than for us to share the rest of our lives together, openly and the way we're really meant to."

Suddenly, they were in each other's arms engaged in an embrace of love and passion. Amanda pulled back a little so that she could look directly into Carrie's eyes just before she gave her beloved a tender kiss on her soft, pouty lips. Carrie made a little noise in her throat as she responded to Amanda's gentle explorations, and the kiss went from soft and tender, to a slight nibble, and on to a full blown deep and passionate lip and tongue tango. They became so lost in each other that it seemed as if they weren't ever coming up for air.

The kissing turned into fondling and caressing, with Amanda gently taking the lead. As she moved her hand underneath Carrie's sweater, she went slowly so as not to scare her, and when she closed her hand over one of Carrie's breasts, Carrie let out a soft gasp of pleasure against Amanda's mouth.

"I'm sorry, baby," Amanda whispered. "Am I going to fast?"

"No sweetheart." Carrie laughed. "I've just never felt anything like this before, and I can't even tell you how many years I've been longing for your touch, so please, don't you dare stop! I don't have any experience with women so you're going to have to show me how to be with you, and what you like."

Nothing had ever turned Amanda on as much as those words did, coming out of Carries pretty, pouty lips.

"I'll be more than happy to show you everything you need to know, baby," Amanda said.

After that, the ice was not only broken and thawed, but now completely boiling between them, and 15 years of pent up passion exploded between them. Amanda pulled Carrie's sweater off along with her bra, and took in the sight of Carrie's beautiful, firm breasts before leaning in to gently suck and tease her pale, pink nipples. Amanda first methodically traced her tongue all along the sides of Carrie's tits before alternately taking each on of her nipples into her mouth and sucking on them tenderly, while she used her thumb and finger to tug and tease the other nipple. Carrie arched her body into Amanda's, as she moved her hands against Amanda's breasts through her shirt, anticipating what her naked skin will feel like in her hands.

Anticipating Carrie's thoughts, Amanda leaned back and stripped herself of her shirt and bra, and placed Carrie's hands on her ample breasts for her to explore. Carrie gently squeezed and caressed her tits as she reached for Amanda's mouth with her own, and Amanda helped guide Carrie's hands with her own as their lips, tongues and hands created urgent sensations of arousal to ripple through their bodies.

Amanda pulled away from Carrie slightly, and gently guided her to lean backwards against the couch, so that she could continue her sensual exploration of Carrie's delightful body. Amanda unbuttoned and unzipped Carrie's jeans and slowly peeled them off her legs. Carrie was wearing a pair of pretty black panties, and as Amanda gingerly slid her fingers inside of those panties, she was rewarded with first the sensation of smooth, velvety bare skin, then the feeling of moistness and a sweet aroma of honey muskiness, that was a sure indication of Carrie's excitement. Amanda tugged off Carrie's panties, and using her fingers, she parted the smooth fleshy petals of Carrie's pussy and quickly located her stiff little rosebud of pleasure. Amanda started making little circles around Carrie's clit and when she leaned down to pleasure her with her tongue, Carrie let out a soft primal moan while clutching either side of the couch cushions.

Having Carrie totally naked on her couch was a dream come true for Amanda, and she couldn't count the number of fantasies she had had about this moment. She wanted to please Carrie in every way possible, and show her what passionate love making is supposed to feel like. Slowly, she parted Carrie's thighs open further and Amanda then slid in two of her fingers into Carrie's soaking wet pussy, and glided them in and out while licking and sucking on her erect clit.

"Oh my god!" Carrie cried out, as her body stiffened and started to shake.

"That's it sweetheart, let go and enjoy." Amanda directed, before returning her attention back between

Carrie's smooth thighs.

She used her tongue to slowly lick around the folds of Carrie's pussy lips, while she continued to glide her fingers in and out of her most intimate area. Carrie's entire body responded in rhythm to the movements of Amanda's tongue and fingers, and she started to rock and press her hips up against Amanda's mouth. Amanda could feel the wetness in her own pussy while she tasted and enjoyed Carrie's. Both of their bodies started to rock in unison as Amanda could now feel Carrie's inner muscles starting to contract around her fingers, and she kicked all of her pussy-loving talents into high gear. When Carrie's orgasm hit, she started to cry out over and over again, getting louder with each sound and Amanda kept a tender, tight hold of her as she relished the feel of sensual climax electrifying Carrie's body.

Amanda caressed Carrie's curves as she waited for her to fully integrate her first lesbian experience and orgasm. She smiled at the satisfied look on Carrie's face, and Amanda couldn't wait to show her more about the fine art of Sappho love. The women eventually moved upstairs to Amanda's bed where Carrie received her first lesson, which was how to caress, lick and taste Amanda's pussy, and Carrie was amazed at how much of a turn on it was to watch Amanda squirm with pleasure from her efforts. They continued to excite each other over and over again throughout the night, until they fell asleep in each other's arms exhausted, but oh so happy.

Amanda and Carrie didn't wake up until mid-morning, and when they were both fully awake and enjoying their cups of morning coffee, they tried to take in the surrealness of the situation, and the reality that they were actually totally and fully together, as they should be.

"You know I thought about you on my honeymoon," Carrie confessed shyly.

Amanda was quiet for a moment and then she reached out to grab a hold of Carrie's hand. "Look, I know this is all very new to you, but you've got to remember that I've been in love with you for years. And, if all this is too soon for you, all you have to do is say so. But, I honestly don't feel like this is all completely new, but rather a new chapter in our lives together. And, if you think about it, we've actually been together for 15 years already. I want nothing more than for you to move in with me, so we can share and adventure the rest of our lives together."

Carrie smiled at Amanda, and kissed her lovingly on her coffee-scented lips.

"Mandy, I meant what I said last night. I've known deep down that I have loved you for a very long time. I'm totally sure about us, and I'm more than ready to commit to you, too. The sooner I move in here the better!"

Carrie's answer left a glow around the both of them, as they kissed and spent the next hour intimately expressing their newly found commitment of love to each other.

Spirited Sapphire Publishing

STORY 22 – LIPSTICK LESBIAN LUST: CARNAL CANDIED KISSES

Jessie rested her slender body against the doorway to the room where all of the holiday excitement was happening, and simply stared in awe for a moment. This was literally the coolest, most avant-garde thing she had ever seen! Whoever had come up with this type of holiday fashion show was a genius! Looking around the expansive and bustling venue, Jessie's eyes saw human sculptures that were either nearly nude, or completely nude, and covered only in glittery, bright works of body paint art. In the center of the ballroom, she spied several beautiful women wearing nothing but glittering pasties on their firm, round tits with matching thongs twirling around on aerial devices, as well as swinging from trapezes. Oh my god! Jessie gasped as she turned and spotted what could only be described as a human sushi table. The 'sushi table' was actually a gorgeous and completely naked woman, and on top of her curvaceous body were arrangements of various kinds of sushi. Seated around the lovely human sushi display, were a handful of well-known female celebrities, and Jessie couldn't help but blush a little as she recognized most of the women. Aren't we all just primal creatures in the end? Jessie thought to herself.

"Hey girl!" Jessie felt an arm slide around her waist and she turned to greet her friend, Eleni.

"Hey back," she said. "I was starting to think that you weren't going to get here!"

"Oh, you know me," Eleni said, as she gave Jessie a quick kiss on the lips. "I wouldn't have missed this for anything. Wow! Can you believe all of this? I'm so happy we both managed to get this gig! It's going to be so much fun!"

"Oh, I agree! Have a look at that sushi table over there," Jessie said. "Isn't that girl beyond yummy?"

"God yes! Forget the sushi! I'll just eat her!"

The girls giggled together as the both openly ogled the human sushi bar. As they looked around at the crowd of guests, they started recognizing some very famous lesbian faces. This holiday party was one where all of the guests could be comfortable in public showing their sexuality. There were even lesbian celebrities in attendance who were still "in the closet" publically speaking. That was one of the many reasons that lesbians from all over looked forward to this combination holiday party and fashion show each year.

Suddenly, Eleni turned to really get a good look at Jessie, and took in her costume, her beauty and her oozing sex appeal.

"Well, look at you!" she exclaimed. "Aren't you the sexy holiday vixen!"

Jessie returned Eleni's comment with a coy smile. She was dressed as a sultry snow angel, and her costume was a brilliant, almost blinding white, with of course, an abundance of glittering silver accents. She wore her light blonde hair down, and paired with her big blue eyes, she truly had the appearance of one breathtaking angel. The costume consisted more of fluffy feathered angel wings attached to her back, than anything else. The rest of her outfit consisted of a see through halter top over her perky but delicious looking breasts, with silver snowflakes covering her nipples, and a see through G-string with only a single silver snowflake strategically centered on the thin fabric. Her feet were encased in silver stiletto heeled boots, and the exposed parts of her legs sparkled with airbrushed silver snowflakes.

"I'd love for you to be my guardian angel," Eleni teased, while looking deep into Jessie's eyes.

"Well, what about you!" Jessie flirted back. "In that

candy cane outfit, you look good enough to eat."

Eleni was dressed in a white sheer body suit with glittery red candy cane stripes encircling her shapely nude body that was underneath it. Her round little breasts were only just barely covered with one of the stripes of red, as well as her bare mound. She wore glittery red stiletto heels and a huge red bow in her raven black hair, which she had put up for this event. The daring and baring costume accentuated Eleni's long legs, which were very shapely with slightly muscular dancer's calves. Her lips bore a red textured candy cane lip gloss, and she was most definitely a heavenly body in sultry holiday attire.

The girls stood back and had a good look at each other before dissolving into more giggles, with lots of flirtatious touching. After a few more minutes of flirting with each other and scoping out the crowd of gorgeous women, they decided it was time to start working the room. It was their job to keep the guests entertained and excited throughout the evening, as well as to promote the risqué holiday fashion show, which they were both to be a part of later in the evening. So, with a parting kiss, Jessie and Eleni separated and blended into the crowd of party goers.

Jessie moved liked a coy cat through the people, touching women on the arm, putting her arms around them, offering little kisses on the cheek, and engaging them in brief snippets of conversation. She knew she looked hot, and these women were definitely appreciating her appearance. As Jessie wiggled her way through the crowds of women that were standing in little groups drinking, eating and engaged in chit-chat, she felt many hands caress her cute little ass. And, a few times she had women drape their arms over her and sneaking little feels of her tits. Jessie didn't mind, and in fact, it was actually quite arousing. As she continued to travel and mingle throughout the expansive ballroom, she kept looking around for her sexy friend Eleni, hoping to get a glance or two of her luscious body.

As Jessie's eyes scanned the crowd, she finally spotted her beautiful friend flirting outrageously with a short, busty red haired woman. The woman was busily licking Eleni's costumed body as if she were, in fact, a true candy cane. Jessie giggled as she watched the way Eleni seemed to be encouraging this woman to keep licking and caressing various parts of her body. Eleni's body was quite the beautiful specimen, and it was also a bit of a turn on for Jessie to watch Eleni get licked and fondled by another woman. In truth, Jessie was getting more than a little excited at the wishful thought of Eleni licking her own body. Shivering a bit, Jessie started to make her way over to the group of women that Eleni was successfully entertaining. As long as she was playing her part along the way, the show's promoters didn't care where she was standing in the room.

Jessie walked up behind Eleni, pressing the entire front of her body against her back and teasingly licked the side of her neck, while strategically resting a hand dangerously close to Eleni's innermost thigh. Eleni glanced over her shoulder to see who was doing that to her and smiled when her eyes met with Jessie's.

"So, the sexy Snow Angel wants a taste of the candy cane," she teased.

"You better believe she does," Jessie whispered back.

The group of women that was circled around the girls loved the overt flirtatious actions between the two seductive party hostesses, and soon efforts were made by the on-looking women to join in on the fun. There was groping and kissing and baring of breasts, and the pod of wanton females were having quite the time. It was then that Eleni noticed that the promoter was gesturing to her and Jessie, so that meant that the fashion show was just about to start. The girls excused themselves by giving each of the women in their group a memorable kiss and scurried off.

Once they were backstage, the girls had to change before they could hit the runway. Jessie glanced over as Eleni was wiggling out of her candy cane outfit. Her perky tits were so damn inviting, and Jessie wanted nothing more than to suckle them in her mouth. Jessie's eyes scanned down further over Eleni's taught stomach, long legs, and of course, she didn't miss the beautiful view of Eleni's smooth pussy mound. Quivers shook Jessie's body as she fantasized about what it would feel like to enjoy Eleni's naked body under her own. Eleni caught Jessie watching her undress, and then redress, and winked at her knowingly. Jessie smiled back as she heard the pre-show music start, which meant seating was taking place around the long ballroom runway. It also meant that Jessie would have to wait for another time and chance of hopefully enjoying Eleni's body, touch and kisses.

Eleni was also enjoying the view of Jessie, as she stripped out of her Snow Angel costume. Her body was amazing, and her facial features were literally breathtaking. Jessie truly did have the heavenly face of an angel, Eleni thought. One very, very sexy angel! Eleni was pretty confident that the feeling of intense sexual attraction was reciprocated judging from the way Jessie had been acting with her tonight.

Suddenly, the music changed and got louder, which meant it was 'show time'. The girls each took a last look in their dressing table mirrors and turned to each other.

"Ok, it's time!" Eleni said.

"Let's go hot stuff," Jessie replied back.

The next 45 minutes went by in a flash, with pumping rock holiday music, flashing lights, falling snow, and lots of near naked women on display. Both Jessie and Eleni loved doing these avant-garde shows, and the crowd tonight was of particular interest to them since they were all women, each beautiful in her own right. This show was a little different as well because of the blatant lesbian theme it carried, and all the ladies that were part of the show served as some serious eye candy for the all-female audience.

Each time Eleni and Jessie passed each other in between their turns down the runway, they silently interacted with one another through knowing, coy smiles, in fact, smiles that were becoming increasingly more blatant and lustful. Eventually the two girls weren't able to conceal their desires, and they both pranced up and down the runway like two cats in heat. Jessie was even starting to have some trouble with her tiny outfit underwear pieces, because her pussy was getting wet at the site of Eleni and thoughts of how her pretty little pussy would taste. Eleni was having troubles of her own, and she couldn't keep her eyes off of Jessie's pouty, gloss covered lips and perky bouncing tits.

By the time the show ended, both of them were dying to have a private place to go. After the girls took their part of the runway bows, they got their wish. One of the other show models was going to an after party and didn't need her hotel room. She was one of the few lucky models that had managed to score her own private room, and now she was offering it to Jessie and Eleni if they wanted to use it for changing clothes or just to hang out and relax for a bit. Either way, she didn't care. She wasn't going to be there.

Eleni and Jessie exchanged looks and instantly took the model up on her offer. Jessie grabbed the room card with one hand, and her bag of clothes with the other, and off the girls went to have an 'after party' of their own. When they entered the room, they couldn't believe all of the things it contained. There was a long table littered with diamond accessories, sexy lingerie, seductive perfume and various other items that had been sent up from the sponsors of the show. It was a virtual toy land for all things sexy and sassy.

"Oh wow," Jessie exclaimed. "Would you look at this?"

"Oh my god!" Eleni chimed in, as she fingered the sparkling jewelry pieces and satiny lingerie ensembles.

The girls poured themselves some champagne that was chilling in an ice bucket, and started trying on all the extraordinary and very expensive lingerie pieces. Eleni looked positively mouthwatering in the candy apple red, see-through teddy that she chose to put on. And, the flowing red feathers that lined the bottom of the teddy just barely covered her beautiful ass. She put on some satin red heels that almost perfectly matched the hue of her nipples, and, the color contrasted beautifully against her long dark hair and big green in her eyes. Eleni sashayed around the room like she did when they were on the runway, performing some model poses for Jessie, who had just donned an emerald green corset with lace up stays. As she took another big sip of champagne, Jessie slipped on a pair of matching green stilettos that showed off her amazing legs to their best advantage, and Eleni smiled with deep approval. Each girl then finished their look by trying out the expansive makeup palette, with a finishing touch of sparkling candy cane lipstick. The fragrance they chose to spritz on each other was of an intoxicating and seductive scent that only served to amp up their excitement.

As the heavenly bodied women gave into the primal desires they had been feeling all evening, Jessie leaned in towards Eleni and touched her tasty lips to hers. The fire of desire was then immediately escalated, and their tongues feverously explored each others mouths, while hands caressed and squeezed tits and ass. Becoming weak in the knees, the girls fell backwards onto the queen sized feather bed and their entangled bodies continued to kiss while their hands continues to explore. Eleni freed Jessie's tits from her corset and began sucking and tugging on her pink, erect nipples while Jessie trailed her fingers with a feather light touch up and down Eleni's sides and just over the roundness of her ass. As Eleni was getting ready to pull off Jessie's thong, she happened to catch sight of a bow-topped box over on the comp table that was filled with all those sponsor goodies. She got up from the bed and started over to the table, pulling Jessie with her.

"Hey, Jess," Eleni said, holding up the box. "Look at this."

"Hmm, what do you think is in it?" Jessie asked as she walked over to join Eleni.

"Only one way to find out," Eleni said. With that, she opened the box, and inside, nestled against a bed of pink satin material, was a metallic pink vibrator tipped with a cluster of tiny little plastic pearls. Eleni reached in to remove it from the box, and held it up so that Jessie could see it.

"Why don't we see how well it works," Eleni said, smiling slyly at Jessie. Putting a hand on Jessie's chest, she gently pushed her back onto the plush sofa. Eleni tugged off Jessie's thong and spread her thighs wide apart as she started to slowly brush Jessie's pussy lips with the turned off wand. She kissed Jessie fully and passionately on her candy glossed lips, while spreading Jessie's other lips with her fingers and taunting her pussy with the tip of the pearled vibrator.

When Eleni felt Jessie's pussy become wet, she turned on the vibrator and began circling the pearled head gently around the outer part of Jessie's stiffening clit. She moved it around in tiny gentle circles, and as she did, Eleni could see Jessie's wetness increase as her love juice glistened off the metallic surface of the vibrator. Jessie started to moan and move her hips in a way that told Eleni what she wanted. Instead of giving it to her right away, Eleni turned up the speed on the vibrator a tiny bit, which just made Jessie only crazier with desire, and she stuck her head deep between Jessie's thighs so she could pleasure her clit with her mouth while continuing to tease her outer pussy lips with the shiny hand-held appendage.

Eleni could feel Jessie's whole body begin to tremble beneath the touch of her mouth and hands, and uncontrollable moans started to escape from Jessie's mouth. Realizing that Jessie was getting close to climax, and ready to receive more, Eleni increased the speed just a tad more, and glided the pearled-tip vibrator deep inside Jessie's soaking little pussy. Sliding the vibrator rhythmically in and out of Jessie's love tunnel while suckling on her hardened clit at the same time, took Jessie right over the edge, and she bucked and rode both the vibrator and Eleni's mouth, as wave after wave of climax rippled through her body.

"Oh my god," Jessie breathed, as her body relaxed against the sofa pillows. "That was....wow!!"

"Yeah," Eleni agreed. "You did seem as if you were enjoying yourself."

The girls took a brief pause to sip from their champagne glasses, and Jessie leaned in towards Eleni and began to kiss and nibble on her mouth and neck, before moving downward. Eleni let out a faint moan, and Jessie was eager to return the favor, so she took control of the shiny pearled vibrator and the moment.

"Let's go enjoy a hot bubble bath sexy, and then it's my turn to show you just how great this little holiday toy is," Jessie said as she waved it at Eleni.

After a sensual bubble bath and another couple rounds of intimate pleasures, the sun started to peek through the window and cast a glow over the two naked girls entangled with one another on the bed. They were both smiling with an erotic 'after glow' as they drank mineral water and fed each other pieces of fruit from the mini fridge, both of them knowing that this was only the beginning of something wonderful and hot between them.

STORY 23 –
LESBIAN ROMANCE:
COLLEGE GIRLS FIRST
LESBIAN EXPERIENCE

So this is college, Jenny thought as she hugged her arms around her chest and looked around her bare dorm room. After her parents had helped her carry everything up to her room, they had taken her out to lunch and then set off back for home, a several hour drive away. Jenny had spent some time putting her things away and settling in, and was now sitting on the edge of her twin-sized dorm bed contemplating her new surroundings, her newfound freedom, and the new chapter in her life that she was about to embark on. Jenny had been anxiously awaiting this moment for a couple of years now, and now that she was actually here, in this moment of incredible transformation, she couldn't help but feel slightly apprehensive.

As all these thoughts raced through her mind, one thought in particular seemed to stand out. That thought was of Jenny's wrestling with a part of her identity the past couple of years, and her struggle to explore this curiosity, or perhaps it was an innate need. Whatever it was, Jenny was starting to become consumed with these feelings and desires that had surfaced so dominantly in her psyche, and she was hoping that college life would allow her the freedom to search and discover her sexual identity.

As Jenny continued to get settled into her dorm room, she noticed herself anxiously waiting for her roommate to arrive, and was hoping that the two of them would get along easily in the small quarters that they were about to share for the school year. Jenny hadn't really shared a room with anyone before, and she was silently wondering what the boundaries were for close quarter living. Thankfully, the room was actually larger than she had thought it would be, with plenty of space between the two twin-sized beds, a small refrigerator and microwave, two small desks and chairs and a private bath.

That last part was a relief to Jenny because she had feared sharing a communal bathroom with the other dorm girls. In fact, ever since Jenny had started to become aware of her possible sexual orientation, she became quite apprehensive in gym class throughout her last two years of high school, most especially when she was in the girls locker room. She didn't know how to act, she wanted to stare at the other girls, she was sure she was obvious as hell, and worst of all....she didn't want to be 'outed' by some straight girl who might claim to feel violated to the school principal. So, Jenny kept a tight lid on her newfound feelings and desires, and those feelings and desires have been bottled up tight inside of her for the past two years, waiting to explode like a volcano.

Previous to the past two years, Jenny had allowed herself to think back to the only boyfriend she had tried to have during her sophomore year of high school. Evan had been cute, very sweet and had treated her like she was a queen. Jenny had genuinely liked Evan, but therein lie the problem. She only liked him, as a friend, as a great companion to hang out with, and there was absolutely no attraction on her side at all, even though she did have sex with him a few times.

During those times, she was shocked to find herself fantasizing about girls in order to fake that she was enjoying herself. And, when those sometimes girl fantasies soon became all-the-time girl fantasies, Jenny realized that she was being unfair to both herself and to Evan, and so she ended the relationship about halfway through their sophomore year. Even though it had only lasted a few months, her time with Evan helped Jenny come to the realization that maybe she would never, and could never, be attracted to the opposite sex in any type of romantic or sexual way.

Sharing her revelation was something that Jenny couldn't bring herself to do, though. While she did attempt flirting with other girls sometimes either at school, or at after school events or parties, she didn't really know what she was doing, and never knew if the girls were just being friendly or if they might also be interested in girls the way Jenny was interested in girls. However, now that she was far away from home and in college, Jenny had hoped to make a new life here and maybe find her very first girlfriend. And, since it was a liberal environment and she didn't know any people here, she felt it would be a safe place to 'come out'.

Sound of footsteps approaching her doorway suddenly snapped Jenny out of her semi-trance state, and she was slightly paralyzed with a moment of apprehension. Those footsteps could very well belong to the girl that she would be spending the next year living with. All sorts of doubts suddenly swirled through her head, and as Jenny turned towards the opened door, a beautiful creature stopped directly in front of the doorway that stopped her breath. A girl with the most amazing long, dark brown hair with matching sultry brown eyes stopped in the doorway and looked up at the room number. After looking back down to check the piece of paper she held in her hand, she turned and spoke over her shoulder to someone behind her.

"Yep, this is it," the girl said.

The beautiful creature entered the dorm room with a loaded backpack on her back, while pulling a suitcase behind her, and a man and woman entered right behind her carrying boxes marked with the word 'college' on them.

"Hi, I'm Katie," the girl said as she walked into the

room and meeting Jenny's eyes.

"Hi, I'm Jenny."

They smiled, shook hands, and Katie introduced Jenny to her parents.

There was an exaggerated moment of silent communication between the two girls, and then Jenny excused herself from the room to give Katie and her parents some time to settle her in.

Katie settled in, college classes started just days later, and through all the chaos Jenny and Katie became great friends. Such great friends, that during the first six months of college the girls spent most of their free time together. Whether the girls realized it or not, they both were of immense help to the other in the fact that they found an avenue to express and understand who they each were, and what they truly desired. They both not only boldly expressed their truth, but they also both expressed their support of each other, thus creating a foundation of trust and open communication that unbeknownst to them at the time, would lay the groundwork for future revelations.

Unlike Jenny who had pretended to like guys out of confusion and overt family and society pressures, Katie was always fully aware of her sexual orientation, even though she never really followed through with any possibilities. While Katie never actually had a relationship, there was a particular girl that she flirted with all throughout her senior year of high school. And, while she hoped that something might manifest between her and her female target of flirtations, nothing ever happened beyond that.

The two freshman beauties lives became entangled with one another, and soon, in addition to becoming the best of friends, both of the girls found themselves harboring secretly held emotions and feelings for the other. This created yet another layer of complexity to their relationship, and that was a layer of growing sexual and romantic tension. However, neither girl spoke of these feelings to the other out of fear that those feelings and emotions might not be returned, and that it might also ruin the close and wonderful friendship they had built. So, both Jenny and Katie danced that dance that lesbians often do, when two women are both consumed with a mixture of insecurity, fear, and unexpressed emotions that prevents them from exploring the possibilities of a relationship with one another.

Was this as far as things would ever go between them, Jenny often thought to herself. After all, wasn't the freedom of college life supposed to give her the platform to be out and open with other young women? It was, and it did. However, what college life hadn't guaranteed Jenny was the courage to take those first steps. So, Jenny tried to think of a way to create an opportunity in which she could tell her roommate Katie how she feels. And, regardless of the outcome, Jenny knew this was a necessary step in her evolving into her grown-up lesbian shoes.

Spring break was coming up and both Katie and Jenny had decided to not go home, or join the masses at one of the random spring break destinations. Both girls had elected to stay on campus and just enjoy a laid back week of no classes, no exams and nothing in particular to do. Jenny was ecstatic when Katie had told her that she too was planning on staying on campus during spring break, and Jenny was suddenly struck with the thought that this might be the opportunity she was seeking.

Jenny was secretly thrilled to have Katie all to herself for a whole week without the interruptions that a class schedule brought on, and Jenny decided to commit to telling Katie how she felt, and hopefully Katie would mirror back at least some of those same feelings. After all, there was no denying the growing sexual and romantic tension between them, and many of their friends have been making comments about it for months now. It was obvious to their friends, and it was obvious to them. And, since this is no longer high school, it was time to end the sweet, shy banter and make a move.

Most of the college campus was empty the first night of spring break, due to the fact that the majority of students had either gone home to visit family, or set off to one of the spring break party destinations. Katie and Jenny both noticed the shift of energy, not just on campus, but between themselves. Was it the unspoken anticipation of what the relaxed week alone together might bring? There certainly seemed to be a lot of nervous eye contact going on between them, and a little uncertainty about what they should do with their time. To entertain themselves on their first evening alone with no studies or other commitments, the girls bought some wine coolers and rented a DVD of the cult movie favorite 'Personal Best'. The story line of the two main girls in the movie had some seeds of familiarity that resembled the true life story line of Jenny and Katie. In the movie, the two young girls were newly best friends who met at school, and developed a romantic and intimate relationship. As Jenny read the movie description on the DVD box, she couldn't help but wonder if Katie had chosen this particular movie deliberately or if this movie selection was just a little 'nudge' from the universe.

As the girls drank their wine coolers and watched the movie while sitting side-by-side together on Jenny's bed in the dimly lit dorm room, the intense emotional and sexual overtones of the movie were causing both of the girls to squirm and become consumed with emotional and sexual overtones of their own. Jenny was secretly looking for a way to at least hold Katie's hand as she watched it rest just a couple inches away from her thigh, as they sat propped up against the headboard of Jenny's bed. Their shoulders were touching as were their bare feet, and the tingles that this sent through Jenny's body was almost too much to bear. Jenny noticed her breathing had altered slightly, as she took in the scent of Katie's skin and was imagining her own hands slowly caressing Katie's toned, smooth thighs. At some point, Jenny had completely lost focus of the movie, and her imagination took over completely as she envisioned a full-on body contact experience with Katie.

Katie's thoughts were also not on the movie, but on Jenny's cute little breasts, and Katie was imagining her hands, mouth and tongue exploring them eagerly and tenderly. The more the wine coolers loosened the hold on Katie's inhibitions, the more she was hypnotized and drawn to Jenny's full, pouting lips. They looked so soft and so kissable, and Katie thought she would explode if she didn't kiss Jenny soon.

Jenny happened to sneak a glance in Katie's direction at the exact same time that Katie was fully contemplating the beauty of Jenny's mouth, and their eyes locked in an intense, lustful stare. No more shy glances, no more cute innuendos, and no more 'accidental' touches. Passion was now taking the upper-hand, and feelings and emotions that have long been held unexpressed, were about to indeed be expressed.

Katie took the lead, and leaning in awkwardly, but sweetly, kissed Jenny's lips, noticing that they were every bit as soft as she imagined them to be. That tender meeting of their mouths was all it took for Jenny's body to respond fully and instantly, and what started out as tender, timid kisses quickly turned into a hungry melding of lips and tongues.

"Oh my god," Katie suddenly burst out apologetically. "I'm so sorry, Jenny! I didn't mean to make you feel uncomfortable."

"Seriously?" Jenny asked sounding a bit disappointed. "Are you really sorry for kissing me?"

"No baby, I'm not sorry that I kissed you." Katie replied. "I've been wanting to kiss you for what seems like forever, but I just never knew if you felt the same way, and I don't want to do anything to upset you....or, lose you."

As the girls stared into each other's eyes, and an undeniable moment of truth flashed between them, Jenny broke the brief silence and let out a soft little laugh.

"The only thing that will upset me about this moment, and this kiss, is if you don't finish what you've started." Jenny replied. "I too have been dying to kiss you and touch you for months, but was too afraid to tell you or do anything about it. And then, I started to become afraid of what would happen if I didn't do anything about it."

"Really?" Katie asked incredulously. "That's exactly what I've been feeling!"

"I've never had a girlfriend, as you know, but I really, really would like for you to be mine." Jenny confessed, as she deposited a passion-filled kiss on Katie's mouth.

"Wow!" Katie exclaimed while reeling from Jenny's soft, tender kiss. "I've pretty much always known that I'm a lesbian but I've never had a real girlfriend, either, and I would so very much like to be yours."

"So, what you're saying is that we're both lesbian virgins, in more ways then one?" Jenny laughed.

"I guess so," Katie replied while joining in on the laughter. "Maybe we should do something to change that."

"Oh, I totally agree." Jenny said softly, as she gently pulled Katie's mouth to hers to commence their intimate initiation.

Jenny had only minimal clues as to what to do with a woman sexually, but she did know that both her mind and body responded at the sight, scent and thoughts of a woman, especially this woman. As their tongues explored each other's mouths, first tentatively, then feverously, the growing pitch of their excitement seemed to silently command and control their moves and intentions, helping to orchestrate the sexual union for these novice sapphos.

Katie had been secretly watching lesbian porn, so she had pretty good idea on how to touch another female, so she gradually took the lead by slipping Jenny's t-shirt over her head and unhooking Jenny's bra, as they continued to kiss and caress each others delicate curves. Jenny thought her heart was going to beat out of her chest when she felt Katie's hands on her breasts for the first time. Jenny gasped in pleasure as Katie gently tugged and pinched her nipples, and traced her fingers ever-so-lightly around her soft, nippled mounds.

Katie's excitement mirrored Jenny's, as she slowly made her way down to where she could wrap her mouth around Jenny's pink, hardened nipples. Katie could feel her own pussy responding to the pleasures of Jenny's body being felt beneath the touch of her hands and mouth. Oh yes, Katie thought, this is where I belong, as she suckled and licked Jenny's tits. She then felt Jenny's hand come around and nestle gently at the back of her neck, and she knew that their bodies were indeed finding their own natural intimate rhythm.

Jenny loved the way that Katie was licking and nibbling her breasts, but she was also now very eager to explore Katie's naked flesh, so she gently pulled Katie's body towards her. As they moved into a lying down position, they rolled over onto their sides facing each other, and Jenny quickly tugged Katie's shirt off so that she could do some touching and tasting of her own. The second her hands touched Katie's perky breasts, she felt a sudden heat rise up in her belly and between her legs. Jenny's fingers pulled on Katie's dark nipples, and as she traced Katie's plump, perky breasts with her tongue, Katie's body began to writhe back and forth in pleasure.

As Katie enjoyed the touch of her beloved, her body was responding with a level of arousal she had never known existed. Katie then felt Jenny's hands move down across her tits and stomach, and somehow managed to swiftly remove her shorts and panties. The foreign feeling of a naked female body pressed against her own, nearly caused Jenny to black out with pleasure, and her eyes momentarily rolled upwards as she let out a heavy, wanton sigh of pleasure.

Katie was feeling the same pangs of desire as she once more took the lead, and quickly stripped Jenny of her jeans and panties, leaving her beautiful body fully exposed for her pleasure. Moving her hand lightly across Jenny's bare stomach, she slowly trailed her fingers down to Jenny's secret pleasure zone between her soft thighs. As Katie gently guided a single finger between Jenny's fleshy petals, she found that Jenny was very wet and her finger easily glided around her clit and pussy lips. Jenny's head fell back with a loud moan, as Katie continued to caress the soft, smooth folds of her lips.

Now that she had Jenny revved up, Katie got up her nerve and started to slowly make her way down so that her face was between Jenny's thighs. Using her tongue as she had seen done in the porn movies, she used it to gingerly tease Jenny's swollen clit. Jenny was caught by surprise, and her ass bucked upward against Katie's mouth due to the erotic currents that were coursing through her body. The more Katie licked and teased the delicate folds of her pussy, the more concentrated and intense the heat and buzzing sensations grew in Jenny's lower stomach. Holding Katie's head in place with her thighs, Jenny suddenly started to ride against her mouth and tongue in total abandon, as all the blood in her body felt like it was rushing towards the innermost folds of her thighs.

Her orgasm slammed into her before Jenny even realized what was happening, and her body lost all last remnants of control. Crying out again and again, she moistened Katie's face with the evidence of her pleasure and satisfaction. As the last tremor rippled through Jenny's body, she was able to let her thighs fall apart to release Katie's head, as she lay still and took in long, deep breaths.

"Oh my god," was all Jenny could breathe out in a raspy whisper. "It was better than I could ever have imagined!"

Katie giggled as she made her way back up Jenny's body to give her a kiss, and Jenny got a sampling of her love juices left on Katie's mouth. The taste of her arousal gave Jenny a burst of new energy, and she suddenly flipped Katie over onto her back, anxiously ready to experience the reverse roles of giving and receiving.

"Ok baby, now let me see what I can do for you," Jenny said wickedly as she glided her way down Katie's amazing body. As it turned out, Jenny was a fast learner, and she mimicked all the sensual moves Katie displayed previously on her. The two beautiful sapphos twisted and contorted their naked bodies around each other on the bed, and Jenny brought Katie to the most mind-blowing orgasm as she sucked gently on Katie's clit while softly squeezing her pretty, plump ass. As Katie's body jerked in climax, Jenny kept thinking of how sweet Katie's pussy tasted, and how good it felt to trace her tongue across Katie's smooth lips.

As the girls lay naked together with their arms around each other, sharing the last wine cooler while the credits were rolling on the half-seen movie, Jenny suddenly jumped off of the bed and went over to her jewelry box. After rummaging around in it briefly, she returned to the bed and told Katie to hold out her arm. As Katie did, Jenny took hold of Katie's hand and fastened a pink & silver bracelet around her wrist.

"That's to say that I'm officially, and happily, your girlfriend now," Jenny said, smiling.

"Well, then I have to give you something, too," Katie exclaimed.

She presented Jenny with a silver chained necklace that she fastened around her neck, as she lovingly kissed the curve of Jenny's neck. The two girls cuddled up together on Jenny's bed and turned the movie back on to try and give it another go in watching it to the end, while basking in the glow of their newfound world of romance and sapphic sexual intimacy.

STORY 24 –
LESBIAN SEX:
COWGIRL SEDUCTION AT THE
WILD WEST RANCH

Jennifer was so happy to finally be away from her busy, demanding job and arrive at this all-inclusive wild west ranch she had booked a vacation at, that she literally couldn't stop smiling. Jennifer loved her job as a media marketing specialist in Seattle, Washington, and she was definitely a Seattle girl through and through, but she hadn't had time to get away for some much needed fun and relaxation time in close to three years now. So, when one of her co-workers showed her a website outlining a vacation package to a wild west ranch located in New Mexico where she could ride horses, hike, prospect for gold, mingle with the ranch owners and ranch hands by day and relax around evening campfires by night, she jumped on it. Even though Jennifer thinks of herself primarily as a 'city girl', she has always been fascinated by the happenings and life of the wild, wild west. Jennifer had been anxiously looking forward to her trip to the state of New Mexico ever since she booked the vacation package, and she was even more excited about partaking in all the fun activities she anticipated having at the ranch. And, now that her feet had actually touched the tumbleweed covered grounds of the desert, Jennifer's spirit was soaring, which was evident by the ear-to-ear grin she wore on her face.

As Jennifer's feet guided her through the sandy dirt amongst the many barns, cabins, ghost town looking shops and corrals, she observed an equal mix of both animals and guests, along with plenty of ranch hands running around to guide and take care of them both. Ranch guest accommodations consisted of lovely rustic little cabins situated in rows away from the ranch's main barn structure, and Jennifer was quite thrilled with the décor and ambiance of her cabin. She was treated to a patch quilt-covered queen size bed, as well as a small private bath with a shower and tub, a kitchenette, and a sitting area adorned with two wooden rocking chairs on either side of a small table with an oval braided rug underneath. But, what she loved the most was the earthy stone fireplace centered in the cabin wall directly across from the sitting area. A warm, crackling fire on a late September evening would most certainly be cozy, not to mention, very romantic.

Jennifer settled into her cabin, unpacked and changed from her traveling clothes into a pair of form-fitting denim jeans, a black long sleeved t-shirt and a denim jean jacket. She topped off her new cowgirl look with her first ever pair of genuine cowgirl boots. Jennifer's friends had warned her that she better 'break' them in before expecting to wear them all day, let alone every day, on her vacation. So, that's exactly what she did, and Jennifer wore them everyday to work for the entire month prior to her vacation. Her efforts paid off, and despite the first week of painful heel blisters, the boots were now efficiently 'broke in' and quite comfortable on her feet. Plus, Jennifer thought they looked quite sexy, and would go well with whatever she chose to wear, whether it was jeans, shorts or even a sundress during her solo cowgirl retreat.

Now that she was dressed in her official ranch clothes, Jennifer was ready to walk around, explore the ranch, and get a bearing on where everything was and make a mental list of the activities she'd like to do while she was here. Pulling her cabin door shut and locking it, Jennifer then pocketed her cabin key and set off on the dusty path that led back to the central hub area of the expansive ranch

The first thing that caught Jennifer's eye was a large, well maintained barn. Immediately to the left of the barn, was a fenced in area where a young horse was being put through its paces by what Jennifer assumed to be one as of the ranch hands. And, that ranch hand just happened to be one of the most drop dead gorgeous women that Jennifer had ever seen. Model tall, she had long dark blonde hair that wafted back and forth in the wind underneath her cowgirl hat, and a body that just wouldn't quit. Jennifer could tell that this woman's long legs were firm and toned by the way her tight jeans molded around them. Jennifer's heart skipped a beat as her eyes continued to roam upwards over the beautiful horse trainer's body, taking in the sexy curves of her firm, round ass, slim waist and ample breasts that pressed against a tight fitting flannel shirt.

Jennifer rested against the split rail fencing as she stood in a lustful trance and watched the woman's lithe body twist this way and that as she worked with the young, resistant horse. After a few minutes, Jennifer was snapped out of her trance when one of the male ranch hands approached her and offered to show her around the ranch, and give her the official guest welcome tour before dinner. Jennifer followed the lead of the male ranch hand, making a note to herself, to come back again to the horse barn to see if she can make acquaintances with the stunning female horse trainer.

The male ranch hand introduced himself as Brad, and he showed Jennifer which buildings around the ranch property were used for dining, entertainment, various guest services including outfitter excursions, and shopping. There was a general store where guests could purchase a small selection of groceries, and dinner was usually a communal affair with all of the staff and guests eating together as one big happy family in the dining hall. After dinner, there was various nightly entertainment scheduled in several of the barn buildings, along with the nightly bonfire and marshmallow roasting located in the square just outside the dining hall of the ranch.

As Brad was leading Jennifer down a dusty path across from the horse barn, Jennifer's curiosity got the best of her, and she inquired about the beautiful woman she'd seen working with the horse earlier when Brad had approached her.

"Oh yeah, that's Anna," Brad answered. "She's our expert horse trainer and main trail riding guide. I gotta say she's really something when it comes to those horses. Between her good looks and natural ability to calm and handle the horses, her guided trail ride excursions always book up. Some people even call her a horse whisperer."

"I just bet they do," Jennifer murmured. "How do I get in on one of those trail rides?"

"There's a daily sign-up sheet in the main house, and guests need to sign-up the night before. Anna heads the group out daily usually just after lunch, and they leave from the horse barn where you were watching her work with the horse earlier."

"Thanks, Brad," Jennifer said. "I'll do that. You've been so helpful in showing me around. I really appreciate it."

During her guest welcome tour of the ranch, Jennifer could tell by Brad's overt flirtatious gestures that he was more than a little interested in getting together with her, but she was able to politely detour his intentions without hurting his feelings. It wasn't usually evident to people that she was a lesbian, so warding off flirtatious advances from men was something Jennifer was quite accustomed to.

Jennifer wandered over to the main house to find the sign-up sheet for the guided trail rides, so she could add her name to the next days riding list before heading over to the dining hall for dinner. Unfortunately, the guest trail ride list was full for the next two days, so Jennifer was going to have to wait until her third days stay to enjoy that adventure. Boy, Brad wasn't kidding. Anna's guided trail rides were definitely popular with the ranch guests.

As Jennifer entered the dining hall to grab some evening chow, she was happily surprised to see Anna already enjoying her dinner at one of the tables, and engaged in conversation with her fellow dinner companions. Judging by the look of rapture on the faces of both the men and women at Anna's table, she guessed that they were just as enamored with Anna as she was. With no more empty chairs at Anna's table, Jennifer was going to have to find another opportunity to make the acquaintance of this cowgirl beauty.

Later that night after dinner, Jennifer attended the nightly ranch bonfire, where she recognized members of the staff in attendance, along with a good number of guests. Jennifer roasted some marshmallows while enjoying the acoustic guitar melodies offered up by a few of the musically inclined ranch hands. Jennifer certainly didn't overlook the fact that Anna was also in attendance, and this time, she seemed to notice Jennifer sitting directly across from her on the other side of the roaring fire. Anna's smiled and winked at her, and Jennifer returned the smile as warmly as possible while holding Anna's very direct, and dare-she-say, sensual stare.

Jennifer's body was absolutely twitching to go sit next to the cowgirl goddess and make conversation, but the evening bonfire was filled with music at the moment and not conversation, and it would have been rude for Jennifer to interrupt that. Jennifer and Anna continued to exchange many a flirtatious glance during the guitar serenade, and just when Jennifer thought there might be a break in the music and an opportunity for direct contact with Anna, another ranch hand approached Anna, and the two of them disappeared in the direction of the horse barn. Damn it, Jennifer thought. She was realizing that between Anna's ranch duties and popularity with the guests, getting acquainted with her dream cowgirl just might be more challenging than she initially thought. Disappointed that she didn't get to talk to her before it was time to return to her cabin, Jennifer left with the rest of the bonfire attendees once the fire died down, and enjoyed the chilled evening air and distant barks of the coyotes as she strolled back to her cabin. Tomorrow would be her first full day at the ranch, and Jennifer looked forward to the day's adventures.

Jennifer slept soundly that night in her cabin, her dreams filled with visions of Anna riding bareback on a striking black horse amongst the desert terrain of the wild west vista. In her dream, Anna's long blonde hair was blowing in the wind behind her, and her beautiful full breasts bounced gently up and down to the rhythmic motion of the trotting horse. Jennifer awoke hungry and horny early the next morning, and after masturbating to the visions of Anna from her previous night's dream, she made some strong black coffee in her little kitchenette and ate a light breakfast of toast with honey. After breakfast, Jennifer showered, dressed in a cute country looking sundress along with her new cowgirl boots, and headed out in the direction of the horse barn, where she was hoping to connect with Anna. Jennifer's intentions were intercepted by Brad the ranch hand, and she was coaxed to go with him and a group of the guests to both watch and help in the milking of the cows, and feeding of the pigs and chickens. Once they were fed, Brad headed them out to gather fresh eggs from the hens, and they all returned to the dining hall-kitchen with plenty of fresh milk and eggs needed for the ranch's meal preparations. Jennifer was really enjoying herself, and was looking forward to sharing her morning experience with Ann, if she ever got a chance to get some one-on-one time with her.

Lunch was a very interesting affair, as any of the guests could help in the cooking and food preparation if they wanted. Jennifer decided to give it a go, and she whipped up a little dessert magic by preparing a couple of fresh country apple pies, using a recipe she had memorized from when she used to make them with her grandma. Lunch was served promptly at 12:30 PM, and as the lunch bell was being run outside by one of the kitchen staff, Jennifer was excited to see Anna enter the dining hall and head over to one of the smaller dining tables with her meal.

This time Jennifer worked faster, and she managed to grab an available seat next to Anna at the table. Anna looked over when Jennifer sat down, and gifted her with the most beautiful of smiles that made Jennifer's heart skip a beat in her chest.

"Hello pretty lady, I'm Anna," she said warmly, offering her hand to Jennifer. "I'm one of the lead staff on the ranch and in charge of the horses."

"Yes, I know. Brad told me when he was giving me the guest welcome tour yesterday before dinner. I was actually watching you work with one of the horses before then. I'm Jennifer, by the way."

The two women shook hands, and there was an unmistakable current of instant and palpable attraction between them. They talked easily with one another during lunch, and walked out of the dining hall together afterwards.

"I hope you'll sign-up for one of my guided trail rides, Jennifer," Anna said, with a hint of coyness in her voice. "I'd love to show you around."

"Oh yes," Jennifer replied. "I signed up last night, and found out that your trail ride seems to be pretty popular around here. I wasn't able to get on the ride list until tomorrow."

"Then I'll look forward to seeing you," Anna said with a seductive smile on her face. "I better get back to work. After today's trail ride, I've got some grooming and training to do later this afternoon."

The women said goodbye, and Jennifer set off to check out the ghost town looking corridor that was home to a cowboy saloon, general store, western apparel boutique, antique shop and other specialty stores that Brad had pointed out to her yesterday. After a couple hours of browsing around, Jennifer took her purchases, along with a hot apple cider toddy, and headed back to her cabin to freshen up and change clothes. After all, a morning of animal tending followed by pie baking and shopping in the dusty dessert had left her in definite need of a cleansing hot shower.

After showering, freshening up her hair and makeup, and changing clothes, Jennifer headed back out about an hour before dinner, which was served every evening at 6:30 PM. She wanted to swing by the horse barn, in hopes of running into Anna. After all, Anna had mentioned to her earlier that she would be there grooming and training the horses after her daily trail ride. Much to Jennifer's delight, she spotted Anna out in the fenced in training area with the same horse she had seen her working with the day before. Anna saw Jennifer climb up on the fence to watch her, and she smiled and waved to her from the other side of the arena.

Jennifer was feeling relaxed after her hot shower and hot toddy, and she sat in awe as she watched Anna work with the horse. Anna did in fact seem to have some magical connection with the horse, and as the colors of the sunset drew down upon the ranch, Anna's curvaceous body looked positively breathtaking against the backdrop of deep orange and red hues that colored the sky. Anna's dark blonde hair reflected against the sky's colors like a shiny gemstone, and the combination of muted colors and shadows caused by the setting sun made Anna's moving body look like a seductive dancer, which Jennifer knew she would fantasize about later. Anna had this unique combination of down-to-earth and exotic qualities about her. She was sweet and genuine, yet seductive and mysterious. She was charismatic and compassionate, and insanely beautiful and alluring. Jennifer felt herself becoming quite hungry, but not for dinner. Instead, Jennifer found herself becoming quite ravenous with desire for this earthy beauty who has consumed her thoughts ever since arriving.

Jennifer was startled by the sound of the dinner bell ringing, and nearly fell off her perch on the edge of the fence. Anna smiled at her, and approached her with the horse following closely behind her.

"Great to see you Jennifer" Anna said with a smile. "I hope you don't mind, I reserved us a couple seats together in the dining hall tonight. Go on ahead. I need to get Midnight back to her stall, and then I'll meet you up there in just a few minutes."

Jennifer's heart about leaped out of her chest. "That sounds great" she replied. "I'll see you up there".

Jennifer jumped down off the fence, and headed over to the dining hall, all-too-aware of the tingling sensations she was feeling in the lower part of her pelvis.

When Jennifer spotted Anna entering the dining hall about ten minutes later, she waved her over to the table, and they chatted all through their meal, while Jennifer was keenly aware of, and slightly distracted by, Anna's thigh up rubbing up against hers underneath the table. The overt flirtatious gestures continued after dinner, as both women attended the evening's bonfire and sat next to each other on one of the large logs provided as seating. After the bonfire concluded, Anna walked Jennifer back to her cabin, and before they parted ways for the night, Anna told Jennifer that she was looking forward to seeing her the next day on the trail ride, and surprised Jennifer with a soft, sensual kiss on her mouth.

Jennifer was so excited about going on the trail ride the next day that she could hardly sleep that night, and when she finally did, her dreams were once again filled with beautiful visions of Anna. This time in Jennifer's dream, Anna was naked except for her hat and cowgirl boots, and she was bathing the black stallion by the horse barn. Vivid images of water dripped from her naked skin and soap bubbles adorned the voluptuous curves of her hips and tits. Jennifer once again awoke horny as hell, and started her day with another round of masturbation followed by strong black coffee, before showering and dressing.

Jennifer dressed in a riding outfit she had bought yesterday afternoon at the western apparel shop. She pulled on a pair of new Levi jeans, and decided to go braless before pulling on her midnight blue, long sleeved flannel shirt, followed by a denim vest, her cowgirl hat and boots. Jennifer put on a little makeup and smoothed on some lip balm before locking up her cabin and heading over to the horse barn. Jennifer was pleased to hear that today's trail ride was going to be in the morning instead of after lunch, which meant that Jennifer would be able to see Anna sooner vs. later.

As Jennifer approached the trail head next to the horse barn, she smiled when she saw that Anna was already there and helping people to mount their horses. The very sight of her caused a rush of electricity to surge through Jennifer from head to toe, as her body yearned to be close to and touched by this wild west beauty that literally hypnotized her attention. Anna smiled at Jennifer when she saw her, and finished assisting a woman onto a horse. Anna then walked over to a beautiful light colored horse and led her over to where Jennifer was standing.

"Good morning Jennifer. Wow, you look fantastic!" Anna said.

"Thank you" replied Jennifer. "I was trying to go for the sexy cowgirl look."

"Well, you certainly succeeded. You're going to be a great view for me during the ride" Anna said flirtatiously. "And, I'd like you to meet Peaches. I chose her especially for you," as she gestured towards the cream colored horse.

"She's beautiful!" Jennifer exclaimed as she petted the side of Peaches' face.

"Do you know how to ride?" Anna asked.

"I've ridden quite a few times in the past," Jennifer replied. "so, I'm hoping it's like riding a bike, and it will all come back to me once we get started."

"Great, just let me know if you need any help from me," Anna grinned. "Now, let's get you mounted" as she helped guide Jennifer up into Peaches saddle, glad for the opportunity to catch a feel of Jennifer's hips as she helped boost her up.

Once all eight of the guest riders were secured on their horses, Anna gave them a brief safety speech, and then off they all went down the trail with Anna in the lead, followed by the eight guest riders, and another ranch hand taking up the tail end of the horse convoy. Jennifer was riding just behind Anna and was treated to a view of her luscious ass as it rocked seductively from one side to the other in the saddle. Anna must have felt Jennifer's eyes on her because she turned and looked over her shoulder. Smiling wickedly at Jennifer, she winked and called out for everyone to pay attention and stay on the trail.

As they rode, the swaying movement of the horses gently stimulated Jennifer's clit, while the rubbing of shirt fabric against her braless breasts caused her nipples to be in a constant state of erection. Jennifer's eyes were more on Anna's body than the desert landscape, and as erotic thoughts consumed her mind, her fingers casually unbuttoned both her denim vest and the top four buttons of her shirt, so that with just the right movement a pair of eyes could catch a view of her bare tits underneath.

Jennifer rode as close behind Anna as she dared, and at one point, when the trail grew a bit wider, Anna came back to ride alongside her. Anna's eyes immediately found their way in the direction of Jennifer's gaping shirt, and Jennifer could literally feel her pussy get moist as she watched Anna staring blatantly and the peek-a-boo titty show.

"Girl, you are seriously making me wish there weren't any other people out here with us right now," Anna said quietly as she rode closer to Jennifer.

"Really? I can't say I disagree with you," Jennifer replied back with a coy smile.

"You look absolutely gorgeous in that outfit," Anna said.

"Would you like to see how I look out of the

outfit?" Jennifer asked as she winked.

"Ohhhh, you're killing me here, do you know that?"

Jennifer laughed, and the sexual innuendos and flirting continued off and on throughout the entire two hours of the trail ride. By the time they all arrived back at the horse barn, both Anna and Jennifer were hot and worked up, and in more ways than one. When Anna came over to help Jennifer dismount, she deliberately let her hands remain on her longer than necessary, as Jennifer's body slid between Anna's hands from Peaches saddle down to the ground.

"Why don't you stay Jennifer, and let me show you the inside of the horse barn?" Anna asked Jennifer quietly.

"That sounds perfect," Jennifer replied, grinning.

Once all of the guests had dismounted and gone about their other business, Jennifer and Anna entered the barn. A couple of ranch hands were finishing up by bringing the last of the horses to their stalls and giving them fresh water and alfalfa. Anna and Jennifer continued to flirt discreetly and playfully with one another as they waited for the ranch hands to finish.

Finally, all the horses were tended to and the ranch hands left the barn, leaving Anna and Jennifer to themselves.

"I thought they'd never leave," Anna said

Anna took Jennifer's hand and slowly pulled her into the nearest empty stall that had just been cleaned, with fresh straw added to the floor. Once she had closed and locked the stall door, Anna leaned into Jennifer and worked her lips and tongue gently against her mouth, while her hands busily removed Jennifer's vest and unbuttoned the rest of her shirt. The kiss quickly became quite passionate, and as soon as Anna relieved Jennifer of her vest and shirt, she slowly guided her down onto a pile of fresh soft hay, so that she could work on removing the rest of her clothes.

As Jennifer lay in the straw, Anna continued to kiss her soft lips, as her hands caressed and fondled her perky tits. Moans escaped Jennifer's mouth as Anna's fingers tugged at her nipples, and she felt one of Anna's knees press up and rub against the crotch of her jeans. Jennifer rocked her hips against Anna's knee, and the gently rubbing friction against her pussy caused insane floods of heat to surge into her pelvis.

Anna leaned back and tugged off Jennifer's boots, before coming up to unbutton Jennifer's jeans and slide them slowly down and off her legs along with her panties. Jennifer had never been with a woman who was both so beautiful, and so experienced, and Anna certainly knew what she was doing as she continued to magically entrain Jennifer's body as skillfully as she entrains her horses.

While Jennifer lay naked against the straw, Anna stood up before her and slowly started to remove her clothes, tossing them aside as she bared her beautiful body for Jennifer. Anna first pulled off her boots, and then guided her jeans down over her curvaceous hips, before stepping out of them and tossing them aside. Jennifer then watched her fingers unbutton her plaid shirt teasingly one button at a time, until her large breasts were freed of the shirt and jiggling tauntingly above Jennifer's eyes. Jennifer could feel her heart pound in her chest, and as Anna slid her panties off exposing her soft, smooth mound, Jennifer thought she'd orgasm just at the sight of Anna's naked body standing above her.

Anna kneeled down between Jennifer's legs and spread them apart so she could kiss and lick her way up Jennifer's smooth legs and thighs. Jennifer's ran her fingers through Anna's long thick hair as her head and mouth nibbled their way closer and closer to Jennifer's pussy. Spreading Jennifer's legs apart even further, Anna slowly glided her wet tongue along the innermost crease of Jennifer's thighs, as Jennifer's hips started to rock back and forth. Eager to taste the sweetness of Jennifer's pussy, Anna then ran her tongue ever-so-softly between the folds of Jennifer's pussy lips, making teasing passes across the pretty rosebud of a clit that hid underneath. The musky honey taste drove Anna wild, and she reached down between her own legs with one of her hands, to gently caress her own smooth pussy. Anna then parted Jennifer's pussy lips open wide with her fingers, and gently began to suckle on her erect clit, as Jennifer gently rocked her hips against Anna's mouth.

"God, you taste delicious!" said Anna from between Jennifer's thighs. "Here, let me show you." And with that, Anna slid up Jennifer's body and kissed her fully and slowly on her mouth, allowing Jennifer to taste the sweet dew of her pussy on Anna's lips.

The kiss quickly grew from soft and tender, into a passionate tongue tango and lip nibbling frenzy. As their lips and tongues danced with each other, Anna slid a couple fingers into Jennifer's wet pussy and glided them in and out, while her thumb teased circles around Jennifer's clit. Anna could feel Jennifer's hard nipples poke against her own tits, as their bodies pressed against each other on the straw-filled horse stall. At the same time, she could also feel Jennifer's pussy start to contract and pulse around her fingers as she continued to finger fuck her.

Anna rode her pussy against one of Jennifer's

thighs as she continued to kiss and finger fuck her, and she thought of how Jennifer's naked body felt like heaven pressed against her own naked skin. As her fingers tickled Jennifer's G-spot while her thumb still caressed circles around Jennifer's clit, Jennifer's body began to stiffen in her arms until a cry of ecstasy escaped from her mouth and her hips and body trembled and bucked against the efforts of Anna's touches.

Anna gently began kissing Jennifer's orgasm-fatigued body from head to toe, as Jennifer's fingers stroked Anna's worship-worthy body with her eyes still closed and a smile on her face.

"Please let me return the favor" said Jennifer.

Anna rolled Jennifer's body on top of her own, and Jennifer first enjoyed Anna's breathtaking tits with first her hands, and then her mouth and tongue, while Anna kept hold of Jennifer's hips and pressed them against her own, rocking their pelvises together in rhythm. As Jennifer made her way between Anna's soft thighs, she gently spread her pussy lips open with her fingers and licked slowly all around Anna's love hole and clit. Even the scent of Anna's pussy was intoxicating, and Jennifer's own again growing arousal caused her to lick and suck Anna's pussy faster and faster until Anna's hips pushed up suddenly against Jennifer's mouth. As Anna's body shook in climax, Jennifer continued to suck her clit as she slid a finger deep into Anna's pussy. Anna's hips pressed against Jennifer's hand, as she rode the waves of her orgasm to its end.

Jennifer looked down at Anna, as she lay like a beautiful naked angel against the straw, and leaned down to taste the salty moistness of her mouth while Anna's breathing slowly returned to normal. As Anna returned Jennifer's soft, tender kisses they heard the chow bell ringing loudly across the ranch. Quickly, the women sat up and got dressed, because they didn't want anyone coming to look for them to let them know dinner was ready. Once they were dressed and on their feet, they embraced and kissed one last time before heading out of the horse barn and towards the dining hall.

"So, would you like to come to my cabin tomorrow night? It's my last night here, you know," Jennifer said on their walk to the dining hall.

"It's a date," Anna laughed. "You can tell me all about city life in Seattle. I might just need to visit sometime and would love for you to be my very own personal tour guide."

"You've got it!" Jennifer said, grinning as she was already looking forward to her last nights stay.

STORY 25 –
LESBIAN ADVENTURE IN THE SKY: SAPPHO SEDUCTION INTO THE MILE HIGH CLUB

Dori generously tipped the cab driver who had just picked her up from her apartment and dropped her off curbside at Denver National Airport, for her red eye flight from Denver, Colorado to Miami, Florida. With her laptop and over-packed suitcases in tow, Dori was excited about her journey and highly anticipating connecting again with her sister. The main reason for the trip was to attend her sister's college graduation, but Dori had planned her stay for a full two weeks so she could enjoy a bit of fun and sun in the 'Sunshine State'.

After checking in her bags and getting her boarding ticket, Dori made her way through the airport security line and then on to the boarding gate area where her flight was to depart from. Sipping a hot cup of coffee she picked up at a coffee shop along the way, Dori settled into a seat facing the boarding line and pulled out her laptop to work on the writing outline of her latest novel as she awaited her boarding call.

Dori was a semi-famous mystery novel writer, and she always traveled with her laptop, squeezing in moments of writing time every chance she got. Through past experience, Dori had discovered that long flights, especially middle of the night 'red eye' flights, offered her the perfect opportunity to work on whatever current writing project she was involved in. Being confined to an airplane seat for hours at a stretch typically forced out the usually distractions that caused writers block, allowing the creative ideas and words to magically flow from her mind, through her hands and keyboard, and out the other end as formed sentences, paragraphs and exciting story plots. Dori knew her flight was going to be long and quiet since it was a 'red eye' flight, which meant a perfect opportunity to enjoy a couple glasses of wine and write away while the majority of the other passengers were sleeping.

Dori quickly got lost in her writing as she waited for passenger boarding to be called, and she was so wrapped up in her thoughts and typing that she almost didn't notice the sudden activity around her near the boarding gate counter. Something drew her eyes upward, and as Dori scanned the boarding gate area, her eyes locked on an incredibly sexy flight attendant pulling a carry-on tote and walking crossing the waiting area along with a couple more flight attendants. They were obviously the flight attendants assigned to her flight, and it appeared that they were getting ready to board the plane ahead of the passengers.

The flight attendant that captivated Dori's attention was not only drop-dead gorgeous, but she had this air of mystery about her, and a sort of dominant, dangerous sex appeal that Dori was attracted to. The flight attendant had long dark brown hair, big brown eyes, a curvaceous figure that made her uniform look like the sexiest piece of clothing on the planet, and a teasing, seductive smile that Dori was sure served like a beacon in the night, drawing attention and suitors to her wherever she went.

Dori mused at how the object of her attention would make for a perfect character in one of her future novels, not to mention, her own private fantasy when she masturbated. The flight attendant must have felt Dori's eyes on her, because she suddenly turned around and looked right at Dori. They exchanged smiles and a surprisingly long and lingering non-verbal moment of communication. The sexy flight goddess finally turned away to speak to the male flight attendant standing next to her, as he appeared to be getting ready to start take the passenger's boarding tickets at the gate.

Dori's body warmed as her eyes took in the gorgeous features of the sexy flight attendant as she turned and disappeared down the jet way. I sure hope I get to see more of her during the flight, Dori thought to herself. As she was thinking this, she heard the male flight attendant's voice make the announcement for passengers who were ticketed in first class to begin boarding. Dori noticed that there were only a few passengers who responded to the First Class seating call, and once they all made their way onto the plane, the rest of the passengers were then called to board.

Even the number of coach ticketed passengers didn't appear to be all that large. This was a relief to Dori because that meant there would be more open seats and less chance of spending the flight next to a well-meaning yet chatty passenger, allowing Dori lots of undisturbed time and space to allow her to work on her latest novel. She closed her laptop and stood up to gather her carry-on bag and purse, and then headed over to the short passenger boarding line. When Dori made it to the front of the line to where the male flight attendant was taking the boarding tickets, he smiled at her and handed her an alternate boarding ticket.

"I've got some good news for you Miss," he said. "Since we're traveling kind of light tonight, one of our flight attendants has upgraded you to First Class seating at no charge. Enjoy your upgrade and your flight Miss."

"Wow, what a nice surprise. Thank you so much!" Dori replied.

Dori boarded the plane and searched for the new seat assignment that was stated on her boarding ticket in First Class. She located it quickly, put her carry-on bag in one of the overhead compartments, and as she settled in her large, comfortable seat, she noticed that the sexy flight attendant that had captured her attention in the gate area was tending to some of the First Class passengers a couple rows up from her. It appeared that the gorgeous flight goddess was assigned to First Class, and Dori smiled at the thought that her wish came true, and she would indeed get to see this gorgeous creature quite a bit more during the course of the flight. Leaning back in her last row seat, she loved the fact that there was a wall behind her that separated her from coach class seating, and there were no passengers across the aisle or for two rows up from her. As long as she could discipline her attention away from the sexy flight attendant and focus on her novel outline, the seating arrangement made a very conducive environment for her to get some serious writing done during the flight.

As Dori was bending down to retrieve her laptop from its sachet case, she heard a sultry voice from above her.

"Welcome aboard. May I get you a cocktail before we take off."

Dori sat back upright in her seat and looked up to meet the eyes of the sexy flight attendant. Dori squirmed a little and was consciously trying to keep her composure, as she was all too aware of the gorgeous, voluptuous body standing just inches from her face.

"I'll have a glass of merlot and a bottle of water please" Dori replied, feeling herself blush, and suddenly wondering if she was going to be able to concentrate and actually focus on her writing during the flight.

The flight attendant briefly disappeared behind the curtain of the First Class galley, before returning with Dori's drinks. "Here you are," the attendant said, handing Dori her wine and water. As the flight attendant handed Dori her drinks, a surge of lustful electricity bolted through Dori's body as she gently brushed her fingers against Dori's and allowed them to linger longer than was needed.

"Well, if there's anything you need during your flight, you just let me know" said the flight attendant, removing her hands from Dori and turning to attend to the other First Class passengers.

"I'll be sure to do that," Dori replied, giving her a shy coy smile, and enjoying the view of the flight attendant's tight curvy ass as she walked up the cabin aisle.

Within the next five minutes, the captain made the announcement that they were ready for take off, and after the usual video and visual demonstration of emergency plane procedures, the pilot guided the plane down the runway and up into the air. Once they were airborne and the fasten seatbelt sign was turned off, Dori opened up her laptop and proceeded to work on the novel outline she had started earlier. Dori was just getting into the rhythm of her writing zone, when someone quietly sat down in the seat beside her. Dori looked up from her laptop, to find that that 'someone' was the intoxicatingly beautiful flight attendant.

"Hello again, am I disturbing you?"

"No, not at all," Dori said as she smiled broadly at the beautiful woman sitting next to her. She was surprised at how fast her body and mind responded to the sight and attention of this woman, and once again surges of electricity pulsed through Dori's body as she tried not to squirm in her seat.

"I'm Becky" the flight attendant said, introducing herself. "What are you writing so industriously there?" she asked Dori.

"A pleasure to meet you Becky, I'm Dori. I was actually just working on an outline for my next book. I write mystery novels for a living."

"Oh really? I love mysteries! Have you written anything that I may have read?" Becky asked.

"Well, I'm not sure." Dori recited some of her more bestselling books to find that Becky had actually read three of them.

"Oh you're good! I love that PI series you're doing! Camilla is such a strong female character!" Becky enthused. "Hey, if you don't mind, I've got to look after some passengers here, but I'd like to come back and visit with you some more."

"Sure, I'd like that" Dori replied.

Giving Dori a sexy wink, Becky got up and went to tend to the other First Class passengers. Becky made short work of serving the few passengers that were in First Class with cocktails, pillows, blankets and other incidentals, and in no time, she was back sitting next to Dori.

"So who or what is in Miami?" Becky asked Dori.

"My sister, actually. She's graduating from college and I'm flying in for the ceremony. I extended my vacation time while I'm there, so I can get in some fun and relaxation while I'm there. I don't get back home often, so I like to make the most of it."

"Sounds like fun," Becky said. "I get lots of layovers in Miami. It's a great place. Do you have a boyfriend there or something?"

"Nooo, I don't have a boyfriend there, or anywhere else for that matter," Dori laughed, feeling herself blush.

"I don't believe there's not someone special in your life as gorgeous as you are," Becky said, as she touched Dori on the knee, fishing for a direct or indirect clue to

Dori's sexual orientation, as well as her relationship status.

"Well, I'm kind of at loose ends right now," Dori said, unsure if she should be more honest or not, and how much she should say, or not say.

"What's your type then? Maybe I know some single guys to introduce you to," Becky said in a teasing tone.

"Ok, you want to know my type?" Dori replied. "That would be someone about my height, with long dark hair and seductive brown eyes. I really like voluptuous figures, with curvy hips and full breasts. Long, toned legs also really turn me on. I'm also attracted to confidence and an air of mystery and danger. So, do you know anyone like that?" Dori said as she boldly looked Becky straight in her eyes.

"Ohhh I just might," Becky said, almost purring after having gotten the answer she was seeking. "I've got a question for you."

"Hopefully, I'll have an answer."

"Have you earned your wings yet?" Becky asked, with a look on her face like a hunter aligning its attention and appetite on its prey.

"Earned my wings? What do you mean?"

"Your wings for the Mile High Club. You know, where you have sex on a plane while it's flying high in the air."

"Oh." Dori started to laugh. "Honestly, I kind of thought that was all a bit of a myth or something. Do you mean that people actually do that?"

"They certainly do," Becky said, leaning in closer to Dori. "Listen, most of the passengers are going to be turning off their lights pretty soon, and going to sleep since this is a 'red eye' flight. I not only know someone who meets the description of your fantasy, but I'm also more than willing to help you earn your wings this evening, if you'd like" Becky offered, giving Dori an intense look of lustful hunger that Becky knew was having the desired affect on Dori that she wanted.

"Well, how can I even think about turning down such a tempting offer like that," Dori said quietly, as surges of heat now pulsed throughout her body. Dori knew at that moment that she would not be getting any writing done during the flight. This evening, the adventure would be played out in reality for Dori, instead of vicariously through one of the characters in her novels.

Becky winked at Dori as she reached over and gave her hand a teasing, gentle squeeze before getting up to see if any of the First Class passengers needed anything before they started to settle in for the long night flight. Dori's mind was pulsing with mental visuals of her induction into the Mile High Club, not to mention, the deep, throbbing pulses she was all too aware of happening between her legs. She anxiously waited for Becky to make her round with the passengers, and every time Becky walked near her, she gave Dori a sultry smile full of promise.

After it appeared that Becky was finished tending to the passengers, the pilot had dimmed the cabin lights, and all but one of the First Class passengers had also turned off their private overhead lights to presumably go to sleep. In the now dimly lit First Class passenger area, Dori saw Becky emerge from behind the galley curtain and make her way towards her.

"Come with me," Becky whispered quietly to Dori, as she approached her.

Dori got up from her seat, her legs shaking slightly in anticipation, and she followed Becky back up to the flight attendant's galley area as Becky pulled closed the heavy curtain that separated it from the passengers. After holding a finger to her lips, that signaled Dori to be quiet, Becky pulled Dori's body against her own and delivered a slow, deep and very passionate kiss. Dori immediately responded to Becky's soft lips and tongue, and her hands hesitantly started to explore the outline of Becky's amazing curves as their mouths hungrily, yet sensually. explored one another.

Suddenly Dori pulled back slightly as she whispered to Becky, "Shouldn't we go in the bathroom?"

"No, gorgeous," Becky answered. "As long as we're quiet, we'll be fine right here. Plus, there's more room here for us to enjoy each other's company. Damn, you're so beautiful" Becky finished, as she moved back in to get another taste of Dori's sensual pouty lips.

As Becky's mouth licked and nibbled its way down the side of Dori's neck, she slid her hand up underneath Dori's sweater and didn't stop until she reached the swell of Dori's full, firm breasts. She was thrilled to find that Dori's bra had a front closure, which she was expertly able to unhook in a matter of a second, unleashing both of those luscious orbs from their clothing confinement. Becky lifted Dori's sweater up over her tits, and leaning forward, her mouth quickly found Dori's dark nipples, and wrapping her lips around them one at a time, she nibbled and sucked on them until they became erect in her mouth.

Dori's head fell back and she moaned softly in her throat. She loved the way her nipples responded so instantly and intensely to the attentions of Becky's mouth, which caused a similar reaction within her pussy, which was now noticeably warm and tingling. Using her own hands, Dori slid her fingers down and around the curves of Becky's hips, as she then tugged to lift Becky's form fitting skirt up over her lovely, firm ass cheeks. Surprised by the fact that Becky was wearing a garter and stockings, Dori's fingertips immediately enjoyed the feel of Becky's smooth skin on the tops of her thighs. Dori's fingers then found their way between them as she gently grazed her fingers across the crotch of Becky's satiny smooth panties, pressing the fabric softly against Becky's pussy lips.

Grabbing the sides of her hips, Dori pulled Becky up against her as she gently ground her pelvis against Becky's mound. Becky reached a hand around Dori and pulled the lever that released the double seated jump seat that flight attendants used to sit on during takeoff and landing. Becky sat down in one and started to pull Dori down next to her, when suddenly the plane hit a bit of turbulence, causing Dori to slip onto the floor in front of the jump seat that Becky was seating on.

They both giggled a little and then Dori decided since she was already on the floor that she might as well take full advantage of it. Moving to her knees, she spread Becky's thighs apart and leaned forward to bury her face in Becky's crotch. Discovering that Becky's panties were now moist in the center, only served to spur Dori on. Using a finger she moved the silky fabric aside and used her tongue to first part the soft folds of Becky's moist pussy, before moving on to make soft, slow circles around Becky's hardening clit. Using then what she knew worked so well, Dori then took Becky's erect rosebud in her lips and suckled on it ever so gently, causing Becky's hips to rock against her mouth as her legs squeezed together trapping Dori's head between

Becky's thighs.

"Oh god, Dori," Becky cried in a whisper. "That's so fucking good!"

"Let me give you more baby" Dori said in a muffled voice from between Becky's thighs.

"Yes, give me more, I'm gonna cum!"

As Dori's lips and tongue continued to lick and suck Becky's clit, Dori could tell by the growing tenseness in Becky's thighs that she was close to cumming. As Dori began to suckle just a tad bit harder on Becky's clit, she slid in a couple fingers deep inside Becky's wet pussy and flicked the tops of her fingers against the inside wall of her honey pot. Becky's thighs tightened against Dori's head as she bucked her hips upwards and Dori could feel the spasms of climax ripple throughout Becky's body. Becky's head was thrown back against the galley wall, and she was obviously trying to suppress the moans and groans that were trying to escape from her mouth, as her body twitched in orgasmic pleasure.

Turbulence then suddenly hit once more, causing Dori's body to bounce over to the other side of Becky's legs. Becky helped her to get up from the floor as she started unfastening and unzipping Dori's slacks, eager to explore what was underneath of her new Mile High inductee's clothing.

Sliding Dori's slacks and panties down to the floor, Becky told Dori to hold on and stay standing as she spread Dori's legs wide apart. With her head positioned between Dori's legs, Becky started to tease Dori's smooth pussy lips with her fingers. Parting her pink folds, Becky traced her fingers ever so lightly all around Dori's pretty pussy lips as Dori's legs started to get weak, and she had to grip tightly onto one of the galley cabinets for support.

Becky was anxious to get her mouth where she so badly wanted to be, already able to smell the sweet musky scent of Dori's wetness. Expertly fielding those fleshy petals that hid Dori's pleasure center, Becky started to return the pleasure that Dori had already so skillfully given her. Dori wasn't as successful at suppressing her cries of ecstasy as Becky slid her fingers into her cunt and started to finger fuck her, and unbeknownst to Dori, her moans of pleasure were being heard by the now awakened First Class passengers.

Becky was also unaware that their Mile High escapades were now the in-flight entertainment of the First Class passengers, and she continued to finger fuck Dori while licking her erect clit, until she had to help Dori stay standing as volcanic waves of climactic pleasure trembled through her body from head to toe.

What neither Becky nor Dori were aware of, was that midway through their Mile High encounter, the turbulence had knocked one of the cabin phones from the cradle, and was broadcasting their encounter to the First Class passengers. The previously darkened cabin filled with sleeping passengers was now filled with wide-eyed voyeurs, who were treated to the audio delights of the Sappho seduction happening just behind the galley curtain.

Becky stood up next to Dori and gave her one last kiss. "Welcome to the Mile High Club sexy," she whispered.

"Thanks for inducting me," Dori whispered back against Becky's lips.

Becky and Dori straightened their clothing, and Becky stayed behind in the galley area while Dori went to return to her seat. As Dori walked quietly down the aisle, she caught some odd looks from the First Class passengers, all of whom seemed to be awake now. Back in the flight attendants area, Becky's eyes widened as she saw that the First Class cabin phone was dangling from the hook. Frowning, her heart raced a little, wondering if any of the First Class passengers had overheard the encounter between her and Dori. Putting the phone back into the cradle, Becky decided there was nothing she could do about it, and went about to check on the needs of her passengers, hoping none of them would mention anything.

The rest of the flight went smoothly, and Dori spent the time making adjustments to her novel outline, working in her Mile High induction into the storyline. Just before they were to land, the pilot came on.

"Welcome folks to sunny Miami, Florida" he said over the cabin intercom. "Today's expected temperature is 82 degrees, with clear skies and plenty of sun. Please put your trays and chairs in the upright position, and make sure that your seatbelts are fastened to prepare for landing. We hope you enjoyed your flight as well as the unexpected in-flight entertainment, and we look forward to you flying with us again."

Dori and Becky exchanged looks after the pilot's last comment. Dori couldn't believe what she had just heard. Surely, no one heard them! But, what Dori didn't know, that Becky did after their encounter, was that the cabin phone had been knocked off the hook.

After the plane made a smooth landing and the passengers started to disembark, Dori lingered behind, as she deliberately wanted to be the last passenger to get off the plane. As she passed Becky, who was guiding the exiting passengers, Becky handed Dori a slip of paper with the phone number of the hotel where the flight crew would be staying for the next couple of days. Becky then winked at Dori, as Dori took the piece of paper and continued her way towards the plane's exit door.

Going through the door that lead into the jet way, Dori passed by the pilot and co-pilot, who were both grinning so widely that their faces looked like they were about to split.

"Hope you enjoyed the flight, Miss. Please do fly with us again." The pilot said to her.

Dori decided she didn't care if they heard or not. That was one of the most sexually adventurous experiences that she has ever had, and she would certainly do it again if the opportunity presented itself. Who knows, maybe next time she'll be the one helping some beautiful woman earn her 'wings'!

STORY 26 –
LESBIAN COP:
UNLAWFUL STRIP SEARCH

Danni paused to checked her reflection in the full length mirror once more before heading out the door. Her blue spaghetti strapped sequined dress was perfect with its form fit and mini length, which served to emphasize her firm, round ass and long, toned legs. The blue satin heels she had chosen matched her dress beautifully, and its deep plunging neckline drew attention to the perky breasts that were jutting out behind the thin sequined fabric. Danni looked smoking hot, and she was hoping to turn some heads when she entered the private nightclub she was attending with a friend later. Her almond-shaped green eyes were adorned with smoky colored eyeshadow and black kohl liner, that transformed them into a sultry retro look. With a final finishing touch, Danni ran her fingers through her dirty blonde hair once more, to give it a tousled, sexy look, and glided on some shimmering lip gloss to accentuate her pouty, full lips.

Yes, Danni thought with satisfaction, I look pretty damn hot! Grabbing her purse, she set the house alarm and was out the door. Tonight was going to be hugely exciting for her. She had been invited to attend a party at a very exclusive private nightclub in Los Angeles. Her friend, Annabelle was a member there, and had invited her to come along. She had told Danni to 'dress to impress', because you just never knew who you might meet, and besides, all sorts of wild things tend to happen at these private parties.

Danni was meeting Annabelle at the address that she had given her that afternoon. This was so exciting for her because she had always wanted to attend one of these much talked about private parties, but she didn't have enough money for the exuberant membership dues. Danni had been amazed to find out just a few days prior that Annabelle was a member there, and thrilled when

Annabelle had invited her to come to the party tonight.

She had chosen to take a cab rather than try to drive so that she could be assured of having a great time, and Annabelle was waiting for her in front of the club as her cab pulled up. Danni exited the cab and joined Annabelle at the building entrance, which was swarming with gorgeous people and mammoth-sized security personnel. The women hugged in greeting and each told the other how great she looked. In truth, Danni was more than a little excited to see her sexy friend Annabelle, and she had been hoping to catch her attention for a while now. Maybe the ambiance of the evening would give her the chance to see if she could make something happen between them.

Annabelle showed her ID to the doorman and informed him that Danni was her guest for the evening. Once the doorman verified their status on the guest list, the girls gained entrance and within just a few feet of entering, Danni could hear a live band playing somewhere in the maze of walls, rooms and bandstand areas. That immediately got her excited because she loved dancing. They proceeded down a long hallway lined with scantily clad bodies pressed against one another, their figures illuminated by the red neon color that lighted the entryway, which then ended at an archway that opened up into the main part of the club. Danni smiled to herself, thinking that it felt like they had just entered the 'batcave' for the underground horny, sexy socialites. People were dancing to the music shrouded in colored strobe lights and other intense lighting, and Danni took pause to admire the many alluring female forms dressed in their barely-there attire. The lights seemed to be keeping time with the beat of the music, and Annabelle pulled Danni out of her hypnotic girl watching trance, by grabbing her hand and pulling her to the dance floor.

As it turned out, Annabelle was quite a good dancer. She moved her hot little body in ways that Danni had only dreamed of seeing her do, and visions of their naked bodies entwined with one another were saturating Danni's thoughts. Of course, Danni was no slouch in the dancing arena herself, and did quite well in moving her body in very erotic ways, and right up against Annabelle's sexy, sweet-smelling body. The girls danced and writhed together to the music for almost half an hour, before Anabelle broke their rhythm.

"Are you having fun?" Annabelle shouted to Danni over the music.

"Absolutely!" Danni shouted in answer. She was also really starting to get her hopes over the possibility of the two of them going home together that night.

Danni and Annabelle decided to take a break from the dance floor and go get something to drink, when they noticed a ruckus of some sort coming from the front part of the club. They stopped on their way to bar and tried to figure out what was going on, and they didn't have to wait long. Police came barreling down the hallway and right into the club, guns drawn. It took a couple of minutes for their shouting to be heard above the music, although once the band caught sight of them, they stopped playing instantly. People on the dance floor started screaming and scrambling in terror.

"Everyone stay right where you are!" shouted a cop that seemed to be in charge. "Nobody leaves! If you try to leave, we will detain you at the jail!"

Annabelle and Danni clung tight to each other not quite sure what was going on, but neither of them tried to defy the orders that were given. It was clear that both of them were very scared and nervous about this turn of events.

"What's this about?" Danni whispered nervously in her friend's ear.

"I have no clue," Annabelle whispered back.

"Hey! You two by the bar whispering! We'll start with you since you seem to have something to say!"

This last order was spoken by an attractive and tough femme looking cop, who was heading in the direction of where the girls were standing. The female cop had short wavy black hair with toned arms and rather large breasts that strained against the shirt of her uniform. As she approached them, Danni had a flash of realization that this was a woman she could really be attracted to under most circumstances. However, given the situation, and the fact that the femme tough cop already had a intimidating demeanour about her and was aiming a gun in their direction, all that Danni felt at that moment was something a bit closer to terror.

As Danni's eyes were glued watching the female cop approach them, and was now only several feet away, Annabelle was suddenly ripped away from her by another cop, and Danni was left in the presence of the femme fatale cop who was blatantly sizing her up from head to toe. Suddenly gripping Danni by the arm, the policewoman aggressively escorted her towards the back of the club, where party goers were being questioned and some even being handcuffed and loaded onto the awaiting paddy wagons parked out back. Danni was now paralized with fear and didn't want to push her luck and join the others in the paddy wagon, so she decided to quietly comply.

"What's your name?" barked the policewoman.

"Danni Bartlett."

"Danni? Short for Danielle?"

"No, it's just Danni and not short for anything."

"Are you trying to be a smart ass?" the policewoman asked abruptly.

"No, ma'am," Danni answered. "I'm just trying to answer your question."

"Uh huh," the cop said. "Well, Ms. Bartlett, how often do you come here?"

"I don't come here often at all. In fact, tonight was my first time here. I came with my friend, who is a member here."

"Your first time here? Sure it is. Ms. Bartlett, are you aware that this club is under investigation for illegal gambling and prostitution?"

"No!" Danni exclaimed. "How would I know something like that? I already told you that this is my first time visiting here."

"I'm sure." the femme cop said dismissively, while never taking her eyes off of Danni's body, and still blatantly scanning her up and down. "Hey, Campbell! Here's another one for downtown!" A rather large male cop quickly approached them and took Danni firmly by the arm.

"Wait!" Danni cried. "Where are you taking me? I haven't done anything wrong!"

"That's something we'll sort out down at the station, ma'am," Officer Campbell said as guided Danni outside and hoisted her up into the back of one of the awaiting paddy wagons.

Her riding companions were expressing various stages of fear, outrage, and disbelief. By the time the wagon full of party goers had arrived at the police station, Danni had gone through each of those stages on her own although they hadn't exactly been in that order. Now, she was bouncing around with all three of them, and wondering what was happening to her friend Anabelle.

As Danni was roughly led into the police station, she noticed that there were a lot of other people there she recognized from the club that actually looked as if they might have been involved in something shady. Certainly some of those women looked like they could be high priced call girls. She didn't see Annabelle anywhere, though, and was starting to worry.

Danni was shoved into a holding cell with a lot of other women from the club, but she avoided speaking to any of them, and instead found a seat on a bench towards the back of the holding cell to try and just be by herself. There was something really 'off; about all of this, Danni thought, and something about the way that tough femme cop treated her just wasn't sitting right with her. It was freezing cold in the cell and she hadn't brought a wrap or jacket of any kind with her, so she sat shivering for several tortuous hours when finally, the female cop that had been so rude to her in the club came to the cell door and called her name.

It was obvious to Danni that this cop wasn't interested in men, and under any other circumstance, Danni thought, I would be flirting like crazy with this woman. But, this of course was no ordinary circumstance. Escorting Danni into a private interrogation room, the femme cop shoved her towards the middle of the room and instructed her to sit down at the table. While biting her tongue, knowing she should just keep her mouth shut, Danni's frustration was starting to mount over the situation and she wasn't quite sure she'd be able to do that.

"Now, Ms. Bartlett," the cop began. "What do you know about the activities that take place within the confines of this private club?"

"Aren't you supposed to introduce yourself before you start questioning me?" Danni irritatedly asked. She was horrified that she had just allowed those words to fly from her moving lips the moment the words were spoken, but there was just something about the way the femme cop kept treating her that was getting her riled up. Admittedly, there was some sexual frustration adding to the moment and her growing tension, but this was not the time or place to let those feelings get the upper hand.

"What? Are you trying to be a fucking smartass with me?" the cop said.

"No, ma'am, not at all. It's just that you have me at a disadvantage. You know my name and you know why you've brought me here. I don't know either of those things."

"Are you accusing me of false arrest, Ms. Bartlett?" the cop demanded.

"I'm not accusing you of anything, ma'am," Danni replied. "I'm just trying to figure out a way to communicate with you."

The femme cop stared at Danni intently and seemed to consider this for a minute.

"I'm Officer Lambert," she finally relented. "And you are here for questioning regarding allegations of illegal activities in the club where you were arrested tonight."

"Thank you, Officer Lambert," Danni said.

"However, I honestly cannot help you with your questions. Tonight was the first time I have ever been inside of that club and I didn't even get that far into the club. I never was off of the dance floor until just before you and your friends arrived. I didn't even have time to get a drink."

"What about your friend that you were whispering with? How often does she go to this club?"

"I honestly don't know. We don't talk that often."

"Really? I bet you'd like to talk to her a lot more, though, wouldn't you?" Officer Lambert sneered.

"I'm not exactly sure what you're asking, Officer."

"Never mind. Now, getting back to what you know about that club. If you're withholding information that could help us put a stop to illegal activity there, it's considered to be aiding and abetting and obstruction of justice."

"I keep telling you that I don't know anything!" Danni yelled back, in a combination of fear and frustration.

The exchange between Danni and the aggressive femme cop continued for a grueling animated hour, and took yet another unexpected turn when Officer Lambert slapped a pair of handcuffs on Danni's wrists and hooked them to a cuff ring attached to the interrogation table. Officer Lambert told Danni that she didn't believe a word she was saying and that she was about to be subjected to a strip search to insure that Danni wasn't hiding any drugs or anything.

"You can't be serious!" Danni exclaimed. "I'm not wearing that many clothes. Where would I hide anything?"

"That's what we're about to find out," Officer Lambert replied, smiling to herself as she turned and went over to the interrogation room door and opened it. Another female cop quickly entered carrying a cup of coffee, and sat down in a chair facing Danni.

Officer Lambert locked the door, turned her attention back to Danni and jerked her up from the chair she was sitting on. The femme cop made one long firm sweep starting from between Danni's legs up to her chest, and gave her tits a firm squeeze before ripping her dress from her shoulders and down around her ankles. The femme cop then literally tore Danni's panties off of her and tossed them across the room. Bucking against the shackles that bound her to the table, Danni writhed and squirmed as the fingers of Officer Lambert grazed over her smoothly shaven pussy. "Oh my gosh!" Danni thought, "Oh my gosh!"

The femme cop moved to stand in front of Danni, taking in the sight of Danni's nude and delicious curves. As Danni continued to yell and pull against her constraints, the femme cop licked her lips and assessed the perky roundness of Danni's tits, her diamond hard nipples, and slim taught waist. The Officer then walked around behind Danni, and in one swift movement, one hand grabbed a chunk of Danni's tousled hair holding her head up and back, while the other hand vice gripped around Danni's right tit. Conflicting emotions surged through Danni. Fear was still ever present, yet she was surprisingly aroused and could feel herself getting wet due to the dominating actions of the gorgeous femme cop.

"Mmm, you got a real juicy one this time, Lambert," the other cop said.

"Let's find out just how juicy she is," snickered

Officer Lambert as she shoved Danni's upper body flat against the table and plunged two fingers deep inside Danni's cunt.

Danni whimpered slightly, yet damn if she wasn't somehow enjoying this twisted situation.

"Got a wet pussy, does she?" asked the other cop, as she gawked at Danni's tits pressed against the table and her ass shoved up in the air.

"Fuck yeah!" Officer Lambert replied. "I think she might even be enjoying this just a little bit, aren't you Danni?"

Officer Lambert slid her fingers in and out of Danni's now, inexplicably, soaking little pussy. Danni didn't understand this because she had never felt so humiliated and helpless in her life, yet, at the same time, she also felt highly aroused. As Officer Lambert continued to finger fuck her, Danni actually started to hope that one of those fingers might just stray over to her desperately aching clit.

The other female officer in the room had spread her thighs apart and was openly massaging herself between her legs outside the fabric of her uniform. Her eyes never left Danni's nude body, and what Officer Lambert was doing to it. The voyeur cops eyes seemed to slightly glaze over, and Danni thought that maybe the voyeur sight of her assault was about to push her over the edge of pleasure, but Danni wasn't sure. All she was sure of was that she was drastically turned on now and it was obvious to all three of them.

Suddenly, Officer Lambert withdrew her fingers from Danni's pussy and kicked her legs further apart. Firmly keeping hold of Danni's upper body against the table, the femme cop aggressively started smacking Danni's round ass cheeks, taking pleasure in the jerking movements her captive's body made after each contact and watching the skin color turn from cream to crimson red. Danni caught a glimpse of the voyeur cop from the corner of her eye, and was sure the cop just climaxed at the sight of Danni's heightening assault.

The assaulting cop suddenly stopped spanking her captive's ass, and Danni suddenly felt her pussy lips being pried wide open by the cops fingers. Fingers began roughly massaging her swollen clit, and Danni bit down on her bottom lip as she could no longer resist the waves of pleasure coursing through her body.

The femme cops could tell that their detainee was close to cumming by the way she started to gyrate against the hands of her assaulting Officer. And, just when Danni could no longer contain herself, and was succumbing to the erotic assault she was undertaking, she felt an additional two fingers brutally shoved up her ass. This wasn't something that she normally enjoyed but it was too late. Through the pain, there was also a lot of pleasure, and Danni's body bucked against both her metal restraints and the restraint of her captures hold.

As Danni's body fell limp against the table, Officer Lambert withdrew her fingers and stepped back to enjoy one final view of her detainee's beautiful naked body. The femme cop gathered Danni's clothes from the floor and tossed them on the table in front of her.

"You're free to go, Ms. Bartlett, but I suggest, in the future, that you stay away from that club. Do you understand?"

"Y-yes ma'am," Danni managed to stammer.

The femme cop removed Danni's cuffs, and both cops turned and quickly left the room, closing the door behind them. Danni was shaken, both physically and mentally, and as she donned her two articles of clothing, she wondered if her friend had undergone the same unlawful strip search and interrogation that she had. As Danni exited the interrogation room and walked out of the police station, she could feel twinges of soreness in certain delicate places, yet she couldn't help but smile at the unexpected, bizarre and strangely erotic turn of events the evening had brought.

STORY 27 – LESBIAN DOMINATION: SUBMITTING TO MY LESBIAN MISTRESS

"Hey, sweetie," Meg whispered to her partner, Marisa, who was still sleeping. "I just want to let you know that I'm leaving for work now. Have a good day. I love you."

She leaned further down to kiss Marisa goodbye. Marisa returned the kiss without really opening her eyes. "Love you, too, baby," she mumbled, and with that she turned on her side and went back to sleep.

Meg smiled as she walked out of the room and headed to the door. She was an executive secretary for the CEO of a large corporation, and her day was usually quite full and busy. That was one of the reasons that she liked to get to her desk a little earlier than her 8:30AM required starting time. There was always something that needed to be done sooner rather than later. She stopped to pet their two dachshunds, Minnie and Mighty, and give them their morning meal on her way to the door.

While Meg was already on her second cup of coffee at work, Marisa got up and headed to the shower. She had the rather unique career of being a professional dominatrix. Her hours were varied and she worked at a private dungeon where people, both women and men, paid to have her control them for an hour or two at a time. There was never any sex involved since she maintained the true professional rules of a dominatrix. It was only to fulfill the discreet fantasies of her clients in regards to them being dominated, controlled, bound and sometimes even mildly humiliated. Her clients were very high profile, so discretion was vital. These discriminating clients needed and wanted her services, and they paid handsomely for the privilege. Because Marisa was into the fetish lifestyle herself, she made one hell of a dominatrix.

Sometimes Marisa had to laugh a little when she

thought of how much money she made in half of the time that Meg worked, and honestly, she enjoyed every single minute of it. The scenarios that Marisa got to play out ranged from mild to outlandish, and every once in a while she was taken to new areas of fetish awareness that she never knew existed before. Able to bring that fetish and sexual play awareness into her and Meg's sex life was a key factor in keeping their sex life stimulating, and could be the stuff that movies and books are made of.

Marisa smiled as she thought of what their friends would say if they knew she actually did at work. While their friends and acquaintances knew them on the exterior to be a quiet, loving lesbian couple, maybe even a little bland to the unknowing, behind closed doors, the pair of beautiful lesbians were wild, adventurous and explorers of the vast world of sexual fetish play.

No one really knew what Marisa's job was, and the couple had a cover story they told people, and that was that Marisa worked various jobs for a professional a temp agency. This kept the couple from having to give out a definite company name and occupation to their inquiring friends. And, while Marisa knew that her career as a professional dominatrix would not last forever, she would definitely enjoy it to the fullest while it lasted.

Marisa had even met Meg at a fetish ball, and while neither went with the intention of looking for a partner at the time that is exactly what happened. Both women are very much into role playing and especially roles that involve bondage, domination and submission. So, not only did neither have to hide their fetish desires when they met, they were able to fully embrace the lifestyle with one another in their relationship. Meg was completely ok with Marisa being a dominatrix, and knew that no boundaries were ever crossed when she was 'working'. Plus, the benefits of having a lesbian mistress as a partner were fucking fabulous!

As Marisa finished getting ready and headed off to work, she was mentally looking forward to the party that she and Meg were throwing the next evening. The food and band had already been arranged. The invitations had been sent out and everyone had RSVP'd that they would be attending. People seemed to love their parties, and Marisa and Meg threw some great parties.

When the women returned home from work that day they started to make preparations for their party. This meant cleaning the house from top to bottom as well as making sure that the door to their 'play room' off the main hallway, what they told others was a spare bedroom, was securely locked. That bedroom was only for special times between Marisa and Meg. And, those special times were always a surprise for Meg, and she never knew when she would be entering that room because Marisa was the one that made all of the decisions regarding it.

The party the next night turned out to be a complete success. All of the guests had a phenomenal time dancing to the music of the band, eating some delicious food and enjoying some of the finest wines and alcohol that you can find anywhere. Things started winding down around midnight and guests started to trickle out a few at a time, and by 1 a.m. everyone had gone home.

Meg and Marisa stood in the midst of the leftover party mess and sighed. It had been a great evening of dancing, eating, drinking and fun, but after every great party there is always the after party cleanup. Meg went into the kitchen and returned with a box of large trash bags. She started picking up used cups and plates and putting them into one of the bags as Marisa watched her keenly for a moment. And, before she could get very far, Marisa abruptly ordered her to stop.

"Leave it. Go take a shower and wait for me in the bedroom," Marisa commanded, staring at Meg intently as she took a very commanding demeanor.

"Um, ok, baby," Meg said. She put the trash bag on the floor and walked past Marisa on her way out of the room. Passing by her, she leaned in to give Marisa a kiss but Marisa drew away.

"I told you to go take a shower and wait for me in the bedroom," she said in a stern voice, as she ogled Meg's braless tits through the thin fabric of her sexy, feminine blouse. It was play time, and Marisa has just transitioned from doting, loving partner to commanding, sultry dominatrix.

Puzzled at first, Meg gave her a bit of a hurt look. Then, as if a light had gone on inside of her head, she flashed a quick, shy grin and lowered her eyes to look at the floor. Her mistress had just given her an order, and every good submissive knows to obey the commands and desires of her mistress.

"Yes, ma'am," Meg responded, as she walked past her mistress and towards their bathroom to prepare herself for the desires and play commands that her dominatrix lover would soon be giving her.

Once in the bathroom, she started the water running to warm up a bit while she stripped out of her clothes. Once naked, Meg stepped into the hot, steamy shower and melted into the warm water as it cascading over her naked curves. It had been a while since Marisa had taken such a stern tone with her, and that could only mean one thing....the play room. Just the thought of Marisa taking her into that room turned Meg's insides into pulsing waves of arousal and anticipation. As she was lost in erotic thoughts of possibility Meg soaped up and washed every beautiful square inch of her shapely body, using the sensual, heady spiced body wash that her mistress enjoyed the scent of. Tracing her fingers over her shaved pussy, Meg's anticipation of her mistress's touch grew, and a faint moan escaped her mouth.

Finishing her shower, Meg turned off the water and stepped out onto the bath rug. After drying off with a soft bath towel, she stood still for a moment, staring at her naked body in the mirror above the sink. She snapped back into reality, and remembered that Marisa always laid out certain items she wanted Meg to wear during their sessions, which she was to attire herself with after bathing. So, after toweling her hair off a little, she continued to ready herself by applying some fresh make-up and spritzing on some cologne. Once finished, Meg stood there waiting in the nude in front of the mirror, until her mistress was ready to call for her so she could adorn herself with tonight's chosen attire items for their play time.

While Meg had been showering, Marisa had also been quite busy. First, she had set out a black silk and lace teddy with demi cups and crotchless panties for Meg to wear. She also added a studded blindfold to the ensemble, as well as sheer finger gloves, stockings and black stiletto heels. Once she had readied Meg's outfit, she dressed herself in a form fitting latex suit of all black, and thigh high 'fuck-me' heeled boots that transformed her appearance from sweet lover to femme fatale dominatrix. It was a look that always worked quite well on her clients, and Marisa knew it would have the similar effect with Meg.

A vixen by any definition, Marisa was quite tall and slim, with bouncy, full breasts, long dark brown hair, and piercing green eyes. Whenever her eyes fixated on you, especially when she was in dominatrix role, they had the power to hypnotize you into submission, and make you silently beg for and worship her command. For the moment, she had put her long hair up into a tight French twist, lending her a severe yet ultra-sultry look. Leaving her hair down gave her a softer look that she preferred to reserve for her and Meg's softer moments of intimacy. Glancing at herself in the full length mirror, she liked what she saw. And now, it was time to summon her lovely submissive.

She called for Meg, telling her it was time to get dressed, and as Meg entered the bedroom and walked past her mistress naked and in silence over to the laid out clothes, Marisa took great pleasure in the sight of her lovers nudeness and the sultry scent of the cologne she had obviously spritzed on. Meg had certainly learned a lot about the essence of role play since they began their relationship, and she adapted to playing the role of submissive quite well. Even though Marisa was indeed the dominant during their role playing sessions, the effect of watching her submissive lover had its own dominant effect on her, and she could feel the heat and moistness rising inside her pussy already.

"Slowly put on the lingerie, stockings and heels, and put the blindfold on last," Marisa ordered Meg.

"Yes, Mistress," Meg said quietly, as she complied and began to slowly pull on the silky black teddy. As she dressed, Marisa crossed the room to take a sip of her warmed cognac she had prepared for herself, and watched her submissive kitten dress for tonight's occasion.

Meg was shorter than Marisa by a few inches, with small firm breasts and the most luscious curvy hips and ass. Her naturally wavy hair was long and dark brown, just like Marisa's, and perfectly suited her heart-shaped face, creamy light skin and deep blue eyes. As Meg slid on the sheer black stockings, Marisa admired her long slender legs, and watched with growing hunger as Meg's fingers grazed against her smooth inner thighs as she finished pulling up each stocking.

"Put on the blind fold," Marisa ordered, as she licked the trickle of cognac that clung to her bottom lip.

After Meg had complied, and was now standing before her mistress blindfolded and in silence, Marisa attached a collar and leash around Meg's neck and led her down the hall to their secret spare room. Meg did not speak as she was being led through the house, for she knew that she was only allowed to respond in speech when commanded to do so by her mistress. So, the only sound to be heard in the moment was that of the haunting, alluring music that got louder as they approached the door to the secret room. This music always made Meg feel as if they were walking through the corridors of a Transylvanian castle, and was so strangely intoxicating and erotic to her.

As they entered the space, the dominatrix and her submissive were bathed in low red and purple lighting, which gave the room a haunting dungeness effect. The walls were painted black with long velvety, crimson red curtains covering the windows, and the floor was covered with old creaking floor slats. There were various pieces of B&D equipment and other accessories littering the room, along with a collection of ropes, paddles, ceiling hooks, more blindfolds, nipple clamps, whips, and paddles. There was even a dimly lit cabinet containing various dildos behind its glass antique doors. The main item was located in the very center of the room, which was a mechanical saddle mounted on a wooden sawhorse, and it had a black dildo attached to right behind the saddle horn.

Marisa had Meg stand in an open space near the middle of the room, and pushed her to her knees. Meg was startled by this and nearly feel on her face, but managed to keep her balance. Once Meg was kneeling, Marisa removed the collar and leash, and roughly yanked off the studded blindfold. She threw the blindfold aside and grabbed a handful of Meg's hair. Yanking her head back, she stared down intently into Meg's eyes.

"Tell me how beautiful I am!" commanded Marisa, while continuing to stare into the eyes of her submissive.

"Oh Mistress, you're the most beautiful woman on the earth," Meg enthused.

"What did you call me?" Marisa barked as she picked up a small riding crop and cracked it across the back of her submissive's shoulders.

"Mistress?" Meg stuttered, as she was slightly unnerved by Marisa's reaction, because that's what she has always called her in these sessions.

"You are to call me Goddess from this moment on," Marisa said sternly, as she gave Meg's hair another not-so-gentle tug.

"Yes, my Goddess," Meg answered meekly.

"Get on your hands and knees, and stick your ass high in the air for your Goddess" Marisa ordered, as she released her grip on Meg's hair.

Meg instantly did as she was told, and once on her hands and knees, she arched her back and jutted her luscious round ass up high in the air, which is exactly where her Goddess mistress wanted it to be. With no warning, Marisa brought down the riding crop across Meg's ass cheeks causing her body to ripple with after effect. Even though the strike stung, Meg very much enjoyed this erotic discipline, and it was a sexual treat she didn't think she could ever do without again. Her Goddess mistress had successfully shown her how to enjoy the loving discipline and dominance of B&D role playing. The spanking continued for several minutes with Marisa ordering Meg to beg for each strike of the crop against her ass, and then to thank her after receiving each one. Meg's body continued to tremble after each crop strike, and she was acutely aware of both the hot, stinging sensation in her abused ass cheeks, as well as the hot, tingling sensation in her pussy. She wanted to massage her ass cheeks so bad, and soothe the sting, but she knew better than to move out of position without being ordered to by her Goddess mistress.

When Marisa tired of delivering the spankings, she ordered Meg to get up. Once she was standing on her feet again, Meg was suddenly whipped around by Marisa, and before she knew it, her body was swiftly pulled over to one of the walls and her hands were cuffed into two sturdy wall hooks. Picking up her prized whip, Marisa used it to skillfully and cleanly cut down the middle of Meg's teddy, which seemed to invisibly split right open and fall to the floor, exposing Meg's gorgeous tits to her. With a second swift movement, Marisa tugged the delicate string of Meg's thong, and in a flash her submissive was now fully naked, properly contained, and utterly vulnerable to her mistress's desires.

Walking slowly over to the selection of nipple clamps, Marisa inspected the collection on the table before finally selecting a pair with rubber tipped ends. When she returned to Meg, she clamped one onto each of her erect nipples, and gave them each a little twist. Meg bit her bottom lip to keep from crying out because this was to teach her self-control, and if she showed weakness her punishment would be worse. Her nipples have always been very sensitive, so the clamps served to cause quite a bit of nipple sting, but a sting that also further activated her already throbbing, moist pussy. Meg was always careful to not let her arousal from nipple clamps show outwardly otherwise her mistress would take them away. So, she let Marisa go on thinking that they were more painful to her than she could bear.

Using the handle of the whip, Marisa forced Meg's thighs open and positioned a spreader bar on the floor between her legs. After securing Meg's ankles to each side of the bar, Marisa went over to the lighted cabinet containing the dildo collection, to select a specimen for a delightful assault on her submissive. Marisa's sight locked on one of the larger ones, and after inspecting it closely, she seemed satisfied that it would open up Meg nicely. As Marisa approached Meg with the rather large dildo, she saw her submissive's eyes widened as she caught glimpse of the appendage in her mistress's hand.

Marisa smirked at her slave shackled to the wall bolts. Holding the dildo outward in one hand, so that her submissive could continue to get a look at it, Marisa then grabbed and squeezed Meg's tits one at a time over the nipple clamps. Meg's body bucked and thrashed, and her face grimaced while her mistress abused her tits. Marisa then walked slowly around Meg's body slapping the dildo against her reddened ass, tits and face.

Marisa then stood directly behind Meg, and using the fingers of one hand, spread open her submissive's soft pussy lips while probing and pushing the dildo against her honey hole. Because Meg's cunt was already well moistened, the dildo quickly found its way in and slid upwards a little at a time. Meg had been a little frightened by how large the dildo was when she first saw it, but she soon relaxed as her pussy was slowly expanding to the rhythm of her mistress sliding the appendage in and out of her. And, within just a couple minutes, she could feel her pussy grasping onto the dildo like a cat in heat. At that point, Meg let out an unstoppable groan of pleasure, which very much pleased her mistress.

"You know you like this," Marisa whispered aggressively in Meg's ear, as she continued to fuck her from behind with the dildo. "Tell me how much you like me fucking you with this."

"Yes - Goddess – I – love – the – way – you – fuck – me – like - that," Meg stammered, gasping between each word. In spite of the way the dildo was stretching her, she couldn't deny being racked with pleasure. She could even feel a trickle of her juices on the innermost part of her thigh.

Marisa continued to dildo fuck her submissive for several more minutes, before stopping abruptly. She slid the dildo fully out of Meg's cunt for the last time, and un-cuffed her hands. Tossing the dildo aside, Marisa sauntered over to the center of the room next to the mechanical saddle, while Meg rubbed her wrists which were sore from her thrashing them against the shackles. Marisa then motioned to her submissive with her hand to come join her in standing next to the mechanical beast.

"Get on," Marisa ordered. "It's time for you to take a ride."

"Yes, Goddess," Meg replied meekly. Climbing onto the dildo-horned saddle with her thighs wide apart, caused her swollen pussy lips to spread wide open, and Meg was surprised by how easily the saddle dildo slid right into her soaking wet pussy. She realized that the dildo nestled quite deeply inside of her cunt, because she was literally impaling herself on it. Meg was no sooner in place when Marisa hit the switch that turned the mechanical saddle on, causing her body to buck up and down on the dildo.

Meg was already delirious with whole body arousal, and was quite literally pulsating from head to toe from the spankings, titty torture and dildo fucking. Pussy riding this dildo saddle was going to carry her right over that climactic edge. Meg knew it, and she knew her Goddess mistress knew it. Reaching across her beautiful submissive's tits, Marisa started to twist the nipple clamps left and right as she simultaneously made the saddle move and buck faster, causing the dildo to ram in an out of Meg's cunt with a furry. It was more than Meg could stand, and aggressive waves of orgasm slammed through her body, while her pussy and ass bounced off the fetish saddle. Her juices flowed freely onto the dildo and down between her thighs, as she cried out her pleasure over and over again.

Meg's body fell forward limply when her mistress finally turned the saddle switch to 'off'. Marisa gently helped Meg down from the saddle, and smiled at her lover tenderly, as she brushed Meg's hair out of her eyes.

"I'm going to take a shower now babe," Marisa said gently. "I'll meet you in our bedroom when I'm done."

With those words, Marisa walked out of their secret play room, leaving Meg to catch her breath and clean up from their session. Returning to their bedroom, Meg pulled on a pair of sleeping shorts with a spaghetti strapped top, and nestled against the soft bed covers while awaiting her mistress lover. She didn't have to wait very long. Marisa entered the room wearing a short, silk robe and nothing else. She joined her lovely Meg on the bed, and they kissed gently with their arms tenderly wrapped around one another.

In spite of Meg's soreness in certain areas, the sweet and gentle kissing and touching from her lover caused a second wave of desire to surge through her body. Marisa wasn't far behind, and their bodies moved into a slow, sweet lovemaking that was the perfect end to a perfect night.

STORY 28 –
LESBIAN DOMINATION:
WATER BONDAGE DISCIPLINE

Ally checked her reflection in the full-length mirror one last time before heading out the door, and she was pretty happy with what she saw. The black leather skirt she chose accented her long, lean legs, with a matching low-cut leather vest that drew attention to her ample breasts underneath. In addition to her spicy two piece outerwear, Ally wore a sexy black lace bra and panty ensemble underneath, for the viewing pleasure of any possible late night encounter. Ally styled her long dark brown hair into a loose, messy tousled look, and her flawlessly applied makeup highlighted her big green eyes, giving her a sultry, devilish kitten look. Overall, Ally appeared to be closer to 20 or 21 years old vs. her true age of 28. Ally was sexy as hell, and she knew it, and had no problem using her mysterious sexy looks to engage in many random sexual encounters.

Whenever Ally went out with her friends on the weekends, she was often teased about being a freak, and her friends loved to live vicariously through the re-telling of Ally's sexual conquests. That was ok with Ally because, in all honesty, she was a freak and she was never shy about sharing this part of her character with her potential intimate playmates. There were very few sexual fetishes Ally has not already personally explored, and she admittedly was always trying to find a new fetish or brazen new intimate play partner that could up the ante. Ally had become quite the sexual fetish explorer, and plain vanilla sex just would never cut it for her. While some people got an adrenaline rush by skydiving, rock climbing or racing cars, Ally got her adrenaline rush high during times of sexual fetish encounters. And, likened to a drug addict on the hunt for a 'fix' after coming off of their previous 'high', every week as the weekend approached, Ally would be on the hunt for her next 'fetish fix'.

Tonight, Ally and a couple of her friends were heading out to a club that had quickly become one of their favorites. It was only opened on the weekends, but always brought out a huge and very diverse group of lesbians, and was a two-story total club experience. From pool tables and live bands on the first floor, to a rocking D.J., dancing and go-go dancers on the second floor, it was always 'the' place to be on the weekends. And, even though it was windy and cold in New York City that night, Ally, Tara and Aisha weren't going to let a little cold weather and wind keep them from going out and having some weekend fun. Ally was looking forward to some drinking and dancing, and, on top of that, she was hoping to get lucky and score some wild late night sex; the kinkier the better.

All three of the girls looked smoking hot in their own unique way, and wasted no time attracting the attention of many women in the club. Some were women that they already knew as regulars of the club, as well as some that they didn't know, but were more than happy to get acquainted with, as they ordered their drinks and accepted invitations to hit the dance floor. The D.J. was spinning music of a diverse mix of dance, alternative and slow beats, and the beautiful bodies of the women in the club rocked, gyrated and swayed with and against each other to the pulsating rhythms. Whether you were a participant in this sea of Sapphic dance, or just watching from your seat along one of the many bar stations, it certainly made for a lovely display of tits, ass and curves in all shapes and sizes.

After almost an hour of dancing, Ally was ready to take a break from the dance floor, and she slowly maneuvered her way through the gyrating crowd and headed to the bar to order another drink.

"Hey gorgeous," a sultry voice said in Ally's ear.

"Can I pay for that drink?"

Ally turned around to find a totally hot girl standing less than a foot away from her, and as their eyes locked, there was an immediate and unmistakable sexual attraction that sent a wave of pulsating pleasure through Ally's body. The alluring stranger was tall and slender, about an inch or two taller than Ally, and she wore her dark brown hair in a short layered and choppy style. As Ally allowed her eyes to do a quick head-to-toe scan of the drink-offering stranger, she saw that she wore a tight, long-sleeved button-down shirt, jeans and biker boots. Ally's eyes paused for a moment to enjoy the sight of the strangers erect nipples prominently poking against the fabric of her shirt, and as her gaze traveled back upwards, Ally's own eyes once again locked with those dramatic dark brown eyes staring back at her. Ally made no apology for her lustful and obvious assessment, and already her mind was racing with possibilities as she was most certainly turned on by this gorgeous stranger.

"Maybe," Ally coyly answered. "What's your name?"

"My name's Shane," the alluring stranger replied.

"I'm Ally."

"You're pretty damn hot Ally, but I'm pretty sure you already know that?"

"So I've been told," Ally said with a sassy smile. "You're pretty damn hot yourself."

"Well, Ally, do you want to order a drink or do you want to dance?"

"Can I do both?"

"Sure," Shane replied. "But, why don't we hit the dance floor first for a little while, and then we can grab a drink and get to know each other better. I was watching you dance earlier, and I definitely would like to see that again, but this time a little more up close and personal."

With a wicked little grin, Ally allowed Shane to lead her back onto the dance floor for a few more dances, which ended with a sexy slow tune that allowed them to put their arms around each other. Ally already felt a deep sexual attraction to this girl, and this attraction only intensified the moment their bodies pressed together and swayed in unison to the hypnotic, erotic melody. Ally unbashfully grinded her hips and tits against Shane's, and was already enjoying a silent fantasy in her head of her and Shane engaging in voyeur sex right there in the middle of the crowded dance floor. As the song concluded and the D.J. put a pre-mixed dance tape on to play while she took a short break, Ally snapped out of her mind fantasy and was trying to quickly assess where the rest of the evening might be headed with her new sexy friend. Shane took Ally's hand and led her off the dance floor, weaving them through the crowd to find an unoccupied booth away from the dance floor, where it would be a bit quieter and they could order their drinks and talk.

After finding a great corner booth, Ally and Shane slid into the same booth bench side, ordered some drinks from the waitress, and immediately engaged in some 'just how wild are you' conversation and flirtation. As Ally and Shane drank their cocktails, they exchanged some really wild sex stories, with each girl obviously trying to make her stories the wildest and most over-the-top. While conversation of confessions continued, Ally slipped a foot out of one of her shoes and was stroking it along the side of Shane's leg. Simultaneously, Shane was frequently touching Ally on her thigh and arm closest to her, and during this x-rated conversational exchange, there was definitely an air of 'I want you' and 'I dare you' oscillating between them. Ally revealed to Shane some of her craziest fetish exploits, while putting just a bit of a spin on them to make them sound even crazier. Shane also told some pretty outrageous tales of her own, but, in her case she wasn't exaggerating. In fact, Shane was beginning to think that Ally wasn't quite as experienced in the world of sexual fetish play as she claimed to be, and Shane was contriving of a plan to have some kinky fun with Ally, while at the same time exposing her to some true over-the-top fetish play.

Suddenly, Shane put a finger against Ally's pouty, pink lips to stop her from saying anymore, and stared intently into Ally's sexy, green cat eyes. Intrigued, Ally licked the tip of Shane's finger and awaited Shane's next move.

"I've got an idea gorgeous," Shane said. "Why don't you come back to my place and you can show me just how fetish savvy you are? You think you're up for that kitten?"

Ally grinned back at Shane as she shifted her hips against the booth seat. Her body was continuing to respond to the growing cascade of sexual endorphins, and she was finding it harder and harder to sit still.

"I think that's a great idea," Ally replied. "I just need to go find my friends and let them know that I'm leaving with you, and I'll be right back."

Ally located her friends, whom were having the time of their lives at one of the bars, told them that she was going home with Shane, and that she would just catch a cab ride home later. Ally's friends smiled and gave her some friendly barbs, for they knew there would be a juicy tale for Ally to share with them come Monday morning. Ally returned some of the banter, and then quickly returned to the booth that she was sharing with Shane.

"Ok, I'm ready to go anytime you are!" Ally declared.

"Then why wait?" Shane said playfully, and stood up to lead them out of the club.

Once Ally and Shane had found their way outside into the chilled air of the night, Shane flagged down a cab outside of the club. The two women rode the several miles to Shane's place in a comfortable silence that must have intrigued the cab driver, because Ally noticed that he was continuously glancing back at them in the rear view mirror. It turned out, that Shane lived in an expansive loft displaying an unusual theme of dark colored furniture, along with freaky and kinky sculptures, paintings and other fetish décor items. Ally was temporarily rendered speechless as she spun about the large open area rooms taking visual inventory of the most bizarre, and at the same time, most intriguing place she has ever seen, or been in.

Thoughts raced through Ally's mind, as she tried to process the sudden sensory overload. Ally had always considered herself to be extremely sexually adventurous, and she was always looking to discover the next heightened fetish experience. However, Ally was suddenly feeling like she might be a fetish amateur compared to Shane if her suspicions were true, and Shane's freaky sexual desires matched her freaky décor desires.

Ally's fascination and silence was interrupted when she heard Shane speak to her from across the room.

"Hey Ally, why don't you make us something to drink. Everything you need is on the bar over there on that wall. While you do that, I'm going to go set some things up for us in the other room so we can play. It won't take me long."

"Oh sure, sure," Ally stammered. "I can do that."

Shane disappeared into another part of the loft, as Ally made her way over to the wall bar and prepared a cocktail for Shane and herself. Ally sipped at her drink while she wandered around the loft, taking in all of the visual excitement that she was surrounded by and wondering where Shane had acquired such a unique collection of fetish décor items. These were not your everyday fetish paintings and sculptures and décor pieces, and not a single one of them depicted a male in any way shape or form. After the initial shock of witnessing such a brazen collection wore off, Ally found herself getting quite aroused at the depictions portrayed amongst the art pieces.

When Shane returned from her mysterious play preparations, she took her drink from Ally and they both sat down on a dark red suede couch shaped like a pair of sexy plump lips. Directly across from where they sat on the couch, was a life-size black statue of a naked woman wearing a strap-on dildo aimed downwards between the open legs of a second woman laying on her back with her knees bent up and thighs spread wide open. Forget unique coffee table books, this two woman sculpture demanded your attention, and Ally found herself staring back and forth between Shane and the life-size erotic statue. They sat with legs entwined, sipping at their drinks and continuing their risqué conversation from where they left off at the club.

Ally, usually the 'hunter' of all her sexual exploits, was suddenly feeling much more like 'prey' for the first time, and she could feel her elevated heartbeat pound inside her chest while listening to Shane talk with tones of growing sexual hunger in her voice. Ally had to admit that she had in fact recently wished to experience the next evolution of elevated fetish play, and she began to realize that maybe that meant she wasn't going to be the one in control and in charge of how things played out. Ally was now half listening to the words Shane was saying, and half listening to the words swirling around in her own head, when Shane suddenly whipped out a black fabric blindfold and stood up next to the couch in front of Ally.

"It's time for us to play little fetish girl. Get up and turn around, Ally," Shane commanded.

Shane's voice had suddenly taken on a very different tone, which Ally took immediate notice to. Ally also took notice to the fact that she was obviously going to be the submissive during their play time, a role she was not accustomed to, and she was just minutes away from her orientation. Complying with Shane's command, Ally stood up and turned her back towards Shane. She felt Shane's fingers position the blindfold over her eyes, and it was quickly tightened with a firm tug, immediately taking away one of Ally's senses….her sight. Plunged in darkness and not knowing what was coming next, heightened all of Ally's remaining senses. Adrenaline started coursing through her body, and she could feel her heart start to beat faster, her skin started to tingle and her breath escape her lips in short, faint pants.

"Put your hands behind your back," was Shane's next command.

Ally wobbled a little as she tried to comply. Shane quickly grabbed Ally to balance her and pulled her hands behind her back. She expertly tied Ally's hands with a thick cord and led her into the other room. The room she had prepared for their play time while Ally had made them drinks earlier. Ally instantly noticed that this room felt cold and damp, and her body went from overheated to chilled in a matter of a minute. Ally also noticed that the room smelled like a damp, musky basement would, but they certainly weren't in any basement. Right?

"Now, we need to get these clothes off of you little bitch," Shane said in a low, deep voice, as she roughly ripped off Ally's clothes and tossed them to the side of the room.

With her clothes gone, Ally now stood blind and bound, and the cold, damp air quickly permeated into her naked body. The floor was cold, damp and hard under her bare feet, and it felt like she might be standing on a concrete floor. Ally could hear Shane moving things around, and with her other senses heightened, she caught the distinct sound of chains, along with the sound of something heavy being dragged across the floor. Something else that caught Ally's attention was the sound of water. It kind of sounded like it was running through a hose or a pipe.

Ally heard Shane approaching, when she felt Shane's hand grab her by her tied-up wrists and lead her across the damp floor. Suddenly, Ally was slammed up against an icy cold wall that felt like stone, and her hands were yanked above her head. She felt chains being locked around her wrists, holding her hands in place above her head, and Ally's mind made the connection from the chain sounds she heard just minutes before. Shane then ripped the blindfold from Ally's eyes, and Ally gasped in disbelief.

Ally's eyes darted all around the room, and her mouth hung open in complete shock. This room looked like it could have been a dungeon in a medieval castle. Constructed completely out of rock, there were shackles, benches and, oddly enough, fire hoses sprawled throughout the room. For the first time ever, Ally was very nervous about what she had gotten herself into, and maybe she wasn't quite the badass fetish freak she thought she was. Shit, Ally thought to herself, who was she kidding? She was fucking shocked and scared.

In fact, so shocked was Ally at her surroundings, that she didn't notice Shane crossing the room to the other side. However, Shane grabbed Ally's attention pretty damn quick, when without warning she turned on a water hose full blast and soaked Ally's nude body with an icy onslaught of water.

"Holy shit!" Ally screamed, as she tried to buck and twist her body away from the forceful bursts of icy water. Of course that wasn't going to work, because she was very securely chained in place to the wall.

Shane remained quiet, as she turned on and off the small fire hose, smirking slyly at Ally's screams as each burst of frigid water hit her naked body. And, oh what a fine ass body she had. Shane was enjoying the sight of Ally's tits bounce up and down as she tried to squirm away from the direct spray of the water, as well as her pretty dark nipples which were frozen into erectness. Droplets of water dripped from her smooth shaven pussy in-between blasts of water, and Shane was definitely looking forward to a closer examination of Ally's pretty pussy lips.

"Please stop!" Ally yelled. "I get it. I'm not such a badass freak after all. Please!"

Still no words came from Shane. Ally's cries were rewarded only with more icy blasts of water being slammed against her body, which now felt like a naked icicle. It took about 10 minutes of this before Ally started to understand what was going on. She was being forced into submission, and being allowed to experience the thought processes of an obedient being dominated and controlled during fetish play. As yet another cold blast of water hit Ally directly on her already stinging tits, she finally realized that she needed to submit to Shane if she was ever going to get this water attack to stop. Screaming and writhing wasn't going to make it stop, but her silence and compliance would, so that's exactly what Ally finally did.

Shane stood staring at Ally for a minute before she finally put down the fire hose and walked over to her.

"So you think you've learned something yet?" Shane asked, as she enjoyed the view of Ally's shivering nudeness.

"Yes. Yes!" replied Ally

Shane threw her head back and laughed for a moment, before releasing Ally from the chains and shackles that held her against the wall. Ally rubbed at her wrists, as Shane once again was leading her across the room. This time she was led over to a large old fashioned bathtub that had been shrouded by some of the many dark shadows that filled the room's corners.

"Get in," Shane said to Ally rather dispassionately, as Ally's eyes widened in fear at the sight of more water.

Alley had to be pushed by Shane, and as she stumbled forward into the tub, she found to her relief, it was filled with warm water. Shane quickly went about securing more shackles on Ally, in a way that left her spread eagle in the tub, and Ally soon found each of her hands and ankles were tied to the outer legs of the tub.

"Now, just so you're not tempted to do any more of that fucking screaming, this should keep you quiet," Shane said, as she shoved a ball gag into Alley's mouth and fastened it behind her head.

Ally's eyes got huge but she didn't even try to make a sound. Instead, she watched as Shane vanished into a dark corner of the room. When she returned, she was carrying a large dildo, and Ally watched Shane carefully as she approached the bathtub. The size of the dildo both frightened and excited her, and she didn't have to wait long to see how Shane was going to use the rubber appendage on her. Kneeling next to the tub, Shane leaned in and used her fingers to spread Ally's pussy lips wide apart as she rubbed the dildo head in circles around Ally's hole. With no warning, Shane plunged the dildo deep inside of Ally's cunt all at once, forcing Ally to rock her hips upward so that her pussy would take the dildo without pain. Not pausing, Shane continued to fuck Ally with the appendage, until it was all Ally could do not to make some sort of grunting noises against the constraints of her mouth gag. Shane stared hungrily at Ally's bound body in the tub of water, and reveled in the sight of her naked submission. Watching the dildo appear and disappear inside of Ally's cunt made Shane's own pussy wet and throb with desire.

When Shane was finished with the dildo assault on Ally's cunt, she removed the ball gag out of Ally's mouth, released her ankles and wrists, and then told Ally to get out of the tub. Yet again, Ally was being led across the room, and this time they came to a stop in front of a small, padded table. Using the table as a prop, Shane bent Ally over it, as water dripped off of her naked body and onto the floor. Shane then picked-up a cat o' nine tails, and began to tease Ally's back and ass cheeks with alternating gentle and aggressive swipes of the whip.

After all her previous assaults Ally now found herself completely subservient to Shane. Her body and mind were now no longer resistant, but rather willing and open to whatever experience Shane was going to offer up to her next. Ally knew she had crossed that threshold, because her body was responding with obvious sexual desire. Her wet pussy throbbed between her thighs, and she was actually now physically aching for Shane's touch. Ally couldn't imagine what Shane could possibly have planned for her next, but she was hungry to find out. Moaning ever so slightly as she received the whip strikes against her ass, Ally edged her reddened ass up in the air even further, hoping to invite Shane's fingers towards her cunt. Shane took notice and smiled, even though Ally didn't see it, and Shane put down the cat o' nine tails.

"Get up, Ally," Shane said. "We have one more place to go."

Ally stood upright against the edge of the padded table, and Shane turned her around and showed her a bed that stood in another corner of the room. With all the sensory overload going on, Ally hadn't noticed the bed until now. Putting her hand in the small of Ally's back, Shane nudged her towards the bed. Ally went willingly, and once they reached the bed, Shane was once again securing Ally's wrists and ankles to the four bed posts, in a spread eagle position. Only this time, it was on a comfortable bed rather than in a bathtub.

Shane stripped out of her clothes, wet from the backlash of water, and did a slow cat crawl from the foot of the bed to that sweet spot directly between Ally's thighs. Parting Ally's pussy lips wide with her fingers, Shane's practiced tongue quickly found Ally's stiff bud, and as Shane gently wrapped her lips around Ally's clit to suckle on it, she simultaneously slid two fingers inside of Ally's warm, moist cunt. Gliding them in and out, Shane finger fucked Ally until her body was writhing uncontrollably against her restraints attached to the bed.

Ally's responses excited Shane and she leaned down to lick rapid little circles around Ally's clit, while she continued to finger fuck Ally's cunt with her fingers. Ally's body and mind had long since stopped resisting, and she allowed her body to fully give in to the pleasurable assault it was now receiving. Her orgasm hit suddenly and hard, and as waves of pleasure rippled throughout her entire body, Ally cried out over and over again, as her pussy moistened Shane's face in the process.

While Ally's body lay limp catching her breath, Shane got up and retrieved some thick, warm blankets that she brought back over to the bed. She released Ally's bonds, and covered up both their naked bodies with the blankets before turning off the lights. As they cuddled together on the bed, Ally's exhausted body pressed against Shane's, they quickly fell asleep in the darkness.

The next morning found both women smiling and happy. After dressing and calling for a taxi, Shane walked Ally out to catch her cab for her ride home. Before shutting the cab door, Shane leaned in and kissed Ally and handed her a slip of paper with her phone number on it.

"Feel free to give me a call the next time you want some real fetish fun gorgeous," Shane whispered after she kissed Ally softly on her mouth. Then she closed the cab door and smiled as she watched it leave with her new fetish play mate.

STORY 29 –
DIAL "M" FOR MISTRESS

Audra sat quietly contemplating behind her desk, the light from lunchtime London filling her spacious corner office. Clean lines, glass walls, a view of the whole city stretching beneath her as though it was hers to admire. The Queen herself surely didn't have this to look at on her lunch break: the river Thames reflected like a diamond vein in the light of the sun, the bustling people below appeared like ants, and then there was the money, Audra mused. She had made it. She made it big and she made it young. The board of directors, were finally starting to trust her; pretty, blonde, 34. Her counterpart in Marketing was the closest one to her in age, and he was 49. Her office stood high above the bustling city streets – twenty-first floor, leather furniture, expensive wall art, panoramic views – all physical trophies of her professional accomplishments. Audra Kennedy, top City executive, and a damn good one, too!

It was 12:14pm, Friday. The rest of her department would just be sitting down to eat lunch together. Audra hadn't taken a lunch break since she accepted this job 18 months ago; she believed in efficient multi-tasking and consumed her quick meals while at networking events, office meetings, while reading through résumés and taking conference calls. Every year, on January 1st, she penned "Fail to prepare, prepare to fail" on the first page of her new yearly diary, where she journaled her goals throughout the year. 12pm on a Friday was just another hour on the clock, and a brief opportunity to plan for the afternoon. Although today, she was feeling differently.

Audra eyes glanced at the bright yellow piece of paper stuck to the side of her laptop computer. 'Two people', the post-it note said. How could she possibly fire two people? She had hand-picked her business team, and they all worked together perfectly. She liked them, and they loved her. What would it do to morale, to lose two people? She hated having to make this decision, but it needed to be done.

"With power comes great responsibility." She smiled, ruefully. The choice would be made by close of business that day, and she inwardly hardened her heart to any protest. Being fair had got her a good team, but being able to handle the unpleasant components of her work had made her the boss.

After she had signed off on the two names of the employees that had to be let go, Audra stood in front of the bathroom mirror in the ladies restroom located down the hall from her corner office. The office was still bare of people; they'd be paying the waiter at the restaurant by now, jackets slung over their shoulders, taking that last gulp of the wine from their glasses. She had about 15 minutes before the office staff all filtered back to their desks, and the shrill rings of the phones started up again along with all the emailing and faxing of documents and proposals back and forth. Audra smiled back at her reflection, dirty blonde hair falling neatly over tailored shoulders, a pencil skirt fitting over her slim thighs. She turned to look at herself side on, the outfit finished by black high heels, their red soles flashing money as she walked past her employees. Yes, her employees. Would that ever get old? Audra pulled out the small pot of gloss from her bag, touching up the peach color on her plump lower lip. The lip that…

…A brief pause, and a flashback that felt like electricity, shot through her thighs. Audra immediately reached into her large purse digging for her cell phone, buried underneath organizers and folders and calendars. Leaning on the sink, she scrolled through her contact list, her manicured nails clicking against the screen. 'M'. Just the letter - a simple, single letter – and oh how it made her pussy warm. 'M'. Audra momentarily forgot all about her employees, New York clients, and her never ending inbox. Her clit was tingling, remembering. 'M'. She'd already seen her once, Tuesday, and she'd… Audra felt herself get light-headed and closed her eyes, exhaling slowly as she heard the first of her chattering colleagues walking down the corridor just outside the bathroom. She was wet. She was in need. She pressed dial.

"Good afternoon," a voice answered.

"It's Audra." She sounded like a frightened little girl, a girl who knew she'd done wrong but was admitting it anyway. Her heart felt too big for her body, and the moistness in her panties was making her shift in her skirt.

"What are you phoning for, you bad girl." Her voice was like warm honey and whiskey.

"I-I'm sorry Mistress. I was wondering if I could perhaps see you again, tonight."

"It's your lucky day. I can do eight thirty."

Audra's mouth was dry and she whispered, "OK". The line clicked off just as a grey-suited girl from reception opened the door to the bathroom. She smiled. "Good afternoon, Ms Kennedy."

Audra straightened herself up, pulled herself together. She smiled back at the girl and nodded her head in silent greeting. Audra was momentarily too worked up to verbally respond to her. The flush was still hot in her cheeks, the flush from the voice of the woman who would later hurt her, tease her, and then make her cum. She wanted it to be now, she wanted Mistress Raven's dungeon to be on the other side of that bathroom door. Audra made her way down the hall, her heart racing and face pink, back to her office and a scheduled 2pm meeting. Taking a moment to recompose herself once back in her office, Audra felt her heart rate slow and the flush slowly leave her cheeks. She would just have to wait. Yes, 8:30pm would be here soon enough.

Audra tucked her heels under the chair and stirred the ice cubes around in her glass with a drinking straw. The ice clinked together in the water, as dark green seaweed, white rice, and pieces of slippery pink salmon rolled slowly in front of her on the revolving sushi bar. Audra loved sushi, loved how pretty and artistic it was, and how delicate and organized each little roll looked. Her last date, which was months ago, had been at this very restaurant, and she had tucked her heels under the chair in just the same way, and swished her ice around in her glass in just the same way, and ended her dating relationship in just the same way in which she would this time around. Audra was in complete control of her life, just as she was in control over which mouthful of food she would take next, picking jobs and partners like it was a choice between white or brown rice. She had power, she had money, and she had confidence that dripped from every fingertip. And this is what all the women she had ever been with, had liked about her. The woman who was sitting next to her now, picking up bits of sushi with her fingers, that too is what she likes about Audra. She likes confident Audra, who decides where to go for dinner, who books the cabs, who takes her shopping and plans their social calendar. She is attracted to the Audra in charge, and will want the same later on, after they eat sushi and the high heels and panties come off. Audra attracted submissive girls, and she never had the heart to let them down. It was easier to just let them go.

They ate, Audra paid, released her companion from

their casual relationship, and then she left. Within the hour, her legs were curled up underneath her, as she lounged on the black leather couch in the dimly lit reception area. Audra had changed into a white lace lingerie slip under a sheer dress, leaving her feet bare. The door to her Mistress's room was closed, the light from underneath a thin strip flashing black shadows as murmuring voices slunk past. Audra closed her eyes and wiggled her body on the couch, the wait and anticipation always feeling like foreplay.

"Are you ready?" a voice called.

Audra had once dated a model. She had been well over 6 foot tall, as pale and aloof as a swan. She had literally been stunning. People would forget their words when she came through the front door, holding martinis and mojitos unsipped as they stood frozen by this woman's beauty entering a room. Everyone, man and woman, had experienced this woman like a slap in the face. Everyone, except Audra, that is. Now she understood how everyone else had felt when faced with the model. Audra opened her daydreaming eyes and was stunned.

Mistress Raven stood at the door to her dungeon room. She was tall, not as tall as the model but curvier, sexier. Audra had never known hair like her Mistress's; thick, black, glossy, it ran down her back like an oil slick. She stood in front of Audra, black corset wrapping around her curves, her cleavage deep, and her legs long toned and stockinged. Audra's heart fluttered when she saw her Mistress's boots, polished and dangerous. She stood there in impossibly high heels and leather, her red lips frowning sexily as she looked Audra up and down. "I said, are you ready?!"

"Yes, Mistress," Audra finally responded.

"Good. Then hurry up." She clicked her fingers, nails polished bright red.

Mistress Raven turned away and beckoned her to follow. Audra stood up off the couch, as though her Mistress was pulling her on puppet strings.

"No. I want you to crawl." Audra's mistress commanded.

Mistress Raven's eyes were on fire as Audra dropped to her knees. Her blonde hair fell around her face as it reddened, and her heart thumped wildly in her chest.

"Look at me now." Audra lifted her eyes to meet her Mistress's. She knew her cheeks were pink and her pupils wide. "Good girl."

"Thank you Mistress."

Audra followed Mistress Raven into the dungeon on her hands and knees, watching those boot heels push down into the carpet. When she reached the middle of the room, Mistress Raven closed the door behind them. Audra sat back on her heels. The room was cool and her pert little nipples poked through the silk and lace.

"Did I tell you to sit up?"

Mistress Raven turned round and stared down at Audra, cocking her leather-clad hip to the side. A black paddle was gripped firmly by those red tipped fingers, slapping down on one of her palms. It was a provocation, a temptation.

"No Mistress." Audra answered timidly.

"Then back on all fours!" Her Mistress was firm, harsh almost. She brought the paddle down on her palm as Audra went back on her knees. "Do you know what happens when you don't do as I say?" Audra went quiet, breathing fast, as Mistress Raven slowly stepped closer to where she was kneeling, heel toe, heel toe across the floor. "Do you?"

"Yes, Mistress." Audra felt her elbows and knees weaken and she closed her eyes, her hair falling in a curtain around her face. She bit her lip, held her breath, her body tense and taut. She could feel her Mistress's presence behind her, a stilettoed shadow of sex, and the slapping noise of the paddle the only thing breaking the silence. Audra held her breath for longer, longer, longer. Her lungs were full and her jaw clenched, desperate for what she knew was coming. Desperate for...

... Mistress Raven brought the paddle down hard on Audra's ass. The breath Audra was holding burst out in a shriek, and she bit down hard on her lip. The taste of her own blood slipped between her teeth as she felt her ass turn red and warm. Mistress Raven pulled Audra's lacy panties down quickly, roughly, ripping them off her legs and throwing them into the corner of the room. A light touch on her pussy from those red-tipped fingers made Audra's body ripple like an electric shock, and she whimpered as her clit began to throb...

Mistress Raven bought the paddle down harder, again, twice more, three times. Each time Audra cried out, her nipples hardened and her pussy juices moistened the top innermost parts of her thighs. Her ass was warm, hot even, and painful, but her Mistress kept bringing the paddle down and spanking her over and over.

"You must not do anything without me telling you to again." Spank.

"Yes, Mistress." Audra moaned as the paddle hit her ass cheeks one more time, her clit hot and desperate to be touched. She felt Mistress Raven's arm plunge forward to spank her again, and stop, hovering the paddle inches above her raw skin. She flinched as her Mistress gently touched the paddle to her ass, stroking the sore, bruised flesh.

"Am I doing well, Mistress?" Audra twitched with pain and need, as mascara tears ran across her cheeks.

"You're OK, I suppose." Mistress Raven slowly, gracefully flowed over to the wall where all her toys were hanging, and hung the paddle up. Audra was too scared to move, yet she desperately wanted to admire her Mistress's markings in the mirror, and view her bruises and ass spanked red. But she stayed as she was, on all fours, as Mistress Raven ran her painted fingertips teasingly over her tools. Her hands stopped on a curl of thick black rope, deliberately being as slow as possible in front of Audra's pleading eyes. She picked the rope up.

Without turning around to look at Audra, Mistress Raven commanded of her slave, "Stand up now."

Audra quickly stood, wincing slightly at the sting of her spanked skin. Her Mistress took her by the hand and led her over to a long bench. "Lie down," she ordered. Audra lowered herself onto the bench, the cool metal stinging the assaulted flesh of her ass. As she lay herself down, Mistress Raven spread her legs, pushing Audra's dress up to bunch around her waist, as her smooth pink pussy spread open like a beautiful and vulnerable flower. Limb by limb, Mistress Raven tied her to the bench, ankles and wrists, tight and firm. Audra was desperate to wriggle, to buck her hips to show her Mistress how much she wanted her fingers in-between her thighs, but instead she stayed still. Her body was statuesque, and cool against the metal. The only things she moved were her eyes, following her Mistress's deliberate movements as she bound her body to the bench.

"Close your eyes," Mistress Raven commanded. Audra did as she was told, yet reluctant to shut away the image of her corseted Mistress and her jet black hair sliding forward like silk, as she further tightened Audra's restraints. "That's a good girl. There will be no looking, do you understand me?"

Audra felt her eyelids flickering, wanting to open them to follow the sound of Mistress Raven's voice. "I said, do you understand me?" Her Mistress was almost shouting now, tying the rope around her wrists tighter, each wrench of the knot pulling at Audra's skin.

"Yes Mistress," Audra replied obediently.

Audra felt her Mistress's hands slip underneath her dress, running her fingers across her body and pulling her pert little tits out of her bra. Mistress Raven suddenly pinched the raspberry pink nipples in her fingers hard, making Audra take a sharp breath and whimper. Audra struggled to keep her eyes firmly closed, as she concentrated on the sensations of her skin wherever her Mistress was touching, tapping, slapping. She then heard Mistress Raven slowly walk off, the heels of her boot hitting the floor in a languishing rhythm, yet she dared not open her eyes to see why her Mistress had left. Several minutes passed and Audra was restless and tense, as her body squirmed against the rope. She suddenly felt the supple leather of a spanker whip, trace slowly up her stomach and over her chest. The whip stroked her breasts, circling each nipple with slow, deliberate movements. Audra moaned softly, bucked her hips upwards and......opened her eyes! "Oh shit!" Audra thought silently to herself.

Mistress Raven was looking down at her, and they made eye contact immediately. "You're a bad, bad girl."

Audra closed her eyes again, screwing them shut at

tightly as she could.

"No! Too late now, you naughty little slut!" Mistress Raven brought the whip down across Audra's nipple, softly at first. She tapped and tapped, harder and faster, until Audra could feel the warmth in her pussy, feel herself getting wetter and more desperate for her Mistress's touch. Her hips started grinding against the bench and her clit was throbbing, as she felt her whole body pulling against its bindings. Mistress Raven ignored her, an ice queen, bringing the whip down across her pert nipples softer, harder, faster, slower. Audra was going to cum just from that, she knew it. Her breathing was fast, slow, stopped, started, matching the rhythm of the whip strikes against her tits. Audra whimpered and moaned, her body protesting being tied down and forced to stay there.

"Please, Mistress. I'm sorry for looking."

"Oh no, it's too late you naughty slut!" Mistress Raven barked, as she walked off, leaving Audra panting hard. Audra could feel the dampness on the inside of her thighs, and this time she could see what her Mistress was doing by her wall of toys, hanging the little black whip back up in its place. Her Mistress then took down a silk blindfold, and wound it seductively around her hand.

"If you can't keep your own eyes shut, I'll shut them for you." She jerked Audra's blonde head forward, rough and sudden, wrapping the silk around her face. The fabric was cool and smooth against Audra's skin. The room went black again, and all Audra could do was wait, tense and trembling, for her cat-quiet Mistress to come back to the bench. She could just hear the pad-pad-pad of the boots on the floor, the creaking of the corset leather, the soft puff of air as her Mistress walked past her. And Audra was tied there, blind, helpless, and desperately turned on.

"Are you going to be good for me now, little slave?" Mistress Raven's voice was close by her ear, sounding both soft and dangerous.

"Yes, Mistress."

"Good." Mistress Raven ran her fingertips over Audra's thighs, tantalizingly close to her pussy. She spanked the inside of Audra's thighs once, stroking them and pinching them. She inched ever closer to Audra's clit, tapping and stroking, tapping and stroking. Audra moaned now, panting, her hips riding upwards towards her Mistress's hands.

"Let me see how wet you are." Mistress Raven edged her finger into Audra's pussy. Audra cried out with relief, with pleasure, with pain as her Mistress's other hand dug its nails into her thigh. Mistress Raven knew Audra's body like none of her previous partners, even those from her longest relationships. No-one before had worked out that her wet pussy lips were so sensitive, that a light slap would send electric shudders through her body, bringing her to the edge of climax over and over. And, only her Mistress knew that the half-moon nail marks on the softest parts of her body, tiny little purple lines, would turn Audra on every time she saw them until they faded. Mistress Raven's current grip on her inner thigh, sharp over the week's earlier bruises, was driving her mad. She writhed her hips, lifted her still raw ass off the bench in an effort to get her Mistress's finger to go deeper.

For once, Mistress Raven obliged. She curled her long, slender finger around, expertly finding Audra's G-spot. Again, another thing her Mistress knew almost instinctively. None of her previous partners had ever got near it. Audra cried out, moaning as she rode Mistress

Raven's finger, feeling another one force its way in to her soft, damp warmth. She bucked back and forth as her Mistress deftly rubbed the little mound inside her pussy, feeling a build up of pleasure and tension in her belly and thighs. A flush shot down through Audra's body, turning her cheeks, her chest, and the small dip in between her collar bones a deep red. Everything felt hot, her face felt hot, her cunt felt hot. She was wet, wet enough for her Mistress's fingers to slide in easily, bringing her closer and closer to the edge of climax. She was going to...

...Mistress Raven pulled away. She slapped Audra's pussy lips lightly, fingers wet from her juices. Audra moaned pleadingly, pulling against the ropes. The world was still dark behind the blindfold, and she wanted her Mistress. She wanted her Mistress's fingers back inside her, she wanted to orgasm tightly and loudly around those fingers playing at her G-spot. Her Mistress had walked away again, silent. Audra was too aroused to be tense and taut now, so her body lay impatient and longing, waiting for the return of her Mistress.

"I don't think you're ready." Mistress was as cold, as calm, and as in control as ever. She ignored Audra's writhing hips and heavy breathing.

"Please, Mistress." The sound of her Mistress's composure was making it even more thrilling and frustrating.

"You can beg better than that."

"PLEASE, Mistress!" Audra pleaded.

"Try harder!" Mistress Raven slapped Audra's pussy lips, flushed dark pink and damp with desire.

"Please, Mistress. Please make me cum!"

Audra finished her sentence with a sharp gasp, as

she felt the dildo thrust up into her. Mistress Raven forced it in two, three more times, then drew it out, soaked with Audra's juice. She rubbed it on Audra's clit, in between her legs, all over her lips, upwards, tracing it over her body.

"Suck it," her Mistress ordered.

Audra obediently opened her mouth, feeling the dildo on her tongue. Mistress Raven forced her to suck her own wetness off the toy, tasting the sweetness of herself. The dildo found its way back to her pussy lips, slapping them, mixing her saliva with her juices. Audra felt it pounding her, she wanted to shout out directions to her Mistress, tell her to go faster, slower, softer, harder, but she dared not. Mistress Raven had her under whip and chain, tied beneath ropes and blindfolds, so Audra had no confusion as to who now had complete control.

The thought thrilled Audra, bringing her closer to climax. She was moaning and sighing now, losing herself in the blind sensations of her Mistress's dildo, wanting to cum but holding herself back to make it last longer. This was another thing special about Mistress Raven. Audra had had sex before. She had had quite a lot of sex before. Sometimes she had enjoyed it, other times less so. Yet, she had never, never enjoyed sex like she did with her Mistress. She had never forced herself to keep away from climax to make their time last longer. Audra had never dissolved herself to the will of someone else, completely lost in her senses, and relinquished of her self-control. It seemed so simple. Just a beautiful, take-charge woman, some sex toys, and a bit of rope, but she had never experienced pleasure, arousal, and the powerful sexual releases that came with it, any other way. The dildo was soaked now, slippery inside her, and Audra moaned at the idea of her Mistress's hands wet because of her, because she was so very close.

Mistress Raven stopped, Audra moaned again, louder. She breathed "Oh, Mistress!" as her blindfold was suddenly being yanked off. It was bright, and Audra squinted, wanting to shield her eyes.

"No, look at me," her Mistress ordered.

Audra opened her eyes, watering make-up down her cheeks. Her Mistress's hands were squeezing her breasts hard, pinching the nipples erect.

"You have nice little tits; I want to look at them better." Mistress Raven began untying Audra roughly. Audra's limbs felt stiff, her hands and feet numb. "Stand up. I want to look at you."

Audra stood up slowly, flexing her aching muscles. "Quickly!" Mistress Raven had a whip in hand, bringing it to Audra's ass with a smack. Audra shrieked and then moaned, her body bending forward involuntarily.

"Good, good." Her Mistress was pulling on elbow-length black gloves, sensually, sexily. Audra watched her, eyes like a wolf. "Kiss my hands." Mistress Raven commanded, as she held out her gloved fingertips, and Audra bent closer to touch her lips to them. The whip came down again, cracking, lurching Audra's face closer to her Mistress's hands.

"Do you want me, little slave?"

Audra said yes, yes she did Mistress.

"Do you want to show me how much you want me, how much you worship me?"

"Yes, Mistress."

"Then back on the floor." Audra felt her back being pushed down by the heel of one of her Mistress's heeled boots. There she was on all fours again, her ass exposed to her Mistress's whip and the floor inches from her face.

"Show me how much you worship me. Kiss my boots." The whip slapped down again, lurching Audra forward towards the floor. The tip of Audra's nose touch the pointed black leather as she felt the end of the whip pushing the back of her head, hair damp with sweat. Her lips inched closer to her Mistress's boots, nose pressed close, inhaling the scent of creaking leather and sex.

"Kiss them all over. Kiss them clean." Mistress Raven commanded.

Audra ran her lips around the boot, kissing the laces, the leather and the sharp pointed heel. She was kneeling down, her ass pink and vulnerable, ready for the whipping that matched her kisses. She wanted to stand up and look at this beautiful, powerful woman. She wanted to run her hands over her curves, over her voluptuous breasts and her long legs. She desperately wanted to kiss her Mistress's mouth as well as her boot heels. Audra knew, however, that this was not allowed, and this is what made this night and all other nights special. She was the one who would cum, who would get everything she wanted by a woman she wasn't even allowed to speak to. It was exciting, it was thrilling. Audra felt herself growing wet again.

Mistress Raven walked away, leaving Audra kneeling on the floor. She circled her slave slowly, inspecting every part of Audra's tanned and toned body.

"Get on the sofa."

Mistress Raven had opened the door to her dungeon room, and was pointing at a black leather couch in the waiting area. Audra looked around for her lingerie. "Without panties." Her Mistress confirmed.

Her Mistress was cold again, calm and frightening. The damp thrill that Audra had felt kissing her Mistress's boots got warmer and stronger, her pussy tingling in escalating anticipation. She made her way to the sofa, white dress, white bra. The whip guided her along, its tense and sexy presence in the small of Audra's back. She sat on the couch, and Mistress Raven used the whip to guide open Audra's legs roughly.

One hand clasping her throat, her Mistress thrust the fingers of her other hand into Audra's pussy. Already hot and wet, Audra moaned loudly, bucking her hips to make her Mistress go deeper, urging her towards her G-spot again. She pressed herself into the softness of the couch, her ass lifting off the leather stickily, as she pushed herself towards Mistress Raven's hands. Audra was gasping for air now, the long fingers inside her pussy knew exactly what they were doing, knew where to touch, and how to move to make her whimper and moan. Her hands and feet were clenching as the woman softly crushing her windpipe was powerfully thrusting two, three, four fingers into her. This time her eyes were voluntarily shut, mouth wide open as she felt herself ride closer to climax, pussy throbbing and hips grinding desperately. Mistress Raven grew faster and faster, perfectly in rhythm with Audra's own body. Faster, faster, harder, harder, Audra felt she couldn't last much longer. She wanted to scream out for her Mistress not to stop but she couldn't, for the hand that was at her throat, was stopping anything but gasps and moans. Audra didn't want her Mistress to stop, and she didn't, pushing and rubbing and... Audra felt herself cum, hard. Her pussy went tight around her Mistress's fingers as she screamed out, hands gripping the sides of the couch. Audra felt her juices soak her thighs, as all her muscles tensed with pleasure. Her own hands pushed down on Mistress Raven's, holding them in her pussy as it squirted the wetness of her release.

Mistress Raven pulled her hands away, leaving

Audra soaked with sweat and juice, as her body lay soft and exhausted on the couch. Mistress Raven walked around, cold and calm, as she then thrust her hand towards Audra's face, pushing her sticky fingers in-between Audra's bitten lips. Audra tasted herself, sweet and damp on her Mistress's fingers, smiling to herself, thinking this was how she is able to leave her mark on her Mistress.

"Get dressed now." Mistress Raven ordered, as she watched Audra ease herself up, faint with fatigue and pleasure, swaying as if she was intoxicated.

Audra slowly dressed herself, wincing as the clothes touched her new bruises and scratches. She smiled after each wince, counting the trophies, and later reminders of her intense experience and orgasm. She felt her Mistress's eyes scrutinizing her, scornfully watching Audra fold her aching limbs into her everyday clothes. The teasing and pleasure might be over, but Audra would be under her Mistress's command until the door clicked shut behind her, and she was back out in the real world again. She heard Mistress Raven's foot tapping impatiently as she finished dressing.

"Was I good, Mistress?" Audra asked sheepishly, uncertain as a girl.

"Look at me when you speak to me!" Mistress Raven criticized.

Audra snapped around as she fastened her belt.

"You did OK. What do you say to me?"

"Thank you, Mistress."

"Is that all?" Mistress Raven's power still took up the whole of the room, her height and her curves filling Audra's senses.

"No, Mistress, that is not all. Thank you, Mistress. Thank you for what you did to me. I deserved it."

"Anything else?" Mistress Raven inquired impatiently.

Audra stood, her purse slung over one shoulder. She reached in, pulling out the money she had kept aside for tonight. She handed it to Mistress Raven, coy and shy as though she felt her Mistress merited more, everything she had.

"Is this it? After all I've done for you? Is this how you appreciate your Mistress?"

"No, Mistress. Sorry, Mistress. I'll pay more next time, for everything you do for me."

Audra hung her head.

"See that you do. Good night." Mistress Raven helped Audra out into the stairwell and shut the door, her leather-clad curves slinking off like a panther into her rooms. Audra breathed deeply, remembering her climax with the ghost of those fingers still inside her, her skin still smarting.

The rain was heavy that evening. Audra strode forward, opening her umbrella as she strode along the sidewalk in those red soled heels, walking with an air of confidence and togetherness that made people clear a path for her. She seemed sleek, classy, friendly, smiling boldly and mysteriously to any damp stranger that caught her eye. They wouldn't ever know, however, that behind that smile was the secret of her night, and how she was going to enjoy it a second time by herself later that evening, once she got home.

STORY 30 – INTERN BY DAY, DOMINATRIX BY NIGHT:

MY JOURNEY INTO THE WORLD OF BONDAGE AND DOMINATION

Spirited Sapphire Publishing

My name is Katie Towler. I'm 25 years old, 5 foot 6 inches tall, slim, strong, and I was a ballet dancer in my teens. My hair has been every color from black to blonde, and the less said about the bubble-gum pink phase in college, the better. I've finally settled on the shade of dark brown that matches my blue eyes the best, and took my nose piercing out about two years ago. I like movies, have a crush on the musician "Pink", go wild for Japanese food, and my favorite color is crimson red. The dream I've held ever since I was 16, was to become a television producer and make the digital age's lesbian version of "Sex in the City". But first, I'm going to tell you the story of how I ended up having my own sex under the city instead. My name is Katie Towler, I am a professional dominatrix, and here's a glimpse of how I found my way into the titillating world of bondage and domination.

****

Clicking on the remote, the TV popped into life. I typically found myself mindlessly flicking through the channels these days, yawning widely as my eyes stung from ten to twelve hours of solid, demanding work. Fetch the coffee, Katie. Can you call my dry cleaner, Katie? Hey, Cassie ["it's Katie…"] be a doll and run down to costume for me? Lunch hours and refreshment breaks were a thing of my glorious and increasingly ancient past. I was tired. More than just tired, I was exhausted. Yes, I was happy, but more and more I had been feeling utterly deflated and used up, like that of a woman three times my age. My mom often called me from Ohio wanting to talk for hours, wanting me to tell her every last detail about LA. Is the weather nice? Are the people loud, or friendly, or thin? I genuinely wanted to chat with my mom and update her on all those little details she yearned for. I wanted to share with her that all was great, I loved my job, that no, I still wasn't getting paid yet, but I had learned more in the last 3 months than I had throughout most of college. I wanted to be home at a reasonable hour, so that I could call my mom and inquire about life back home. But on those rare evenings that I actually got home on time without e-mails pinging all over my phone until midnight, I was just too incredibly tired. After all, I was Katie the intern (or sometimes Cassie the intern), and what is the intern's place but to do ALL of those things no-one else wants to do?

But, what can I say. That was all part of what I needed to do to accomplish my dream. I had worked at this for almost a decade, and yes, it's been hard. I'd been in total control up until that point, even though my life had always been full to the bursting point with to-do lists, goals, aims, and an ever-increasing set of achievements. I have always known where I was going, and how I was going to get there, an independent, ambitious, good-looking woman with the world at her feet. And suddenly, there was a turning point. When I sat in deep reflection of my life, and how I was constantly running around between the production studios and the coffee houses, the unpaid whipping girl for every in-power person at the studios. I loved LA, I loved television, I loved how much I was learning, and how rich my life experience was. But, during my contemplation, there were inner revelations that surfaced as a result of my internship. Who could ever love being at the bottom of the pile? Who could ever love a life never having any sense of control over what they did, what they said, who to be with, who not to be with? And then there were those glimpses of tantalizing excitement I had witnessed within the people who were in positions of power. It seemed incredibly appealing and even sexy from my vantage point. What pleasures might I experience if and when I'm in a position of power? And, at that point, my life took an unexpected turn in that exploration of power.

Let's just take a flashback into my not so recent past, so I can describe to you how it all began.

That day had been no different. There I was slouched in front of the TV I used to love, now skipping scenes in my favorite show because I'd met the actor through the course of my work as a production intern. I now knew how much of a diva he or she was in real life, and how they talked to the 'common people' like they were an inconvenience, like an irritating splat from a bird on their posh luxury car. Knowing someone had an attitude problem in the real world, really made their performance as a sensitive lover a lot less believable. I skipped that channel, then the next, then the next because I was working on the fourth series of that right now and the senior producer was a slave driver. In frustration, I banged the remote hard against the arm of the couch. My burst of anger punched a whole bunch of keys on the remote, and the TV screen went fuzzily black. I put my hands up to my throbbing temples, and closed my eyes. I didn't need the TV. I needed silence. I needed a full nights rest. I needed a vacation.

Just as I took that first deep breath trying to unwind, my phone beeped. My eyelids snapped back open, the pain in my head worsening as through someone had put a vice round my skull. I was in no mood tonight.

Most girls of my age look forward to Friday nights. At 5:01 pm they are swinging out of the revolving office doors, heels on and lip gloss slicking, phones buzzing from friends at cocktail bars, and sushi restaurants, and blockbuster cinema showings. Or else they were jumping into a cab, headed home to pajama bottoms and take-in pizza, or rose-petal bedrooms, or highly anticipated monthly date nights. Those Fridays were another thing lost to my distant past, along with friends, social entertainment and lovers. That shrill ring of my cell on this Friday evening would be a late night favor from a producer, undoubtedly. Or a colleague on their third beer suddenly remembering something vital for Monday morning and 'oh Cassie ["it's Katie…"] could you just…?' Or it would be an e-mail from London or New York pinging in now, late, early, I wasn't sure. It would have been forwarded to me to deal with, incredibly from somebody who was actually getting paid. Somebody who was about to get the free and relaxing weekend I could only dream about, when I later managed to snatch a couple of hours sleep after dealing with whatever real or perceived 'emergencies' needed to be dealt with right that moment.

I groaned, massaging the headache out of my forehead. As much as I wanted to take back control of my own free time, I really did love this internship. However many coffees I retrieved, and the various times the costume director got my name wrong and the 5:30am wake up calls. I wanted to be in this industry, desperately! I just also needed to live, and for that I needed money. And for money, I needed a job. And for a job, I needed experience. And for experience, I needed to grow up and answer my phone. I took my hands away from my temples, reaching to read the message. What had been a frowning combination of headache and frustration morphed into a smile I felt rise into my face like a lazy sunny Sunday morning. My tired, stinging eyes were suddenly wide open and mostly likely reflecting a wicked little twinkle.

She called herself Tina. That wasn't her real name. Anyone who had read a magazine in the last five years knew who she really was. Corn-fed blonde hair, thick down to her waist, her eyes bright blue and lashes long. I met her one painful, eye-wateringly early Tuesday morning as she filmed a musical cameo for a sitcom. I fetched her coffee, along with everyone else's. Soy milk, decaf. She was sitting in make-up, mouthing her lines to herself softly, her plump peach lips moving and pouting as she played through the scene in her mind. She was beautiful, but I'd seen enough glossy beach shoots and album covers to already know that. It wasn't a shock.

We started talking as I escorted her onto the set. What those photographers and agents and personal stylists had never let me see before, was how short she was. She was barely five foot, tiny and girlish. Her bones were like that of a bird, her fragility emphasized by how pretty and sweet she was.

"Thanks." She made eye contact with me, bursting into a smile that undoubtedly made the producer's heart race with fluttering dollar signs. She was like sunshine, as golden haired and bright as the publicists wanted you to believe. My heart lurched in my chest. I wanted her.

The first time she messaged me on my phone, I had no idea who it was. She had signed it "Tina", coincidentally my aunt's name. Only it wasn't my aunt, because the text message was asking me if I wanted to meet up with her that weekend. It went on to say that she had been fantasizing about me fucking her with a strap-on, stripping her down and spanking her for daring to think of me like that. As I read further down, it dawned on me, slowly and excitingly, who this person was. She knew I was the intern; I'd fetched coffee for her, ran her errands and escorted her wherever she needed to go on the production sets. She apparently felt guilty about that, and wanted me to punish her for it. She wanted me to bind her, and whip her, for treating a goddess like me so shamefully. Yes, she was the soy milk, decaf. Sorry, Mistress. How can I repay you? "Mistress, huh?", I thought pleasingly to myself.

My heart felt as though someone had stabbed a needle through my chest and injected it with pure adrenaline. Excitement surged through my body and settled in between my thighs. I felt myself grow wet at the idea of this sweet, innocent-looking woman wanting me to do these things to her. I'd never dwelt on it before, but the thought of reaching my hands round her neck, pulling her head back by her long rope of blonde hair and playing with her little tits made me throb. I replied to her text message…"yes"! My fingers snaked down into my jeans, imagining what I'd do to her, the bruises I'd make on her ass, her wet pussy…

The next day I took a lunch break. As everyone else linked arms and chattered off to a restaurant, I took my boxed salad and stole down to the costume department. I loved everything about this department. There were fabrics of every color and texture, pins and needles and buttons and frantic vibrancy. Every outfit you could want: astronaut or alien, pirate or soldier, beggar or President. I picked out fishnet stockings and a leather garter, a shiny black corset with red lacing, elbow-high gloves, a whip, a paddle, and a couple of pieces of rope. Oh, and some loose pink feathers to complete my prop collection. I then grabbed some deep, blood-red lipstick from make-up and a long black piece of silk as I was walking out the door from wardrobe. Taking it home that evening, my body was buzzing with anticipation and excitement. I dressed myself up, standing in front of the mirror. I wasn't "Katie the Intern" any more. I was powerful and sexually charged. I wanted to eat people alive. I wanted to drive them wild with desire. I wanted to be the fulfillment of their secret yearnings. I wanted everybody who walked through the doors of my apartment to worship me, to kiss my heels, to do exactly as I said. I wanted to watch them cum, and know it was all because of me.

"Tina" had been a little late, but I didn't mind. I couldn't really fault her driver. My tiny apartment was not somewhere Tina's driver would normally have been taking her to. There was no champagne or paparazzi or French chef. Instead, she'd be presented with me, dressed up, dark hair down, lips juicy and red. I was adorned in boots, stockings, and clad in leather, ribbon and lace that showed how strong I was, a sleek, and sordid ballerina. The gloves from costume fit perfectly, and I felt fantastic. I felt sexy. I felt powerful! I just wanted this girl in front of me, right now. Wanting me, and wet for me. I could have fainted with anticipation.

When Tina arrived, I led her by the hand into my bedroom, and I could tell she was nervous. That only fed my need for her, her fear making me stronger, sexier. She was dressed in a light blue baby doll dress, pert tits and pink pussy peaking out from under sheer lace and ruffles. It was perfect. Tina lay on the bed I'd dressed in black silk for tonight, and she slipped down onto it like I wanted to slip down onto her, smooth yet a bit hard. I'd not said a word to her, just led her into the room and pushed her onto the bed. My dancer's legs in those stockings had already made her sheer panties damp. I pulled out my rope and pulled taught my whip, while Tina watched and gasped. Hearing her little intake of air meant that I'd bring the leather down across her soft, white skin sooner vs. later, wanting to hear her moan and call out for more, wanting her to call out my name with equal parts terror and lust. Oh yes, I was alive, and aroused, and in my element.

Spanking was what she had enjoyed the most. The

third time she had come to see me; it was all she had wanted. She knelt on my bed, white skin on black silk, and climaxed hard around my fingers, juices flowing simply because I'd slapped her ass so hard. She loved me using the paddle, begging me to make her skin raw and pink, to tell her what a little slut she was. How disappointed I was in her. I loved watching her cry out with the first hit, watching the color flood her skin. She'd stand upright and sore at the end of each session, naked with bite marks and nail marks and rope marks, admiring the reds and pinks and purples of her fast-bruising skin. She touched herself in front of my full length mirror while I choked her, pressing down on her tender wounds and she'd cum in her own hands with my fingers wrapped round her throat. When she left I would always feel lighter, stronger. I'd strip myself and my bed, and orgasm two, three times at the memory of my manicured nails in her flesh, and her sighing and whimpering under my control. My orgasms would match hers, and I'd be bucking my hips for her to come back. We needed each other, although she would never be privy to that.

And now, on this boring, aching, exhausted Friday night, she had messaged me again. Sunday morning all in white, a punishment for missing Church, a whip, a paddle, a sore, pink ass. I obliged, and lay back smiling in my chair, the tension round my temples slipping away, sliding into memories of my favorite clients.

Tina may have been the first, but she had started a taste for something. I'd find myself at work, staring at TV sets and make-up artists when all I could really see, all I wanted to see, were those half-moon nail marks in a singer's soft skin. The director's boards clacked down and my mind wandered off towards a whip-crack, a pillow-muffled scream that was half climax, half pain. Even when fetching coffee, I fantasized about turning up to work in leather and lace, taking the paddle to my crawling employees, bound and gagged and naked on the floor by my boots. My mind was off my job, and on my secret life of taboo-filled pleasure.

Although, I wasn't really sure what my job was any more. After two visits, Tina had showered me with money. She wanted to appreciate me properly, wanted to give me everything I deserved, she said. She had cum four times, she was weak and tiny, she had handed me a wallet of dollars. I was her Mistress. I was her Goddess. She didn't deserve money. I took it, sternly. I was earning again.

It was actually Tina herself, who introduced me to the woman who paid me best. Not as secretive or furtive as the musician, Holly was wealthy, very, very wealthy. I didn't ever ask what she did for a living, but I knew it paid better than any of my most impossible dreams and it involved taking long business trips abroad. From Europe, Japan, India, she would call me sporadically, often at odd times. Older than me by about ten or fifteen years, she looked fantastic, especially with a leather collar around her neck.

I still grew warm and wet when I thought of our most recent meeting. My clit throbbed at the memory of her, naked except for her hands and ankles cuffed together, kneeling in front of me. I had led her round my apartment, my slave, my kitten.

"What would you like me to do for you now, Mistress?" She purred, kneeling on all fours in front of me, the fine metal links of her leash in my hand. I was wearing my corset and gloves, full make up, eyes smoky and dark. From the waist down, however, I was naked, my legs spread suggestively, dominating the space around her. She knelt in front of me, demure as a nun, black hair cut short to a bob. Her beautiful dark shoulders were exposed, skin like spilt ink. I pulled her chin up so she was looking at me in the face, deep brown eyes locked into my own as tough as steel.

"I want you to lick my pussy," was my order to her.

I put my gloved hands on her head, forcing my slave into my pussy. I felt her tongue search there, finding my clit, so I pushed her in deeper, harder. Her body writhed and bucked, trying to find comfort as I held her face in between my legs. After she stopped moving, I removed my hands, watching this sleek and successful woman lap at my cunt like it was a bowl of milk. Her eyes were closed in pleasure, tasting me as I'd told her to, giving her Mistress the pleasure she deserved. I watched her, eyes fiery, feeling myself tingle and throb as she knelt there.

"Harder, slave!" I stood up, bringing the whip around to spank her firm, toned ass. She was a cyclist in her spare time. Powerful, driven, a sportswoman. And now, look at her. She moaned with pleasure as I stood, legs wide apart, in front of her. I pushed the back of her head back into my pussy, soaking her face with my juice and her own saliva. I could feel her nose pushing into me. She was struggling to catch a breath, gasping with her mouth, whimpering with need.

Her hands still cuffed behind her back and ankles bound, I took my arms away from her head. She moved backwards, stopping, her face sticky and mouth dark red from my wetness. "Who said you could stop?!" I brought the whip back down with a loud crack. She shrieked and nuzzled her face back into my pussy. I held her cat leash tight to keep her face where it should be, pleasuring me, her Mistress.

"Do you like making me feel good, slave?" From

within my thighs she nodded, I could feel her tongue move up and down, up and down inside me. It made me throb even more, as I pulled her in tighter and closer. I looked down to watch her, eyes closed, mouth open, play her tongue over my clit, my flushed pussy lips. I shuddered as I felt that electric thrill jolt through my body again. Oh, if the boardroom could see this now. If her clients in Germany, in Hong Kong, in Dubai should walk in now, see me - a production intern from Ohio – pushing their hyper-successful colleague's face, all sticky with my own cum, into my pussy, calling her my slave, my kitten, my bitch.

"Do you want to make your Mistress cum?" She nodded again, I felt myself getting closer and closer, electrified by her tongue and the image of her suited men and women walking in and seeing her naked, leashed, bound ankle and wrist.

"Well do it then! Don't I deserve it?!" Another whip-crack. Her tongue grew fast, darting across my flushed clit like a hummingbird. I saw her hips start to grind, I knew this was turning her on. I was sharper.

"Then faster! Make me cum, you little slut." She rubbed her face into me; I pulled her collar tighter, wrapping my gloved fingers around it to pull her in closer and closer. My hands went again to the back of her head. I pushed my hips into her as I forced her in, her tongue still buzzing over my clit, my lips, in and out of me. Her moans muffled against my warm flesh damp from her pleasuring me. I looked down at the chains on her ankles, the handcuffed wrists, silver against her raw skin. I could feel myself rise inside, her naked flesh underneath me. She was there only for me, doing everything I wanted...

...I came all over her lips, her face sticky from my

juice. I pushed her head in forcefully, she felt my climax, tasted the juice in her mouth, on her tongue, her face. She moaned louder than I did, her tongue reaching into me to taste my orgasm, the one I'd forced her to give me. I made her go home that night after paying me, her wrists sore and pink from the handcuffs. She had given me three orgasms, I hadn't touched her once. I felt intoxicated, elated.

I had fun with Holly, just as I had had fun with Tina. My favorite time, the time that made those hours at work tick by the fastest, was my first session with Ana. I had by this time put an advert out, and she'd been the first to answer. Ana had a face I thought was ubiquitous, a kind of standard beauty that meant you felt you recognized her even though you'd never really seen her before. Within about ten minutes of her arriving at my apartment, it turns out that I actually did, in fact, recognize her. I'd never really been interested in the kind of films she'd acted in – chick flicks – but I had a feeling she'd found my advertisement through Tina.

She was so timid. Obviously she'd never done anything like this before, but I could tell how excited she was. I made her sit on the bed, picked up a glass of wine and leaned against the dresser watching her for a while, just long enough that she began to get nervous. I took a sip from my glass, slowly, gently, keeping my eyes on hers the whole time. Quickly I put it down and turned around, bending gently forwards to open a drawer. I took out a length of soft black ribbon, and a short leather whip, and held each in either hand. She glanced from one to the other, sugar and salt, sweet and sour, then back up at me, saying nothing. I began to play with the whip, chewing the tails. She'd begun to get comfortable.

"Take off your clothes" I said simply, no fucking around. She made to stand up but I put a hand on her head and pushed her back down.

"Did I say you could get up?"

Stunned, she lay on her back and writhed back and forth trying to take off her crisp white shirt. Just as she had it over her head, I pounced, laying on top of her and pinning her arms in place, her shirt covering her eyes. I could see her nipples harden beneath her thin lace bra, and guessed she was smiling. I wrapped the ribbon around and around her wrists, and then tied it off to the bed. Sitting up, straddling her naked waist, I grazed her breasts with the back of my hand, once, then again, then a third time before I turned my hand over and scratched roughly all the way down her side, leaving a faint red streak from her left armpit to her skirt. She arched her back then, straining to buck me off and cried out in pleasure. I did it again on the other side, one stroke, then another, then another, and then I waited. At the time the fourth would have come she flinched sideways to her left, expecting the same trick. Instead, I scratched the same side as before, making her squeal and squirm under my touch. She laughed and giggled, almost breathless already. I could feel her legs rubbing together beneath me.

As I swung my leg off, I leaned in close to her blinded face, almost touching, but silent. She could sense I was there, and I let anticipation set in before I jumped away and scratched again right down either side her chest, catching my fingers in her skirt and ripping it down. She lurched again and laughed hard, still breathless.

Her skirt was down now, and her matching lace panties showed how wet she was. I pulled them the rest of the way off roughly, dragging her down the bed slightly. I took more ribbon and tied her legs to the bedposts, holding them apart.

"Now we play a game" I said. "It's called; "Where's next?"

She giggled. I brought the whip to her and let the tails drag across her near naked skin. She shied at the tickling sensation, and I knew she was feeling shivers crawl over her body. I dragged the whip across her breasts, and at the same time took a handful and pinched her nipple hard. She moaned and writhed as I took my fingers away and brought them back in a different place, this time her inner thigh, then next her belly, next under her arm. Each time the tickling was followed by a scratch or a pinch, each time she had no idea where it was going to be. She began to pant harder and harder. I could see her legs straining against the ribbon, trying to squeeze herself together. I put my hand near her, so close I could feel her heat and she could tell I was there. She went still when she felt that, arching her back, willing me to put a finger inside her, to touch her inside, to feel her clit. Anything, anything at all, she silently begged of me. I smiled, I was wet too. I took my hand away and she moaned, almost sobbed. I scratched the inside of her thigh for being impatient and she screamed out loud.

I'd gotten myself too worked up, I wanted to play. Standing over her I took off my own skirt and stood naked from the waist down, straddling her. If she wasn't blindfolded she would have been able to see my wet pussy right over her face. I sat down on her again, this time further up, feeling her firm nipples on my naked thighs. I put my hand down into my damp pussy and began to rub myself, noisily so she could hear and know what I was doing. I felt my juice run down over her, and she squirmed and strained to touch herself, or touch me, I wasn't sure. I rubbed myself, and the whole time she squirmed and bucked and fought against her ribbons, desperate to fuck. I didn't take long, cumming silently. I stopped, went down on her and shoved my tongue inside her. She screamed again, bucking so hard that she almost broke free of her ribbon restraints. She was so close already, I barely did anything before she came, her eager pussy gripping my tongue and trying to pull me in deeper, laughing and moaning. I picked up my skirt and put it back on before letting her loose. I untied her ribbons but she just lay there, panting and panting. I smiled at that memory, feeling myself squirm in turn at the thought of her. She was coming again, tomorrow night. We'd progressed to thick, black rope. I was already excited.

And then, my TV screen still dark, and the sun dipping below the high rise backdrop out of my apartment window, I realized. My phone was now silent, my headache gone. I was never excited for the next day at my internship. I never willed the nights to go faster, my sleep to come earlier so I could get to my job as soon as possible. I resented my colleagues. I had no passion at the production studios anymore. My passion was whips and chains now, making girls laugh and scream and tremble, sticky cum and rope burns. My insides went cold as I made the decision, right there as I confirmed Saturday night with my ribboned Ana.

I didn't show up to the producer's office on Monday morning. Instead, I went shopping for furniture for the newest B&D parlor in Los Angeles. The one I decided to name simply: "Cassie's".

FOLLOW SPIRITED SAPPHIRE PUBLISHING

http://www.spiritedsapphire.com

http://www.twitter.com/SapphoLove

http://www.pinterest.com/sapphicscribes

EXCERPT FROM
LESBIAN FICTION –
DARK THEME SERIES:

VAMPIRA:
BLOOD, LUST AND MURDER
(BOOK 1)

Spirited Sapphire Publishing

The music was loud in the club, so loud that it hurt Karenna's ears, but she had expected that as her hearing was super sensitive and she had come prepared. She discreetly slid a pair of earplugs in to block out some of the volume and immediately felt the tension in her body ease. There were many things that made Karenna tense and the wailing screams that paraded as music was one of them. Which, she thought with a smile, was slightly ironic, as one of the things that most calmed her was the wailing screams of her playthings.

On high alert, her eyes carefully scanned around the dimly lit nightclub. It was filled with sweating bodies, jerking and gyrating to the thumping sounds of the music that the DJ was playing. As she looked around, Karenna was fully aware that she was already attracting attention. Considering that she was dressed in a skin tight red leather corset that pushed her already impressive breasts into a cleavage that any man would gladly drown in, paired with thigh high leather 5 inch stiletto heeled boots, with a tiny black leather skirt that molded to the curves of her ass, she of course knew that she drew attention. Karenna enjoyed all the attention she got whenever she went out and she equally enjoyed rejecting the pathetic advances that were made towards her. And, any fool who tried to put a sticky hand on any part of her body was shocked at the speed and agility she displayed as she broke their wrist with a cool emotionless smile.

The club she was in tonight was one of her favorites. Karenna often enjoyed finding her evening's entertainment in the popular nightspots of the big English city, and tonight, as always, she was in search of someone very specific. Tonight's large crowd promised plenty of choice for entertainment and one of the doormen was related to a good friend of hers. When she had arrived at the club he gave her access to a downstairs storage room, and it was just a few minutes of work to prepare for the evening ahead. He knew her secrets, but he had secrets of his own. He had no problem assisting Karenna with her dark endeavors, and in return, she would throw tokens of appreciation in his direction.

Karenna now prowled her way through the throng of bodies, the scent of sweat and sex hanging heavily in the air. Her nose wrinkled in disgust as a couple of drunken men tried to chat her up. They were both over six feet tall, but had to look up at Karenna. Their so called compliments about her tits and ass didn't impress her as much as they had hoped. She strode on past them without a word. Her tastes were very particular, and though some told her she was too particular, she thought she had every right to her choices. Some evenings she left the city center dissatisfied; either having to make do with a second rate selection or still hungry, craving her fill. She could never decide which was worse. But, on most evenings she chose to prowl through the clubs, she found exactly what she sought. And, on this evening, she smiled with pleasure as soon as her eyes locked onto exactly what she wanted.

Karenna took in several deep breaths, as she stood surrounded by a mass of bodies totally unaware of the dangers she presented. Over half of them were completely safe from her, for she had never found satisfaction with a male. But the others were not so safe. Her presence was so completely confident and commanding that a path always seemed to open up for her without her having to make any effort. Every eye was drawn to her, most without even realizing it, while others stared in hypnotic attraction. But, she didn't waste a glance at anyone she had no interest in, she didn't need to. Karenna preferred to play with girls who were completely lesbian, but she had enjoyed some girls who liked cock at times, and then there had been a few very satisfactory evenings she had selected a girl who had never been with another woman. Karenna almost purred as she recalled the pleasure that one little red head had been, as she taught her the joys of being with another girl.

Tonight, she was going to have the perfect playmate, and she smiled as she watched the tall, slender blonde throw her head back as she laughed. A moan escaped Karenna's lips as she saw that long pale throat fully exposed and the lights from the dance floor glitter over it. Biting her lip Karenna contemplated the joys that were ahead for them both. She sighed softly as she held the idea in her head, knowing that she had to hold back a little. Part of her agreement with the doorman was that he got her leavings. It was a pity that she had found such a perfect little toy on the evening she had made that agreement, she thought. Happy to bide her time, she leant against a wall, watching her selection chat and laugh with her friends. She was not cruel, she would allow her little toy to enjoy the company of her friends first, before they indulged in some fun together.

Aware of stares directed her way, Karenna turned towards a man who was walking towards her. She stared coolly at him and smiled, as he suddenly altered his course to pass her instead of stopping. It amused her that the cattle who herded together in places such as this were so easily corrected; just a flick of her eyes and he had known better than to even approach her. Karenna's eyes flicked back to her target, a cold smile forming on her perfectly full lips as she watched the tall, slender blonde. Her hands, she noticed, were delicate and it seemed she was a tactile girl, which made Karenna's blood heat with passion. It was such fun to play with girls who enjoyed touching, and to be touched. She watched the girl run her fingers over the back of one of her friends, an intimate gesture that told Karenna she was a free spirit. Interestingly, as the blonde's fingers caressed her friend's back, her eyes were fixed on the face of a girl opposite of her, her pretty little pink tongue sliding easily over lips that shone a glossy rose pink.

Karenna tilted her head to one side as she assessed the girl; long blonde hair that was used as a sexual weapon, flicked over her shoulders to emphasize what she was saying, that deliciously pale, slender throat with a pulse beating just a little faster than a resting pulse, telling Karenna that the girl was experiencing some excitement and arousal. Karenna briefly cast her eyes over the group of girls wondering who might be causing that excitement in the blonde, but she didn't care enough to spend more than a second taking in the others. They were pretty, but her blonde was outstanding. Her round tits were full and high, and Karenna felt a stirring in her belly as she contemplated baring them. Her ass, too, was round, and perky in the way of girls just into their twenties. Karenna knew that she was much older than her blonde, but then she was much older than everyone in the building. Even her contact at the door was younger, and he had been born over five hundred years ago.

Karenna let out a low chuckle, a laugh that chilled the blood of a group of men just yards away. They didn't know why they all suddenly decided that they needed some fresh air, they just moved en masse to the exit. Karenna raised her eyebrows at the men's departure, for she was always acutely aware of the happenings in her surroundings. It was unusual for her energy to be felt so clearly when she was prowling, but this little blonde was clearly raising her appetites. The blonde girl, totally unaware that she was being observed, was now flirting with a pretty red head who had now joined her group for a night out. Karenna continued to be aroused and intrigued by the blonde, and had plans to make a move soon. She continued to watch as the blonde licked her lips, obviously imagining how it would feel to kiss the pouty lips of the other girl, having no idea that she was making someone else in the room smile for similar reasons.

Karenna ran through the preparations she had made in the store room downstairs. She knew that her contact would be the one to check that area of the building to secure it once the premises closed, so she had no concerns about being interrupted. And even if their fun was interrupted, she was more than capable of dealing with any interlopers. She smiled as she saw the blonde walk towards the women's restroom, hand-in-hand with the pretty red head. Time to make her move, Karenna decided, as she stealthily followed the pair into the dark gothic décor bathroom.

Printed in Great Britain
by Amazon